antipodes

antipodes

stories / holly goddard jones

University of Iowa Press, Iowa City

©University of Iowa Press, Iowa City 52242

uipress.uiowa.edu
Printed in the United States of America

Cover design and typesetting by Erin Kirk

Printed on acid-free paper

Library of Congress Cataloging-in-Publication Data

Names: Goddard Jones, Holly, author.
Title: Antipodes: Stories / Holly Goddard Jones.
Description: Iowa City: University of Iowa press, [2022] |
Identifiers: LCCN 2021040770 (print) | LCCN 2021040771 (ebook) | ISBN 9781609388294 (paperback; acid-free paper) | ISBN 9781609388300 (ebook)

Subjects: LCGFT: Short stories.
Classification: LCC PS3610.O6253 A84 2022 (print) | LCC PS3610.O6253 (ebook) | DDC 813/.6—dc23
LC record available at https://lccn.loc.gov/2021040770
LC ebook record available at https://lccn.loc.gov/2021040771

FOR ERIN

The nation is a boat,
as some have said, ourselves
its passengers. How troubling
now to ride it drifting
down the flow from the old
high vision of dignity, freedom,
holy writ of habeas corpus,
and the land's abundance—down
to waste, want, fear, tyranny,
torture, caricature
of vision in a characterless time,
while the abyss whirls below.

—WENDELL BERRY

contents

antipodes

antipodes

We built the temple on the site of the sinkhole, which had itself been the site of the National Corvette Museum. You may have seen it on the news a few years back, the washed-out security footage: first of the cars, rainbow-colored, gleaming in the low light, entombed like pharaohs—and then the floor disappears, revealing a column of inky nothing, and the cars drop into it. The video is soundless. Peaceful, even. No shriek of grinding metal, crackle of fiberglass, rumble of disturbed earth. No one ever heard the cars hit bottom. The prevailing theory is that they reached the magma layer and melted to nothing, but I picture them falling and falling and falling, dropping through a secret hole on the other side of the earth, then rising, cars-turned-rockets, and shooting up into space. But I am fanciful. Raising kids will do that to you.

There had been talk of rebuilding the museum, but in the end, no one wanted to take the risk. The National Corvette Foundation donated the land back to the city of Bowling Green, and the city promptly put it up for sale. As you might imagine, there wasn't a lot of interest in a thirty-acre lot with a fifty-foot circular abyss in its center. Even developers, who had otherwise leveled the city into a maze of three-bedroom houses with two-car garages, steered clear. (You can be sure the *Daily News* made use of that pun in a headline or two.)

Most big ideas have obscure or controversial origins. Even today, with social media as a record, you can do a digital excavation on the history of the temple and find more to confuse than illuminate you. I am the Historian, and I was one of the founding planners, and even I couldn't say for sure whether the idea for the temple started with Richard or Kesha or D'Shawn or Wendy or Elsa or Connor. Sometimes, it still seems possible that the idea for the temple was mine, and I believe I can remember the night it came to me, when I was lying on the floor beside the baby's crib, arm pinned between slats, rubbing circles onto her hot little belly while she snuffled and hitched. Yes, I can remember that moment vividly, the thin baby blanket across my legs, stuffed animal as a pillow under my head, yeasty smell of the baby's soiled diaper and the question of whether to wake her to change it, and then *it* came to me, whole, a vision: a temple to hide the sinkhole, keep watch over it. A column of white stone, reaching up to the sky, to negate the darkness. It seemed to me for a long time that this was my vision, my message from God, but later, when Richard was appointed Head Priest, I came to believe that my vision was a false memory. And anyway, as Richard says, the concept of "ownership"—even of an idea—runs counter to the whole project of the temple. We may as well just rebuild the Corvette Museum, he says, if that's to be our mindset.

"I'm going to call the meeting to order," Richard says.

There are days when we are confused about our purpose. Are we meeting or are we worshipping? Are we a congregation or a committee? There are seven of us present, as I note carefully in the Minutes—enough to fit around the oblong table in the conference room with five seats to spare. Richard stands at the head of the table. He pretends, gently, to hammer a gavel. He doesn't have a costume or uniform, but he favors on his temple days a priest-adjacent get-up of black button-down shirt and dark pressed trousers. He wears little wire-framed glasses and gel in his short-cropped hair. He reeks of Old Spice.

"Any new business?" he asks.

We look at each other, shrug. It is all new business. And no business. Now that the temple is erected, the holy vision realized, we are trying not to admit that a next step has not revealed itself to us. The agenda Richard emailed us last week had two line items: (1) New Business; (2) Discussion to Formulate an Agenda.

Kesha unscrews the cap on her Coke Zero and it hisses, drawing everyone's attention.

"Yes, Kesha?" Richard asks.

"But I wasn't—" She stops, clears her throat. "Well, we could talk about a name. For the temple. Or for us, whatever we are."

"What *are* we?" Wendy asks. "Are we a church?"

"We are still in the process of filing for 501(c)(3) tax-exempt status," Richard tells her.

"*Then* will we be a church?" D'Shawn asks.

"I don't believe in God," Connor says.

Elsa, as always, rolls her eyes. "Why are you even here?"

"Who ever said this has anything to do with God?" Connor asked.

This is the conversation every time. An hour in, D'Shawn, who is the group's optimist, makes a motion to name the temple The Church of the Sinkhole, and Kesha, who seconds everything, seconds him. Richard moves to discussion, and Elsa's hand springs into the air.

"That would be like saying you go to the church of the Devil. You don't name your church after your enemy."

"Who says the sinkhole's our enemy?" Connor asks.

"There's a Church of Satan," Kesha offered.

"Satanists are just atheists trolling the government," Connor says.

"We're here to watch the sinkhole," I say, and a hush falls over the group because I rarely speak. "It isn't our enemy or our friend. Neither is God, for that matter."

"Now you're just being blasphemous." Elsa knits her pale reddish eyebrows. "Of course God's our friend."

"You like your friends. You fear your god," I say. I have brought Stella to the meeting, strapped to my chest in a sling. Stella comes with me almost everywhere, not because I am a proponent of attachment parenting but because I have two older children and too much to do, and I need my hands free. She is about eighteen months old now. Her thin pale hair is pasted in damp strands across her broad, creamy forehead. Her green eyes are closed, lashes heavy against her cheeks, and her right hand is clamped around a blue poker chip, which has become something of a lovey to her in recent weeks. She might sleep for another half hour, if I'm lucky, and I resent spending her precious naptime like this, arguing inanities.

"She's right," Richard says. "We're guardians. Or perhaps gatekeepers. That's what got this temple built in the first place. People need to know someone's worrying about the sinkhole so they don't have to."

"What good can we possibly do?" Connor says. "What does any of this mean? Are we just going to be the first to fall in the hole if it widens?"

"When it widens," Kesha says coldly.

"So we're just watching it," D'Shawn says. He sounds relieved rather than doubtful. He likes the fact that today's talk has produced an answer, however vague.

"We study it," I say.

"We appease it," Richard says.

I was going through what my husband called "a rough patch" when I found myself in a Discord community with Richard and the others who would become the founding planners. It's another thing I can't clearly remember—how I ended up there. I wasn't a gamer, but I did spend a lot of time, in the early a.m. hours, staring at my phone while the baby nursed or fussed, or during the nightly bouts of insomnia I suffered those days. Half-awake, I would click link after link, jabbing my thumb, switching between apps. Facebook to Twitter to Instagram to Chrome. There was a lot of that in late 2016, everywhere: a lot of insomnia, a lot of middle-of-the-night internet searches and desperate conspiring. People looking for purpose. People trying to figure out, via the right Google search, how to stave off disaster.

There is no other way to say this: I became convinced in the weeks after Stella's birth that I had a hole in my head. It sounds like a joke, but it was not a joke to me then, and it still doesn't feel funny to me now.

It started at the hospital, the night of her birth. Money was tight, and we didn't have family nearby, so my husband went home to be with our older kids, Meg and Elias. I didn't mind. I had a book to read, a baby to breastfeed, and I knew to expect a night of regular interruptions from the hospital staff, which would infuriate Joseph and inspire him to a grumpiness worse than the broken sleep. I settled in to endure it.

I was drifting, dozing, the baby on my chest—I knew, in a faraway way, that the nurse would jolt me awake if she found me like this, scold me for sleeping with Stella in the bed—when I felt a sort of itchy, crawling sensation at the base of my skull. Automatically, I put a hand back there to scratch and felt it: a scaly patch, perhaps the size of a pencil eraser. I scratched it gently with my fingernail. The rough skin started to flake away, painlessly. I kept going, wanting it all gone. Wanting to feel smooth nothingness beneath my finger pad. At last, finally, I could feel no more loose skin, but what my excavation had revealed was even worse: a cool, slightly sunken circle of flesh. There wasn't even hair growing out of it. The crawling sensation from before was back, but it was in my brain now, an ugly thought that wormed its way through the folded lobes. It whispered *cancer*, *melanoma*, *tumor*, and I held Stella tightly with my free hand, my breath constricted—what if I wasn't around to see her grow up? What would she do without a mom? The transition from sleepy calm to panic was almost instantaneous, and this, too, seemed like proof. Proof of the truth of my instinct. The feeling was so strong that I had to stop myself from calling Joseph, demanding that he abandon our kids and return immediately to the hospital. I was not able, however, to stop myself from hitting the call button to summon the nurse.

I might have been crying by this point. "My head," I said, leaning over and pointing. "There's something on the back of my head."

She was a big woman, broad and doughy, with hair sculpted into one of those elaborate, meringue-like sweeps you see on Pentecostals. Her lip curled. "Like a bug?"

"No. Just look at it, please. Something's wrong."

She turned on the bright overhead light and, hesitantly, parted my hair. Her fingers gently probed the curve of my skull. "I don't see nothing back here."

I put a finger insistently on the spot. It was there, I could still feel it: unnaturally round and irrefutable. "This," I hissed. "This."

"I just see a tiny scratched spot. Honey, do you want me to take the baby to the nursery so you can get a couple hours sleep?"

"No," I said.

"You sure?"

I mopped my eyes with the back of my hand, then shook my head.

She peered at me. "Do you need anything for pain? It's been six hours since you had a Percocet."

"I'm fine," I whispered.

"You can't sleep with the baby in bed," she said. She took Stella from me briskly, plopped her down in the scuffed oak bassinet, and rearranged her swaddle in three practiced sweeps. "Let her lay here a little bit. It'll do you good."

"I will," I said, impatient at this point to have the nurse out of the room, now that I knew she'd be no help. In another few minutes, she left, though I could sense her outside the door, hovering, her suspicions alerted. I didn't care. I hobbled to the bathroom. The pad between my legs was soaked, and the artificial ice pack had long ago lost its chill, but I ignored the discomfort, rummaging in my make-up bag for a compact. The pressed powder had a little mirror. I wiped the dust off with my nightgown and held it up to the back of my head, neck twisted, parting my long hair to reveal a window of bare flesh. Craning for a glimpse of it, though all I could see was the occasional patch of pink. I don't know how long the baby was crying before the sound finally registered with me. Long enough for drops of blood to leak from my soaked mesh underwear and spatter the bathroom floor. Long enough for my breasts to marble and leak. Long enough that, once I'd finally changed my pad and ice pack and emerged, the nurse was back, patting Stella and hushing her and watching me with deep concern.

"I had to use the toilet," I said. "It hurt pretty bad."

"You need to watch your stitches," the nurse said, handing Stella back to me. "I'll get you a stool softener."

"Could I have some ginger ale, too, please?"

The mundane nature of my request seemed to reassure her. She smiled. "Sure you can, hon."

That night was the beginning—not just of my knowledge of the hole or what I thought of first as the spot and later as the hole, but of my divided self. There was the self that knew that I carried around this wrongness, that I was branded with it. My knowledge of the hole was as certain to me as the knowledge of my love for my children.

And then there was the self that knew, or came to understand, that no one else would ever believe me. Not Joseph, who checked the spot for me dozens of times, always with the insistence, "It's raw because you keep scratching it! If you leave it alone, it'll go away." Not the at-home nurse, part of a county program, who visited me a few times a week to weigh the baby and asked me to fill out questionnaires about postpartum depression. Not my gynecologist, who checked the spot after checking between my legs to see how my stitches were faring, then shrugged with indifference. No one believed me, even though the hole was deepening, ever-so-slightly widening, and by the time Stella was smiling her first smiles, I could insert my pinky finger into it, fully submerging the nail bed. So I learned to pretend. I started taking a hundred milligrams of sertraline and fifteen milligrams of aripiprazole a day and seeing a psychiatrist. The medicine helped. Sometimes I even believed the hole wasn't there, and the idea of it seemed like an absurd dream; I couldn't figure out where that other certainty came from, why it was so insidious and persistent. But that was only some of the time. The rest of the time—and this was also better—the hole was an uncomfortable fact I could choose to ignore, like my family history of breast cancer or the fact that we had still not, after eleven years, managed to start Meg a college fund.

The therapy didn't help at all. Once my medications were regulated, I stopped mentioning the hole to the doctor. I talked instead, vaguely, about sadness, about frustration with my husband over his failure to keep up with his end of the household chores. Joseph had warned me, and he was right: *If you don't get control of yourself, they're going to try to take Stella away from us.* And then, when I found the others in the Discord group, it seemed to me that our united sense of purpose about the sinkhole and the danger it posed, our duty to understand and contain it, did for me what therapy was supposed to do. It helped me to compartmentalize my anxiety about the hole in my head, to even think that the hole in my head had led me to that hole in the earth, had revealed my life's real purpose.

I realize I haven't been fully honest. One person believed me.

Stella was perhaps a month old when I was home alone with just her and my eight-year-old, Elias. Meg had gone with her dad to Walmart to get materials for her science project. Stella was sleeping, and Elias, taking advantage of the little window of solitude, had crawled in my lap to watch a Disney movie.

"El," I found myself saying. "Will you look at something for me?"

"Look at what?" he asked.

"Something on the back of my head."

"Okay," he said. No confusion, no demands for clarification. "Where at?"

I lay on my belly on the sofa, and he straddled my back. Cheek pressed to the cushion, I crawled my fingers through my hair until the hole was revealed. The air-conditioned room was cool, and I could feel the chill on the spot. *Inside* it.

"Here," I said, pointing. "What do you see?"

A silence. His hot breath on my neck. Then, a giggle.

"You have a hole in your head, Mama."

My body broke out in goosebumps. Terror, exaltation—I shuddered with it.

"A hole?" I echoed hoarsely.

"Can I put my finger in it?" he asked.

"I guess so," I told him.

Pressure against my skull. He wiggled it, and a nerve somewhere inside me thrummed like a harp string.

"How did you get a hole in your head?" Elias asked.

"I don't know, buddy."

"Do I have a hole in my head?"

"No, I don't think you do."

"Can you look?"

It suddenly seemed urgent that I do just that. I sat up, motioned for him to turn around. I ran my fingers across his scalp carefully in overlapping rows. I folded the short hair apart as if checking for lice. His beautiful little crown, blessedly intact. Not a blemish. Not even a crust of the cradle cap that had plagued him as a toddler.

"No hole," I said.

"Mama, is your hole hurting you?"

"No," I said, and it was true. It hurt me no more than the holes of my mouth or ears hurt me. Was it possible the hole was a part of me? Could an absence, a void, be a part of me?

In that moment Joseph walked in the front door with Meg, found me with my hands on Elias's head, and looked at me warily. "What's happening here?" he asked.

I rubbed my knuckles across Elias's scalp, making him giggle. "Noogies," I said quickly, before Elias could speak. And then, as if she'd sensed my need, Stella cried out from upstairs, rescuing me from her father's suspicions, and I went to her, strapped her to my chest, started to fold a basket of clean laundry.

A different day, a different meeting. We still have not reached a consensus on what to name the temple or ourselves, but we've voted unanimously on which rug runners to order from Amazon, and we've agreed to open the temple's doors to the public once a week for a fellowship session. Not a service in the traditional sense, and Richard won't be delivering a sermon, but he'll say a few encouraging words in the sanctuary, followed by a moment of silence, after which we'll congregate in the conference room for coffee, donuts, and conversation. Our relief at having settled, finally, on a course of action—any course of action—is so palpable that as the committee parts ways for the day, we're giddy, vibrating with positivity and purpose. Kesha, Wendy, and D'Shawn say they're going to head over to Toot's for beer and wings. Elsa and Connor trail behind them to the parking lot, and I assume they are finally going to sleep with each other, which is obviously a terrible idea, but I'm glad they're at last getting it out of their systems. Stella, who will no longer nap through a meeting, is back home with Joseph, and perhaps that's why Richard asks me to hang back.

"Take a walk with me," he says, motioning toward the sanctuary.

The committee meets once or twice a week, but we rarely pass the double doors into this part of the temple. It is a sacred space. It is terrible, in the oldest, purest sense of that word.

Like a tomb, the doors open with a gasp and an exhalation of cold air. It is mild outside for February—low sixties—but the late afternoon sky is clouded over, and the stone walls retain last night's chill. The sky and walls are nearly the same fish belly gray, less color than shadow. The room is silent, save for our footfalls on the polished marble floors, and that sound echoes, seems to spiral up over us and flutter, batlike, against the transparent ceiling.

We built the temple out of limestone. Bowling Green is a karst region, a city constructed on a swiss-cheese bedrock, but one of the country's biggest rock quarries operates thirty minutes southwest of us, so we hauled our temple from there to here, flatbed truck after flatbed truck, rock by rock. Limestone is a rock comprised of the disintegrated skeletons of long-dead marine animals, so we erected a tower of bones, which would focus and amplify the temple's power and further negate the cataclysmic potential of the sinkhole.

Richard is a structural engineer, and he quickly took the lead bringing the project to fruition. He oversaw crowdsourcing, wooed our two major donors, one of them a billionaire eccentric, a bit of a local celebrity, who made his fortune with a chain of climate-controlled self-storage facilities. Richard also assembled and managed the team of subcontractors. He showed us plans on his laptop: white-lined diagrams on a field of black, 3-D renderings with sunlight and shadows and tiny, blank-faced people striding across an ADA-compliant parking lot. We—the other committee members and I—gave him some notes. I recall explaining my vision to him at one point early in the process: how the square-cut stones should spiral skyward, narrowing the column slightly, and then stop before the structure could taper to a point. The roof, flat, would be constructed of clear glass to symbolize the sinkhole's possible bottomlessness. I remember all this, and I remember Richard telling me that it would be impossible to build a watertight and structurally sound roof out of only glass, but we could create the illusion with a gridwork of polycarbonate roofing sheets. Again, though, no one really knows who came up with the idea for the temple, and Richard is the one who presented the vision to us on the laptop screen, making it real before it was real. He is a rare sort of person, driven and charismatic, possessed of what he tells us are "multiple intelligences," which is to say he is creative but can also multiply three-digit numbers in his head. I suspect my own intelligences are also multiple but muted. I am average at many things, unremarkably good at a few, and excellent at none.

And he wasn't wrong about the roof, the illusion he could create. I stand in this space, craning to view that circle of sky, a shade or two paler than the walls defining it, and feel as if I have entered my vision. As if my vision were not an idea but precognition. I could not have brought this space to fruition. I couldn't have even drawn a picture of it.

"I notice," Richard says, "that each time we come in here, you look up. Everyone else looks down."

At his words, I do: look down. There had been talk, briefly, of capping the sinkhole. We could not fill it in or reinforce it, but we could (I think this was Elsa's suggestion) at least hide it and assert our dominance over it by using the space it occupied. The image that sprang into my mind at that was the scene in *It's a Wonderful Life* when George and Mary are dancing on that retractable floor over a swimming pool, and someone, as a joke, decides to open the floor, and George and Mary are so absorbed in that kicking, arm-flapping ritual of new love that they fall back into the water. Startled, then laughing.

In the end, though, no one was comfortable with the thought of letting the sinkhole hide. Watching is our responsibility, our burden.

I approach the guardrail. It's black iron—forty-two inches high, per code, with balusters spaced close enough together to keep even the tiniest determined person from slipping between them. The handrail is nice: polished brass, curved to fit comfortably against your palms. I plant my hands on it, lean over. As always, confronting the darkness, an icy sliver courses through my body. It begins in the hole at the base of my skull, slides down along my spine, jumps, changes directions, and tightens my forearms with gooseflesh. The others have told me they feel it too, or at least something similar. Elsa calls it the presence of evil. Connor talks about magnetic fields, how what we're experiencing is sensitivity to the coming flip of Earth's positive and negative poles, how the changing magnetism is responsible for the preponderance of sinkholes this century and the unprecedented span and depth of Bowling Green's in particular. Kesha blames vertigo, and Wendy says the uniformity of effect is psychological, a kind of mass hysteria. For me, the physical sensation is discomfort that verges on pleasure, like the Percocet-dulled throb I felt between my legs in the days after childbirth. I haven't shared this thought with the others.

Richard's long sleeves are folded to the middle of his forearms, which straddle the railing right next to mine. I can see the knots tightening his flesh, and I point to them, fall just short of touching them. I've grown aware that I have a mild and mildly humiliating crush on Richard, despite the fact that I don't even really like him very much.

"What do you think is causing that?" I say.

"The goosebumps?" he asks. I nod. He stands, rubs his hands and arms vigorously together. "Simplest explanation is just the cold. It's always cold."

It's true. The sanctuary is cool, as I've said, but the sinkhole exhales a deeper chill, as well as a smell, not unpleasant: damp soil and stone, and a lower note that prickles your nose hairs like the smoke of a blown-out match.

"What's a complicated explanation?"

"Which one do you want?"

"The one you buy into."

He shrugs. "I don't know if I buy into it, exactly. But what makes sense to me is that it's primal. It's the part of us that carried spears in jungles. We're attuned to danger. To harmful intent. It's our bodies' way of preparing us to fight or run."

"And instead we're standing here right beside it, looking at it."

"Well, that's evolution," Richard said. "Though I'm not sure our evolved selves are what's going to solve this thing."

"You think it can be solved?"

"I think it has to be. There's no other choice." He hunched down, gripping a baluster for balance, and flapped his hand at me in invitation. "Come down here a sec. There's something I want you to see."

Uneasy, I do.

"You have to look closely," he says. He traces his fingers across the marble tiles that abut the railing. I peer, not seeing at first, and then, as if a new lens has clicked down into place, it's obvious. The marble is creamy colored and veined with thread-thin tendrils of forest green. Among these veins, camouflaged by them, are hairline cracks. An alarming number of them, all coursing toward the hole.

I have to stop myself from jumping back and running for the sanctuary doors. "Jesus Christ," I say. "We only laid this floor a few months ago."

"The damage isn't catastrophic," Richard says. "Yet. Some settling is to be expected. But the uniformity of this damage is alarming. It's the same all the way around the hole. It suggests that a decisive widening will occur."

"A decisive widening," I echo. "Is that an engineering term?"

He laughs without humor. "No. Not at all. Physics has nothing to do with decisiveness."

I feel the beginnings of a panic attack coming on: the familiar flush, the prickling in my forehead and shins, the sensation that my heart is fluttering rather than beating, a moth obliterating itself against a security lamp. "You always talk," I say, "as if the hole's alive. As if it's—" I search for the word. "Conscious," I say, though that isn't exactly right.

"What do you think this has all been about?" He puts his hands up, indicating the temple walls. "If the sinkhole was just a sinkhole, we'd have built a wall around it and hung a Keep Out sign."

"So what are we doing?" I ask.

"Have you heard of the Sacred Cenote?" Richard asks. This is a familiar move of his when a discussion heats up: he pivots toward inscrutability. He knows that I've never heard of the Sacred Cenote, and I don't even bother to shake my head.

"It's a sinkhole on the Yucatan Peninsula," Richard says. "The Mayans used it as a site for ritual human sacrifice to their rain god."

I am trying to find the words now to explain this moment so it makes sense. Here is Richard, his slender fingertips with their buff, neatly clipped nails still pressed against the starburst of cracks on the floor. There is a dusting of dandruff on the stiff surface of his gelled hair and across the shoulders of his black shirt. There's a smeary thumbprint on the corner of his glasses' lens. A little embroidered tag on the pocket of his shirt says GEORGE, which I know to be the Walmart house brand, and there's a plain gold band on his left ring finger, though his wife, whom I've never met and he rarely mentions, is as mysterious to me as the depths of the column of darkness we're discussing. I touch the hole at the base of my skull with the pad of my middle finger. This man, this ordinary man with his musk of discount cologne, has raised the subject of human sacrifice. But—and here's the hardest thing to explain—this fact isn't precisely the trouble. My horror seems quaint, like an artifact of a long-lost time, and this is what bothers me.

"What about it," I say flatly.

He shrugs. "It's just something I've been thinking about. I've been thinking about how it must have been then, not understanding the processes of the world, the weather, the reasons for flood or drought. And then I think, well, we're still there. We still don't understand. We pretend superiority, but we still don't know anything."

"But," I stammer. "But you're not saying—"

"Of course not," Richard says. "But I remember something you said in the earliest days. On the Discord."

I can't help feeling flattered that he remembers something I said then. "What was it?"

"You said—and I remember this was what made me want to be part of this whole thing, what gave me the courage to take it seriously—that we have entered an era of unknowability, of persistent strangeness. That the old rules don't apply anymore."

"I need to get home," I say quickly, and I stand. "My husband's going to be going out of his mind."

"Of course," Richard says, standing up, too. "What's Joseph think of all this?"

I'm torn between my annoyance with my husband and the sense of loyalty I feel I owe him. "He's a Baptist," I say diplomatically. "He finds this all a bit weird. But he's supportive. He likes that it gets me out of the house."

"I suppose it does that much," Richard says. "And the kids?" he adds. We're exiting the sanctuary, and he holds one of the double doors open for me. "How are they?"

"Good. Busy. The bigger ones, I mean, with school. And Stella's talking up a storm."

"You were in college before Stella," he says. "Right?"

I nod. "I'm down to part-time now, but I'll finish in another semester. Only took me twenty years." I try to chuckle, but it comes out sounding like a cough. I feel the old impulse to try to explain my life to him, to wring sense and purpose out of what has been mostly an extended sort of blind meandering, but I bite my lip.

"You've got your hands full."

I say lightly, "Don't we all?"

"I'll be honest." Richard pauses on the temple's front steps and shoves his hands into his coat pockets. The evening is so damp that the air around us is saturated; a sheen settles on his skin. "I'm glad I never had kids. Hell of a world we're living in now. You're brave." But this sounds like an accusation, not a compliment.

I offer that coughing chuckle again, loathing him. "We didn't exactly plan for any of them. But we're glad they're here."

"Of course you are," Richard says.

If you want another example of what's wrong with me, here's a story. My college professor became famous for holding my baby. Maybe you've seen that footage too; the video went viral. In it, a kindly looking, white-haired older man, dressed as you'd expect a professor to dress in a flannel sports coat and tweed trousers, bounces a six-month-old on his hip and, never missing a beat, delivers a lesson on aggregate incomes. With his free hand, the left, he scribbles formulas on a markerboard. The baby watches him, calmly agog. At one point, she reaches out, gently tugs the professor's short beard, and you can hear the class's warm laughter.

What the video doesn't show is me, Stella's mother, forty, exhausted, chewing my thumbnail to tatters, not taking notes because I'm too afraid that the baby might puke on that beautiful flannel coat. I had her with me in class because I'd gotten a sudden call from her daycare: she puked, she has a mild fever, please come pick her up. My husband was at work. It was too late to find a sitter. And Dr. Worsham had informed me already, via email, that another absence would result in my final grade for BUS 349: Macroeconomics dropping by a third of a letter. So, in a panic, maybe even a fit of pique, I brought her to class.

What the video doesn't show is that Stella wasn't crying hard when Dr. Worsham came and grabbed her. Just fussing a little, cheeks hectic; she'd refused the nipple and started shaking her head, emphatic, no-no, and that meant sleep was close. A minute away. Seconds. And then he grabbed her. Could I have said no? It happened so quickly, and he was so decisive. I had nightmares about it later—how quickly I'd surrendered her. How easily I'd capitulated to his silent, confident demand. And yes, I'll admit it: I hated it, seeing him hailed as a hero. This is what constitutes "good news" these days: an old white man holding a baby. How generous of him. How delightful. But Stella's mother, me—I wasn't a hero. I was the middle-aged woman, the failed practitioner of birth control, who'd brought her sick baby to college, disrupting everyone else's learning experience. I got a B– in that class, the worst grade of my college career, and I hated him for that, too.

So that's another thing wrong with me: I surrender too easily. I harbor petty resentments. I make, as my husband tells me, mountains out of molehills.

Over the coming weeks, I Google "Mayan human sacrifice" and "Mayan sinkhole" and a few other combinations, some of which Google helpfully supplies based on other user searches. I do this while I'm supposed to be working. I have a paper due at the end of the semester in Ethical Issues in Entrepreneurship, and I need to assemble a PowerPoint presentation for my marketing class, but I find myself flipping every few minutes between the work tabs and my internet browser.

The Sacred Cenote doesn't look like our sinkhole. It's beautiful, a rock basin filled with turquoise water and fringed from above with flowering vines. I read that it was dredged in the early twentieth-century for artifacts, and researchers discovered the bones of more than two hundred men, women, and children—the children were believed, in their innocence, to be especially desirable—who were surrendered to the god Chaac in times of drought or famine. Feeling absurd, I type into the search field, "Did human sacrifice work?" The first hit is an article in the *Atlantic*, which seems to argue for ritual sacrifice as a kind of "social glue," one that lost prevalence as societies grew larger, more diverse, and more complex, inclined instead toward "reassuring, nonviolent religious rituals." Another article, this one from the *Washington Post*, discusses a study of how sacrificial rituals were a way to reinforce hierarchical social structures. No one entertains the idea—even to play the devil's advocate—that human sacrifices might have literally appeased a god or natural force. I expected as much. But neither is there proof that the sacrifices *didn't* work. I think about strangeness and unknowability and Google "what is in the bowling green sinkhole." Guesses, theories, speculations, but no answers. I go to WebMD and search "hole in head." The most appropriate hit is an article titled, "What causes a hole in your nasal septum?" I try Google and get an article about freshwater fish suffering from a bacterial infection. I touch the spot on the back of my skull, wondering how the dice will roll today. It's there. It has become wide enough, now, that I can slip the tip of my index finger into it up to the first knuckle.

"Quit it," Joseph says from somewhere behind me.

I jump. Drop my hand to my lap. I had thought he was upstairs in bed already, probably sleeping. It's almost midnight, and his alarm is set for 5:30.

"I saw you," Joseph says. "You're still doing it. You're driving yourself crazy. You're driving *me* crazy."

“It’s just a nervous habit,” I say, hurriedly closing the window with the article about the koi fish.

“Maybe you should go on to bed. You haven’t been getting a lot of sleep.”

“I have work due. I don’t know when else you expect me to do it. I have class all morning and the kids all afternoon, and if I don’t do the shopping and the cooking, no one would get fed.” It’s the opening gambit of an argument we’ve had hundreds, perhaps thousands of times, and assuming its familiar rhythms is almost a comfort. It’s our most diligently rehearsed duet; we perform it by heart.

“Maybe if you take a break from the Sinkhole Club,” Joseph says.

“It’s not a club,” I say.

“Cult, then,” Joseph says.

“You’ve never even once come to look at it,” I say. “You can belittle me all you want, but this is in your backyard and you’re utterly indifferent to it.”

“I don’t need to look at it,” Joseph says. “I know it’s there. I know there’s not a damn thing I can do about it. What good’s looking at it going to do? You want to go look at the sinkhole instead of being with your family. Okay, fine. You need a break. I get it, I don’t resent it. It’s been a rough couple of years. You could go to a movie by yourself or maybe do the bunko night at church. Hell, if you were having an affair I’d understand it better. I wouldn’t like it, and I’d probably want to divorce your ass, but I’d understand it. This sinkhole stuff, though. It’s nuts. It’s no different than that head thing you’ve got going on.”

“You’re right,” I say. “It isn’t.”

“I don’t know who you are anymore,” Joseph says. “I love you, but I don’t know you.”

“Neither do I,” I say.

A couple weeks ago, I drove Stella to daycare after dropping Meg and Elias off at the junior high and elementary schools. Mornings were always hard, tempers short. Meg had complained about all the food options I offered her and finally just refused to eat, claiming she’d get an energy bar later out of the vending machine. Elias, who'd snuck downstairs in the night to retrieve the Switch and stayed up until God knows when playing Minecraft, was nearly catatonic, and I had to shove him into his shirt and pants as if he were still a toddler.

Stella, the actual toddler, had chosen this morning to start asserting independence. "Ste-wah do it," she said when I tried to slip on her sneakers. "Ste-wah do it," she said, grabbing at the Velcro closures. When none of us was paying attention, she picked up Elias's glass of milk and dumped it down her front, and when she pooped her diaper just as I'd hustled the older kids out the front door and turned the key in the lock, I decided, *Screw it*. I'd take her to school, play dumb. Let them deal with it.

Stella didn't like this plan. "Ste-wah got butt-butt," she said, patting her bottom.

"It's okay," I told her, grunting, wrestling her into her car seat. "Miss Sherry will clean you up."

"God, Mom, she reeks," Meg said.

"No, no school," Stella said, twisting under the straps as I tried to shove the plastic halves of the buckle together. "Where my po-chip? I got to have it."

"Stella left her poker chip in the house," I said. "Stella can play with poker chip when she gets home."

"Ste-wah wants po-chip *right now!*"

There was a feeling inside me, with the kids sometimes—an unbearable pressure that would build and build and build, the kind that I knew could lead to violence in a person who lacked empathy or control, and it was made worse, always, by my love for them, my terror for them, as if it were their fault they were here for me to worry about. It was worse with Stella, whose arrival had upset our family's delicate balance. There weren't enough rooms in the house to go around. The car wasn't big enough. Our finances, always stretched tight, were on the verge of snapping, and I was forced to scale back to part-time at school when I was only twenty-seven hours shy of my degree. I loved her so much—more, I sometimes worried, than even Meg and Elias—but I couldn't always stand her.

Once the older kids were dropped off, I drove the last leg of the morning's journey toward Stella's daycare—the route that took me past the Temple—listening to her scream, watching in the rearview mirror as giant tears coursed down her cheeks. Then, I found myself screaming too.

Wah!!!! she shrieked, and *WAHHHH!!!!* I shrieked back. I felt out of control and also furiously righteous. I would stop only when she stopped. I could scream too. I could scream and scream and scream!

When I pulled at last into the parking lot of her school, we were both breathless and drained. Shame set in—for me, at least—and it was compounded once I pulled her from her seat and her head dropped to my shoulder, her fingers curled in my hair, and she started murmuring "Mommy Mommy Mommy," and I thought, how cruel this world is, that you have to seek comfort from the one who hurt you. Perhaps it had been wrong to bring her into such a world in the first place. To selfishly keep her here. "I'm so, so sorry," I whispered. Her diaper had leaked along the edges, watery shit that had soaked through her pants, onto the car seat cover, my hands, the bottom of my blouse as I walked her into her classroom.

Tonight, I dreamed I was in the sanctuary, playing a piano. I don't play any instruments in real life, but the dream was so convincing that I awakened confused, wondering if I'd taken lessons and somehow forgotten them, or maybe I was a virtuoso whose talent went undiscovered because I'd never had an opportunity to test it. The physical sensations of the dream were palpable, even in my shadowy small bedroom with the creaky ceiling fan whirling, pilled floral bedspread twisted between my legs, snoring husband a blocky shadow, lying, back to me, on the bed's other side. I could still imagine the flashes of moonlight across my pale hands, which fluttered rapidly back and forth across the keys. I could feel the music as it crashed against the temple walls and sank down into the sinkhole, mesmerizing the sleeping beast lying somewhere in its depths. In the dream, the hole in the back of my head wasn't a wound or an absence or a sign of decay. It was like the space inside a flute or a whistle, a chamber for vibration, a vessel for beauty.

When the dream broke up, I knew what I must do.

I slipped out of bed and dressed quickly, by feel, in yesterday's clothes. Stella's crib was in our bedroom, still, and I paused, hands wrapped over the edge of the rail, and looked down at her. It seemed to me that she belonged, still, on my chest, where she'd spent so much of her short life, her sweet, damp heat wrapped tightly against my thundering heart. I picked her up, considering, and if she had settled down again—well, I might have taken her with me. And it might have been the right thing to do. But she grunted and twisted, trying to roll back onto her stomach, so I kissed her very softly on the temple, hunched down, and let her weight settle back against the mattress. She inhaled deeply, then sighed.

I was almost out the door when I realized my car keys weren't in my purse—proof that the world can be strange, but endings are always ordinary. I found them behind a couch cushion, one of Stella's favorite hiding spots, along with a scattering of her other treasures: a tube of lip balm, one of my old, expired credit cards, a handful of holly berries from the bush in our backyard. And—I had to swallow hard against the ache rising in my chest—her poker chip. I slid the poker chip into my jeans pocket, reassured by the texture of its ridges against my thumb.

I'm holding it now, for luck. I will admit that I am frightened, but I find a small measure of courage in this truth: I lost myself in my children long ago. They are the first abyss I plummeted into. And it still seems possible to me as I stand here, toes gripping the edge of the opening, arms spread along the railings and the fingertips of my free hand bent against the balusters, that Richard is wrong, and the sinkhole isn't some god that demands appeasement. Instead, I will fall and fall and fall until falling becomes flight, and later, from some heavenly vantage point, I will see my children again, and I will know what to do, how to save them all.

exhaust

1.

They had risen early, in the dark, and loaded their car as silently as they could, though the guest room was upstairs, right across the hall from Alan's parents, and the hardwood floors rasped under even the lightest and most careful of steps. Toby followed at her ankles as he always did: downstairs to the car, back up to the room as she conducted her last once-over. When she got on her knees to check underneath the bed for one of Alan's stray athletic socks, which had a way of worming themselves out of sight until every suitcase was zipped tight and stowed away, the dog put his long snout behind her right ear and snorted. Elise laid a distracted hand on his thick collar of fur, scratched.

"All clear," she whispered to him. The dog backed up and came forward again, his long tail making a low, nervous wag, toenails scratching the floor. He followed the progress of the suitcases and stayed close, as though he suspected that Elise would leave him behind, given the opportunity.

She stripped the bed because she knew that Alan would not think to do it. The sheets, she wadded into a pile and set on the floor; the quilt, she folded neatly and centered at the foot of the bed. She tweezed dog hairs off it with her thumb and forefinger, knowing that her mother-in-law would see them later and comment. *That's what you get when your grandbaby's a dog*, she had said more than once, in a voice that was supposed to be joking but wasn't. Cynthia pretended to enjoy Toby—patted her lap when she was watching television in her old blue recliner, winced when the dog took her up on the offer and plopped all forty-five pounds of himself on top of her. *Lord have mercy*, she would say, her face for a single second open and annoyed before contorting into its familiar expression of genial exasperation. Always the same routine.

They had made it to the foyer, their last and lightest bags shouldered, when Cynthia appeared at the top of the staircase in her long pink nightgown, robe, and matching terrycloth house shoes, the kind that slipped on and left her thick, yellowed toenails exposed. She had donned her glasses but was lifting them to rub her eyes, as if she were Cindy-Lou Who and the Grinch himself was traipsing around downstairs, ruining her holiday fun.

“Mom, we told you just to sleep in,” Alan said. “We’re practically out the door.”

“Don’t you want some coffee? Some eggs and toast?” she said. She started heavily down the steps, clutching the banister for support. “I don’t know why on earth you have to be on the road this early, anyway.”

Elise, as was her habit, stayed silent. Alan sighed and glanced between them. “We have to stop twice to charge the car, and we want to beat the bad weather. We told you that. We both have work in the morning.”

“I still don’t understand why you got a car like that. What if the charger’s broke? What will you do then?”

“We have an app on our phone,” Alan said. “Someone used it yesterday with no problem. The charger’s fine.”

“At least take a cup of coffee with you,” Cynthia said, already moving toward the kitchen. “I don’t think I could sleep now if I tried. You hear every little peep in this house.” This, too, was a refrain of hers, and Elise reminded Alan of it every time he tried to put a move on her in the creaky brass guest bed, when he insisted that he’d be really quiet, that no one would know a thing.

“Cynthia, we can just grab something when we stop to charge,” Elise said. “I don’t think I could stomach coffee just yet anyway.”

“I can’t believe the price those places charge for coffee,” Cynthia said. “Four dollars for coffee and milk.”

"Mom, we're not going to spend four dollars on coffee," Alan said. "It won't take five minutes to perk."

Elise played her trump card. "The forecast is looking bad in West Virginia. I know you wouldn't want us driving through the mountains right as the snow hits."

"All right, all right," Cynthia said. She put out her arms and waved her hands at Alan, beckoning him for a hug. He surrendered to her, letting her fold him against the bulk of her heavy breasts and smack his cheek with loud, cartoonish kisses. She subjected Elise to the same treatment, a ritual that had always made her cringe with discomfort. She hadn't come from such demonstrative stock as this. Alan's family—his mother and father, his three older brothers, who had wives of their own and eight kids among them, a mostly pale, red-haired crop of lanky giants like their fathers—were boisterous and exhausting, and they treated holidays and family reunions like performances, as if a hidden camera were trained on them all, recording the fun. To be embraced by Cynthia was so intimate as to constitute a kind of violation: those enormous breasts, so evidently braless through the thin nylon nightgown and matching robe; the oily, artificially sweet scent of the bath beads she used each night in the tub; her damp lips pressed against Elise's cheek, coming so close to her mouth that their noses nearly brushed like lovers in a movie. On the long drive between Pittsburgh and Charlotte, Elise would have time to feel guilty about her distaste for this woman, who, despite her bullheadedness and sometimes outright obnoxiousness, was her husband's mother—and a very good one, Alan had always insisted. But for now she narrowed her shoulders and drew into herself, patting Cynthia's back half-heartedly.

"If only you didn't live so far off," Cynthia said, clutching her, breath as moist against her ear as Toby's was. "I'll never get used to you living down in the South like that. Elise, your parents must be so grateful to see as much of you as they do."

Elise's parents lived in Asheville, two hours from her and Alan's home in Charlotte, and Elise saw them perhaps once or twice a year more often than she saw Alan's parents. This explanation had not worked the first dozen times she had made it to Cynthia, however, so she did not bother now. She just smiled tightly as she extricated herself from the hug and bent down to hook Toby's collar with his short red travel leash. "Tell Steve we said bye."

"It's a shame he couldn't see you off," she said. "But he needs his sleep. Him, he could sleep through the second coming. Me, I couldn't sleep now if I tried. I hear every peep in this house."

"Just lie back down," Alan said. "You might be surprised."

"I won't sleep for worrying. I hate to imagine you on the road all that way. Please promise me you won't speed on those hills. And promise to call me the second you make it home."

"Promise," Alan said, kissing her cheek, and Elise fought an eye roll. *These are little things that she asks for*, Alan had said once to her, and he was usually right. It was a phone call. It wasn't the end of the world. But Cynthia had been hard on her early in her relationship with Alan, and Elise was not good, apparently, at letting go of old grievances.

They made it out the door finally, got Toby situated in his bed in the backseat. The car was toasty warm, the windows defrosted; Alan had thought to start it when he brought down the first of the suitcases. It was one of those marital trade-offs: Alan thought to start the car, Elise thought to strip the bed, and she tried not to be too cynical about how their roles occasionally divided along such conventional lines. Cynthia stood in the doorway, waving, and Elise felt instantly lighter—as if she could breathe for the first time in three days, her every action not scrutinized and commented on ("Why are you in the kitchen, dear? Did you want something?"), her lack of apparent enthusiasm regularly noted ("I sometimes think it would take winning the lottery to get a smile out of this one"), her politics lamented ("And I suppose you think Hillary would have done a better job?"). More than that, she was released from witnessing her husband's indignities, for a man of thirty-three should not have to wrestle off his forty-year-old brother, grappling with him until their shirts pull loose from their belted khakis and the tops of their tidy whities show and they almost knock over their mother's coffee table, should he? Or reassure his mother in four different ways that he had enjoyed the overly salted rib roast she had cooked this year in place of the Thanksgiving turkey. Or defy his usual calm and thoughtful nature, the nature Elise had fallen in love with, to try to rise to the hyperbolic grandiosity of his kin so that no meal was merely good but "the best thing I ever put in my mouth" and no traffic ever bad but "completely at a standstill" and no victory at canasta ever worth less than a triumphant procession around the living room to raucous cheers and boos, invisible scepter in hand? To spend a weekend with Alan's family was to see a side of him that he had kept hidden during the two years of their courtship, a side that he now packed away most of the year like that heavy goose down coat that he bought long ago for a Pittsburgh winter but used only once or twice in North Carolina.

They were approaching the I-79 on-ramp when Alan offered the opening gambit of their ritual eight-hour, post-Thanksgiving bickering. In another thirty minutes it might have been Elise—she might have cracked in the silence and muttered, "Your mother knows good and well that we don't see my folks all that much more often than we see her and your dad," at which point Alan would have rebounded with, "She didn't mean anything by it," to which Elise would have said, clenching the steering wheel and everything else, "When *doesn't* she mean anything by it?" But no, Alan beat her to it this time. As Elise signaled her turn onto the ramp and accelerated as she started looking over her shoulder to check for oncoming traffic—pointless at this ungodly hour, the sun still hours to the east—he said, "You know, I wouldn't have minded having some coffee and breakfast. We should have just let her make it." And something cruel and furious bloomed in Elise, but there was a spiteful joy in it too, and she put her foot down heavily on the pedal, going eighty-five in the empty Sunday darkness, aware somewhere deep, deep within her that this argument would get them at least as far as their first charging stop in Morgantown, and then they could just put on a podcast to pass the time.

2.

Their cell signals were weak in the mountains, so Alan started flipping through radio stations as they got back onto the interstate after charging. They each had coffees from a gas station, filled dutifully in their insulated travel mugs, and Alan occasionally passed Elise a bite of a stale blueberry muffin. Even this, in the acrimony of their recent argument, was a concession to him that she hated to make: taking food from his hand. But she was hungry, and she did not want to try to drive and disentangle the plastic wrapper at the same time, so she allowed it. Finally, with her stomach quiet, her shoulders and the set of her jaw loosened enough for her to say, when he rolled to the strongest signal on the dial yet—"Holly Jolly Christmas," some kind of awful, mixed-up, rock'n'roll version with lots of guitar brandishes—"Well, they don't waste any time, do they?" He agreed that they didn't. The silence became companionable, and Alan didn't change the station, though the subsequent Christmas song was just as grating. It was cheerful noise in the gloom, and though it was a little after 5:00 a.m. now, the sky was overcast enough that there was still not much sun, just a vague haze to the left of them, like the brief glow of a television screen after it has been shut off.

These trips were always stressful. They brought out the worst in her, and though they didn't bring out the worst in Alan—Elise wasn't convinced that he had a truly bad side; his darkest self was the one that cried, "Eat it!" when he beat her hand in a Randolph family penny poker game—they made him a little spacier, a bit less thoughtful than usual. He became, in the presence of his bullying big brothers, her own bullying big brother, teasing and pestering, needling her with comments that he knew would set her off, like one about his mother making coffee and breakfast. And all of this, after eight years together, hit a little too close to home. It was on these long drives to and from their families that their most naked fears about the marriage surfaced. On drives such as these, Elise had admitted tearfully that she resented shouldering most of the burden of the housekeeping, though she and Alan both worked full-time. ("Just tell me what to do and I'll do it," Alan said, sweetly earnest but somehow missing the point all the same.) And Alan, on another trip—or hell, maybe it had been the same one—had said, "I'd appreciate it if I didn't have to have a special occasion and a bottle of wine to get a goddamn conjugal visit." They argued about their jobs, about how to spend their money and where to spend their free time. Less often, they argued about politics—they were more or less on the same page, except when they weren't—and religion, because Alan had the occasional pang of Catholic guilt, most often immediately after weekends among his staunchly churchgoing kin. "I really ought to find a parish in Charlotte," he'd say, fishing for an offer from Elise to join him, and her response was always an even but wary, "Yes, of course you should. If that's what you want."

Alan reclined his seat and closed his eyes. "God. I'm tired."

"You falling asleep on me?"

"Trying not to," he muttered. He twisted in the seat and grimaced. "That guest bed kills me. My back can't take it anymore."

"We're getting old for all of this."

"Old." He snorted.

"Guest beds. Living out of suitcases." She saw the distant glow of headlights in her rearview mirror. "They treat us like children. My parents, too."

"And will until we have children," Alan said.

"So forever, then." She shot a glance at him.

He put his hands out in a "what can you do" gesture, eyes still closed. "Yeah. Probably."

Their small car hummed with eerie silence, and Elise checked the charge. The electric car was her idea and her baby, but range anxiety was real, and the span between here and the nearest supercharger took them to the edge of their predicted mileage. She fiddled with the heater, eyes darting between the road and the accessories panel. If she shut the heat off completely, it looked like they could get another ten-mile cushion.

"We have plenty of charge to get to Beckley."

"I know. I'm just being cautious."

"It's already getting cold in here," Alan said, and Elise snapped, half kidding, "Oh, man up," but he was right. It was in the sixties back home according to the weather app on her phone, but this part of West Virginia had decided it was winter.

The lights in her rearview mirror were approaching with almost startling speed. Elise checked the speedometer—she was going just under eighty, so the vehicle, which was now passing her with ease, must have been doing ninety-five, at least. The car was long, white, not old but not new. Elise couldn't venture a guess at the make, having never been a car aficionado, and it occurred to her too late to make a meaningful adjustment that it was the kind of boxy, bulky, gas-guzzling vehicle that might well be an unmarked police car. She braked out of habit—needlessly, because the car sped off ahead, and she noted before it did that the car had a West Virginia plate. The tailpipe chugged out blue, oily-smelling smoke.

"Fucker," she said. "Hope you break down."

Alan grunted and opened an eye. "Huh?"

"Nothing," she said. "Your coffee's going to get cold."

He had his arms across his chest and his coat covering him like a blanket. Even with the seat set as far back as possible, his long legs were folded awkwardly against the glove box. "Just a nap," he said.

"Uh huh."

"Just some beauty rest, and I'll drive us the rest of the way home, promise."

He was already mostly checked out, so she exhaled loudly and focused all her attention on the road, though there wasn't much to see now that the white car had disappeared ahead. The landscape at this hour was beautiful in a kind of apocalyptic sort of way, everything gray and falling off sharply on both sides of the road, only to rise ominously a bit farther out, carving craggy silhouettes into a dun-colored sky. Autumn, still clinging to the trees back in Charlotte, was gone here. As if in confirmation of this observation, a flake of snow hit Elise's windshield, followed immediately by another, and another—the weather system she had seen forecast yesterday on the news. "Look," she wanted to tell Alan, but his breathing had already gotten nasal and stretched out, and she knew that he would not appreciate the sight as much as she did. Snow had not been a novelty to him growing up—"More of a pain in the ass," he'd told her, "and they almost never canceled school."

She looked over her shoulder at Toby. He too was asleep, gray nose tucked into his tail. Her boys. Her tired boys. She was tired too, so she sipped her coffee and tried very hard not to feel so lonesome. She wanted to turn the dial off the Christmas station and cue up one of her podcasts but was afraid that doing so would startle Alan, so she listened to that waitresses' song with the monotonous hook that she knew she'd have stuck in her head for the rest of the day, a little pleased with it despite herself. The way Alan would have been pleased with the snow despite himself. There were things in a life that you appreciated because they had their time and their place and pretty much left you alone otherwise: snow, Christmas carols, distant family.

She turned a curve and braked suddenly because the taillights appeared out of nowhere, the car they belonged to going slowly enough that Elise wondered for a moment if it wasn't getting ready to pull onto the shoulder with a flat. She signaled and floated into the left lane, heart thumping; she had put her hand on her chest, a prissy, uncalculated gesture that made her laugh at herself a little. "Jesus," she hissed as she went ahead, and she saw that the car was the white one from before, the one that had been going ninety-something and passed her as if she were sitting still. A Chevy Impala—she could read the make as she cruised past. She looked ahead again, feigning disinterest as Alan's window lined up with that of the other car's driver; she didn't want to be caught staring. She was satisfied, though, that the car wasn't pitching to the left or right—there were no obvious signs of distress—so she applied enough speed to get ahead of it and tried to scope out the driver in her rearview. She couldn't see much, but she felt certain the person was male. Probably texting. She hoped that the braking had roused Alan so that she could complain to him, but he murmured and shifted and didn't open his eyes. She resumed going eighty and started watching for the exit to Highway 19.

Alan accused her, jokingly, of road rage. She took other people's driving personally and held short-term grudges; if the car that cut her off in tight two-lane traffic later got caught behind a semi so that she could roll past it, the tortoise to its hare, she cackled triumphantly and told Alan, "That's what you get when you don't have any patience." When a car rode her bumper, she started braking so sharply that Toby would get up in the backseat, circle, and drop with a huff, as though voicing disapproval. It was, like the bickering, something to do, a way to occupy the mind on a long trip; she could admit that much.

But when the lights of the Impala flashed brightly again in her mirror, bearing down on her as quickly as it had the first time it passed her, Elise felt not rage but a tremor of unease. The Impala was fucking with her. Maybe it was her and Alan's bumper stickers, which were a little bit crunchy but not outright political. They'd bought this car after the election, trading in the Bernie Sanders sticker still attached to their old Toyota, and she hadn't had the courage yet to replace it with a candidate for 2020. She had been stupid and optimistic last time; she was superstitious now. So no outright politics, then, though she supposed your average MAGA guy could take offense at BE GOOD TO EACH OTHER and THANK YOU, SCIENCE! and for that matter, your average MAGA guy might take offense at the fact she was driving an electric car, period. God forbid she not perfume the mountains with her blue smoke.

Perhaps, with Alan slumped down so low in the passenger seat, she looked like a woman alone, and that realization made her yet again want to rouse her husband. But no—that was stupid. The exit ramp to 19 was a mile ahead according to the signs, and she could very well make it that far without calling on Alan like a goddamn damsel in distress. What she felt now was the sensation of waking in the middle of the night after a bad dream—she had always been a restless sleeper and even, until her midtwenties, a sleepwalker, and her nightmares were vivid enough to this day that they sometimes left her sobbing—and saw Alan, a foot away that might as well have been light-years, sleeping so deeply that her cries hadn't reached him. She would think about waking him, knowing that he would embrace and comfort her and not even be grumpy about it. But her higher reason always kept her silent and trembling, because she didn't want to disturb his sleep on a work night and because she should, as a grown woman, be able to talk herself out of the heebie-jeebies. It wasn't Alan's responsibility to do that for her. Not then, not now.

She slowed to sixty-five and fixed her eyes ahead as the car inched around her. The driver was taking his time, she thought—she felt his eyes on her, but she refused to even glance to her left. She turned, pretended to fiddle with the dial on the radio, as if there were nothing unusual about this game of leapfrog they were playing on an almost empty interstate, as if the coffee she had drunk wasn't making a bitter bile in the back of her throat. The car finally sped up and pulled ahead, though it was matching Elise's speed now in the left lane. She saw with relief the exit ramp for 19 and, out of habit, out of respect for an ordered universe, put her signal on, bearing the steering wheel to the right. That would be the end of it, she thought. The driver of the Impala had amused himself with her, had made the time pass by frightening her, but his signal wasn't on now—he wasn't even in the righthand lane—so their paths would diverge, and Elise would take the road slightly less traveled by. Goodbye and good riddance.

Her wheels had just grazed the seam between the interstate and exit when an engine revved and a flash of white swooped in from her left, darting across her vision so quickly that it took her a second to register that the Impala had cut her off, was now slowing ahead of her into the 360-degree turn downhill. *Real*, she thought. *Oh my god, this is real.* She could smell singed rubber. As the ramp straightened into the four-lane highway, the Impala put on speed again, a bright square of white in what had become a flurry of fat flakes that melted against the hot glass of Elise's windshield. She put on her wipers and kept her speed low, topping out at fifty-five. She wiped her damp palms on her blue jeans. Ahead, the white car's rearview lights were dwindling, but she didn't allow herself to hope this time that the driver of the

Impala had decided to continue his trip and forget about her. What was worse, she wondered, having him in front of her or behind? Her mind was going wild—she imagined him hidden up ahead, in one of the turn-offs the cops used to trap speeders. Or what if he fell back again, and she had to see those headlights widening in her rearview mirror like startled eyes once more, and instead of passing her, he bumped her? Forced her off the road? What then?

For a while—she didn't register how long—she drove stiffly, hands at ten and two, jaw set. She slowed into turns. The scenery on 19 had always been her favorite part of the trip to and from Pittsburgh, and the snow rendered it more startling, but she could barely look at it; her vision had narrowed to the column of gray road ahead of her, and everything else was dark and distant, her tongue thick and dumb in her mouth. A vehicle approached in the opposite lane of traffic, and she flinched, thinking that he had made a U-turn to come back to her, but the lights belonged to an old green pickup truck with a covered bed and an attached ladder, and it passed on as quickly as Elise had spotted it.

When the taillights appeared ahead again—and she knew them to be the Impala's now, those four red circles like cigarette burns—she was almost relieved. It had been worse not knowing where it was. She slowed, reluctant to pass it again, and shook Alan's shoulder.

"Alan."

"Hmm."

"Wake up."

"Hmm?" He roused in that way he had, abrupt and decisive, rubbing his face briskly, as though he had been caught snoozing in school and didn't want to get the ruler across his knuckles. "What, yes? We stopping?"

Elise saw that she was down now to fifty miles an hour. "No." She pointed at the Impala. "This guy's been screwing with me."

His voice was suddenly sharp, interested. "Speed up and get around him. Leave him behind."

"You don't understand," she said, surprised at the hoarseness of her own voice, the lump in her throat. "I've passed him a couple of times. He speeds up again, gets way off ahead, and then slows down. He's doing it again. He's going to keep slowing down until I have to pass him."

Alan leaned forward and lifted his seat back into position. "Just get around the guy. It's probably some teenager. I'll stare him down as we pass."

"Please don't be confrontational. Please, Alan. He's freaking me out."

"All the more reason. Speed up."

She put on the gas: sixty, sixty-five. The white car sped up, too.

"Just punch it," Alan said.

"I'm not going to punch it."

"Punch it, dammit! Do you want to be dealing with this guy all the way to Beckley?"

She let out a shuddering breath and slammed down her foot. The car lunged forward, again with that weird electric silence, and Toby—she had forgotten about him—barked in his grouchy, anxious way. She was up to eighty now, eighty-five. The Impala stayed two cars' lengths ahead. Ninety. Elise knew that the Impala probably had at least six cylinders, that she wouldn't be able to outrace it if the driver was determined not to let them. They were doing a trembling ninety-five now, and out of habit she glanced at the car's efficiency indicator and saw, predictably, that they were in the red. If they kept this speed much longer, they definitely wouldn't make it to the next supercharger.

"Alan—"

"Keep going. I think he's coming off the gas some."

"Dammit, Alan!" she shrieked, and she was lucky that she had refocused her eyes on the Impala's back end because she saw his taillights brighten in barely enough time to brake herself and make a sharp turn to the left lane. Toby fell heavily into the floorboard with a howl, jostling the back of Elise's seat. "Go, go, go," Alan was saying, and she laid down on the pedal again, not daring to look to the right at the driver or even at Alan, because she heard the first trace of real fear in his voice just then, and that meant that this was serious, that she hadn't just been working herself into a panic over nothing, and she didn't want to see her terror mirrored in his expression.

They raced through a fringe of snow, headlights barely picking out the road ahead. Alan had gotten Toby back into his bed and hooked the seatbelt through the dog's harness (*Why didn't we do that before? What were we thinking?*), and Toby seemed, Alan said, unharmed but terrified. "He's shaking pretty bad," he said, and Elise longed to be somewhere she could hold the dog, put her face into his soft collar of fur, but there was only the road and the snow and the son of a bitch somewhere behind them, and she had no sense of time or distance any longer.

Alan took out his cell phone. Elise kept checking her mirror for headlights.

"Are you calling the cops?" Elise said.

"I didn't get his plate down. I wasn't thinking." He jabbed the home button, his hand shaking, and looked at the screen. "Fuck this state. It says No Service."

"What did he look like?"

Alan shrugged and shook his head. The gestures seemed to Elise more like distracted dismissal than refutation.

Fifteen minutes later they passed a REDUCED SPEED AHEAD sign, and the land started to flatten out in front of them. Elise could see security lights, billboards. They were at Summersville already, the town still sluggish but not sound asleep, and Elise turned off into the parking lot of a shopping center, not bothering to signal, and didn't stop until their car was cloistered among others parked around a McDonald's, which was as well lit and welcoming as any oasis. She would probably feel stupid in another hour or two, as the day brightened and more cars joined them on the road, as the holiday travelers they had been hoping to avoid finally roused from their slumbers and decided, like Elise and Alan, to beat the snow while they had the chance. In another hour or two, her game of cat and mouse with the Impala would have the texture of a nightmare, would break up and become senseless, anecdotal, something she and Alan would share with their friends over drinks back in

Charlotte. The day the hillbilly chased them out of the hills. A dispatch from the land of coal and opiates. But for now, Elise unbuckled her seatbelt and burst into tears, and when Alan tried to put his arms around her she shoved him away. She cried until she was husked out, parched and ravenous, until her hands and legs stopped trembling. When Alan unhooked the seatbelt from his harness and Toby leaped into the front seat and into her lap, she held him tightly and scratched his chest, and his heartbeat was so strong it pulsed under Elise's fingertips. "I'm sorry," she murmured to him. The dog's breath was bad, worse for all the panting he had been doing, but the smell was comforting.

"I'm going in for food," she said after a while. "Do you want anything?"

Alan was looking at his phone. "I have a strong signal now."

3.

Alan took the driver's seat so that Elise could eat. She had gotten him a biscuit, but he waved it off. "Not hungry," he said. After the surprise of her ravenousness in the McDonald's parking lot, Elise found herself only picking at her own biscuit and passing tastes back to Toby, who was finally settling down. The snow kept falling, but the light was stronger now, and they passed or were passed by enough cars that Elise's heart finally stopped thudding at the mere sight of them. She still felt wrong, though—unsettled. She thought perhaps that it was embarrassment, and she could sense this radiating off Alan, certainly; he hinted, in his quiet, careful way, that she had caught him off guard by rousing him from sleep so suddenly, infecting him with her hysteria.

"We both overreacted," he said, but Elise knew that the "we" was politeness. "I woke up with my heart just skittering away. I didn't know what was going on."

She peeled a rind of fat off her country ham and passed it to the backseat. Toby took it from her fingers delicately, never even grazing her with his teeth, then licked the back of her hand.

"I'm not saying that he wasn't some kind of redneck asshole. He was driving dangerously, for sure."

"We almost slammed into him going ninety." She had forgotten to get a drink at the McDonald's, and the dregs of her coffee were cold. She rubbed her tongue against the roof of her mouth, grimacing at the pasty taste of flour and salt. "I don't think I overreacted to that. You were the one telling me to put the goddamn pedal to the metal."

"I've already admitted that I wasn't doing my clearest thinking." This was rare testiness from Alan—his knuckles were white against the steering wheel. "So we might as well let it go."

"And you don't want to call the cops anymore."

"No. I don't want to call the cops."

Alan babied the car, driving a sedate sixty miles an hour, five under the posted speed limit. The snow had already covered the surrounding hills in an unblemished layer, and it blew across the highway like sand. Elise could not believe that it wasn't yet 7:00 a.m., but that's what the screen read, the numbers a reminder of the sane world they had reentered, a world where couples driving home from Thanksgiving faced dangers of a more predictable sort: like this weather, which appeared to be worsening, and the roads, which would soon be getting slick. They were about fifty miles from the supercharger and the car's mileage prediction was sixty-one, with a maximum of seventy and a minimum of forty-seven. They'd shut the heat and the seat warmers off again in Summersville, and her feet and fingers were cold.

"You still want to stop at the Gorge?" Alan asked.

The highway took them across the eerie expanse of the New River Bridge, and their ritual, always on the more spiritually wearying return trip, had been to stop at the visitors' center, which was almost exactly at the halfway point between Pittsburgh and Charlotte, and walk Toby down to the lookout. The lookout was where Alan had proposed to her seven years ago, on the tail end of another trip to visit his family, the first. Later, she would make jokes about test runs and auditions, would accuse him of having to get Cynthia's OK before sealing the deal. The truth of the matter was not so far off from that: He'd had to ask his mother for the family ring she promised him, and Cynthia had not handed it over until the end of the weekend, when she'd told Alan—in his poorer judgment he'd shared this conversation with Elise, though at least not during the proposal itself—"I expect her to give that back if things go sour between you two."

It was a stunning ring, though—a full carat rose-cut diamond set in a delicately filigreed platinum band—and the day he'd given it to her was gorgeous too: summer, very green and lush, vibrating with life. He had not planned to propose at the Gorge, he told her, though the view of the bridge and the valley was pretty enough. He had aimed to take her back to Charlotte, make a reservation and a plan, wear a suit, buy roses. But they had found themselves alone, despite the fine weather, the view, and the dozen cars in the parking lot, and—this is what he had told her, holding both of her hands tightly in his, then fumbling in his pocket for the ring, which his mother had folded into a business envelope with a blue security print on the inside—he didn't want to go back to Charlotte with that secret in his heart.

Now Elise considered his question. She didn't think that they had ever missed a stop to the Gorge on their way back home, and skipping felt momentous, in its way. That Elise was still a little angry with Alan—still frustrated that he had discounted the aggression of the white car as her hysteria—made her less certain that she was qualified to make the choice for them.

"What do you want to do?" she said finally. "I mean, it's bad out. The roads are going to keep getting worse. But Toby hasn't been walked since we left this morning."

"He could hold off until we stop to charge."

They were doing that thing they so often did: putting out neutral comments until they thought they had successfully gauged the other's wishes. Elise suspected that Alan wanted to keep moving.

"That's fine with me. If it's what you want to do."

He drove silently for a moment, his jaw working. "Might as well stop," he said. "I've got to take a leak."

"Visitor's center won't be open yet."

He looked at her and lifted an eyebrow.

"All right, all right," she said. "Do it in the woods, like a manly man." She sat up in the seat a little, surprised at her gladness. "The walkway will be pretty in the snow. We've never seen it that way."

"Well, we should, then."

"Yes, we should."

In another ten minutes, just before reaching the bridge, Alan signaled left. A snowplow was parked on the highway's shoulder, chugging exhaust. One car crossed the bridge in their direction, going a snail's pace, so there was more than enough time to turn.

"We'll have to make it quick this time," Alan said. "I'll feel better when we're over the bridge."

"Looks like they keep it clearer than the rest of the road."

"They have to. I wouldn't want to be the car to get in a fender bender on it."

The parking lot was unblemished when they pulled into it, theirs the first set of tracks. The security lights were still running, but the station itself was dim. Alan parked in a spot close to the entrance.

"I'm going to try the building first," Alan said. "Sometimes these places let you get into the bathrooms even if the other part's closed."

"Want me to wait?"

"Nah." He pocketed the keys and unhooked his seatbelt. "Go on with Toby if you want. I don't think I feel like hoofing it all the way down those steps, anyway. If the building's closed I'll just find a spot behind it."

"You sure?"

"Yeah."

Elise climbed out of the car and slipped into her coat and gloves. Toby, in the backseat, was straining against where they had last buckled him in. "Hold your horses, hold your horses," she said, opening the rear door. She rummaged around the floorboard until she found Toby's leash and hooked his collar. As soon as the seatbelt was unbuckled, he leapt out of the car and pranced in a circle, then plunged his snout into a thicker drift of snow. "I always forget how much he loves this weather," she said. Alan was slamming his door shut, and the lights flashed as he locked all the doors.

"Takes after you," he said. They met at the trunk and exchanged a quick kiss. Alan pulled up the hood on Elise's coat. "Keep your ears warm, woman."

"What about your ears?"

He rubbed them briskly. "I'm used to this weather. I had to walk through it barefoot to get to school."

They split as they approached the sidewalk, Elise and Toby to the right, Alan left, toward the visitors' center. "Find you in a sec," Alan said. His freckled cheeks were already bright pink, and he looked very young. "Watch your step down there."

"I will," Elise said.

She was grateful, following Toby down the plank walkway, that she and Alan had talked themselves into stopping. It was wonderfully silent in the early morning hours, the snow falling in a thick whisper, the Gorge, more visible at this height with the trees shed of their leaves, blanketed in mist. The cold wasn't even that bad; it was one of those utterly windless snows, the flakes in suspension around her as if finely threaded, parting as she walked forward and not melting against her gloves or her warm skin. She bent down to rub the ridge of thicker fur running down Toby's back and into his salt-and-pepper plume of tail, enjoying the smell he got when he ran, a cologne of exertion. He smelled very strong and alive, and he looked it, bounding ahead until the leash stopped him, then jumping up on a bench, sniffing intently through the cover of snow. The world had become a giant present for him to unwrap, secret smells sheathed in cold. His pleasure was Elise's.

The walkway descended steeply down, making sharp twists to the left and the right, and Elise took short, halting steps after Toby. "Whoa, boy," she kept saying, yanking back on his leash, but he was in rare form, the snow and adventure setting off something manic in him. The steps didn't seem to be slippery yet, but she clung to the railing, sweeping snow off it as she and Toby progressed to the lowest level, where the path ended in a platform with an excellent view of the arch bridge and river below, though everything now was obscured in an almost mystical veil of snow—more beautiful, in a way, than the scene at the height of summer. She stopped to rest, arms propped on the railing; Toby, down by her knees, was pushing his nose between posts, head bobbing with the intensity of his breathing. She wished that Alan would join them down here, but the walk up was tiring, and he wasn't as in shape as he once was, back when he proposed to her and they had ascended to the car hand in hand, barely winded. She guessed that neither of them was, for that matter, though she tried to run enough times a week to keep the waistband on her oldest pair of blue jeans buttoned. There were places in the world, and even in a marriage, that you eventually lost the energy to reach. She knew that her own turn would come.

The snow, no longer magic, was melting into her coat now, chilling her. She brushed what she could off her arms and hood and turned with Toby to the steps, bracing herself for the ascent. After four hours in the car, he hadn't yet expended his pent-up energy, and she let him drag her up the first two flights. She moderated her breaths, in through the nose, out through the mouth, and she made it halfway up before forcing Toby to a sit and propping her palms on her knees. She looked up and saw, at the street-level lookout, the shape of Alan. "There's your pop," she told Toby. "Go get him." She unhooked the leash from his collar and laughed breathlessly as he tore up the steps, tags jingling cheerfully, toenails ringing against the wood boards. Much more slowly, she followed. She felt sluggish plodding through the snow, heavy in her winter coat. Her calves and thighs were burning by the time she reached the last flight.

"Not up for a little cardio, I take it," she said when she finally reached the landing, her cheeks warm with exertion, and the words landed awkwardly as she realized that the man bending over to scratch Toby behind the ears was a good foot shorter than Alan and wearing a blue baseball cap. She swallowed against the ache in her throat and took a deep, hitching breath. "Oh," she said breathlessly. "Oh my god, I'm so sorry. I thought you were my husband."

The man patted Toby on the hindquarters and pulled to a stand, smiling in a friendly sort of way. "No problem. We were just visiting."

"Thank you," she said, not quite appropriately, sure that her face was redder than ever. She clapped her hands at Toby. "Over here, boy." Panting in that way that looked like an ear-to-ear grin, he obliged, and she snapped the leash to his collar before he could get away from her. "I hope he didn't pounce on you. He doesn't know a stranger."

"If he knew a stranger, then he wouldn't be strange," the man said.

Elise laughed politely. "You make a good point."

The man hunched down and held out a bare hand; the other, gloved, was clasping the glove's mate. Toby came forward tentatively, as if Elise's presence had made him self-conscious, and sniffed. "That's fine, boy, c'mon," the man said, and the dog leaned against his knee, angling himself into the scratching hand. The leash was taut now, marking a line of six feet. Elise felt, as she often did when people she didn't know showered this kind of attention on Toby, a mixture of pride and discomfort. It was somehow like those hugs from Cynthia: too intimate, too presumptuous. And yet she felt a sense of obligation to strangers that she didn't feel to Cynthia or even to her husband, so she watched quietly as the man kneaded his fingers into the ruff of fur around Toby's neck as the dog lifted up his face to lick the man's chin.

"What's the breed?" the man asked, now scratching Toby's chest.

"Some kind of shepherd mix," Elise said. "I found him wandering along a highway back when I was in school." She found herself not wanting for some reason to say graduate school to this man, as if to do so would be bragging. He was short, perhaps even shorter than she was, and ropy with muscle. Still brown from summer, or many summers—he had the ruddy, spotted skin of a lifelong day laborer, startling next to his very bright blue eyes. He was handsome, in a way. The thick, dark hair emerging from beneath his cap, due a cut, was only faintly threaded with silver.

The man stood, slipped his hand back into the glove. "A hitchhiking shepherd. I like these stories. I like it when a dog finds its person."

"Do you have one?"

"Did," he said. "I'm on the road too much now to have a dog."

"For work?"

He plunged his hands into his pockets and rocked back on his heels a little. He was dressed for work, Elise thought: jeans, boots, a quilted flannel jacket of the kind that a hunter would wear. Still a leash's length away, she thought she could smell the yellowed edge of tobacco, the odor that would have soaked into the skin between his first two fingers and the damp tissue of his mouth. "No. Family, actually." He produced, as if in response to her thoughts, a pack of cigarettes. The glove came off again; he pulled a ribbon of cellophane loose and let it drop at his feet so brazenly that Elise was shocked, then irritated at her own surprise. She'd had an elementary school teacher who encouraged Elise and her classmates to point and yell "Litterbug!" if they saw a person put trash in anything but a "proper waste receptacle." She bit her bottom lip now and watched the cellophane drift a couple of inches and then snag in a crust of snow. "My dad lives up in Morgantown, and his health's poor. I do a lot of back and forth."

"Where's home?"

"New Orleans, for now. Long as this job I'm on lasts."

"What kind of job?"

"Pipeline," he said.

Elise glanced up the path, wondering whether Alan had gone on back to the car to wait for her. "You've got a long drive back, then."

He shrugged. "I don't think about it much anymore." He motioned past the railing, toward the bridge, and Elise noticed that he had wiped the snow clean from the information placard. "How about this thing, huh? I'd have hated to be on the crew putting that baby up." He had propped a cigarette in the corner of his mouth, and now he waved the pack at Elise. "Want one?" he said around it.

One of the things she never would have guessed she'd miss about smoking, much as she'd complained at the time, was doing it out in the cold, with a stranger. She remembered being twenty-five and huddled beside a garbage can on the campus quad. Instant, fleeting camaraderie. Overdisclosure. The art students were in the building across the sidewalk, and there had been this one with white girl's dreadlocks and an eyebrow piercing who announced things like, "Well, he wanted to fuck me in the ass last night" or "Whose cock do I have to suck to get a match?" and Elise had love-hated her so much that she was a little obsessed with her, would think about her when a class got boring and pretend to herself to dread their next exchange. She nodded now at the man before she could second-guess herself, and he tapped the pack so that the end of a cigarette slid out. Elise accepted it, then his light, puffing to start, just tasting the smoke.

"This is a bad thing you've done," she said. "I haven't had a cigarette in four years."

"Then it's a service I've done," the man said. "A cigarette's a dependable pleasure. I don't see why you'd deny yourself a dependable pleasure."

"Cancer?"

"Everything gives you cancer," the man said. "Even this sweet mountain air's probably got something cancerous in it." He took a deep drag and exhaled to prove his point. "Such is the risk of modern living." His voice had an inflection that was old-fashioned, vaguely Southern.

Elise inhaled too, and her arms broke out in goosebumps of pleasure at the warm, tickly fingers in her chest. "Whew," she said slowly, spilling smoke between her lips, feeling not just light-headed but practically aroused. "Lord Jesus." She thought about Alan again, but guiltily, wondering whether there was any way possible that he would miss the smell of this on her when she got back in the car. As if she were a child, sneaking smokes behind Dad's back.

"Now see," the man said. He turned and leaned against the placard, smoking with an easy, even elegant masculinity. "I don't know you from Adam, and I've just made you the happiest woman I've seen in a long time."

"You've made me the happiest I've felt in a long time." She coughed, but even that felt good, cleansing. It was nice to be without her husband for a few moments—nice to get some air, to enjoy something that he had never understood or shared with her. “It’s been a long day.”

“Day’s barely begun.”

“You make another good point.” It occurred to her that they were flirting. “But I’ve been up since before three.”

“That’ll do it.”

“So I earned this,” she said, lifting the cigarette. She flicked some ashes, not realizing for a second that Toby was standing beneath her again, and had to brush them quickly from his fur. She jerked her chin to the right. “You heading down there?”

He shrugged. “Probably not. I can look just as well from up here.” He winked. “A view’s a view.”

“So what made you stop in the ice and the snow for it?”

“I feel trapped if I’m alone in the car too long,” he said. “It’s hard on my nerves.”

Elise thought about the white car cutting across the lanes to beat her to the off-ramp—the way her forehead and shins had prickled almost painfully, the same sensation that hit her whenever she tripped and lost her balance while out for a run, in that second before she knew whether she would catch herself. In a less logical world, this man, this stranger between Elise and the path back to the parking lot, would be the driver of the Impala. She couldn’t help but consider the idea, to tease herself with it. To feel—was it possible?—a measure of excitement at the thought, an excitement that was fed by her earlier fear. He was darker than Alan. Leaner, older. The lips pursed around his cigarette filter were oddly full, even lovely, against the angles of his face.

Her own cigarette was almost gone. She took a last, long drag, already wishing for another, and stubbed it into the snow-covered railing. “Well, I should go find my husband. Thanks for the smoke.”

“Want one for the road?”

She laughed and shook her head. “I wish. But no. Enjoy the view. You should try the other lookout. It’s worth the walk.”

“I’ll think about it.”

“Let’s go, Toby,” she said, and they started up the path back to the parking lot. The snow had slackened to almost nothing in the time it took her to come up the steps and talk to the man—just flurries now, fine and coarse as salt. The first thing she noticed emerging from the wooded walkway was that the car's wipers were unmoving, and a layer of powder covered the windshield. She stopped, pulling Toby to a stay, and looked around.

"Alan?" she called.

She went ahead to the car and tried the driver's side door. Locked. Alan wasn't inside. She tried the button—the lock should have automatically released, sensing her key fob—but nothing. She rummaged in her coat pocket for the keys and came up with nothing, but she realized that Alan had simply switched seats with her in Summersville, and the keys he had pocketed when they parked here were Elise's own. Both sets, then, were with him. Wherever he had wandered off to.

A trill of annoyance coursed through her. What an easy emotion it was to access: the sense of having been wronged, of having been subjected yet again to Alan's thoughtlessness. She strode up to the visitors' center, rattling off to herself a litany of his bad habits, of the ways that he failed to expend an iota of energy anticipating how his actions would affect her. She thought about how he always locked the car when he got out to pump gas, even when Elise was sitting inside of it the whole time, yet he so often forgot to lock it when they both left it unattended, and one time Elise's iPad was stolen. She thought about how he would tell her in the morning that he'd call her about meeting for lunch, and she would wait until 1 or 1:30 to hear from him, then leave a message or two on his phone, only for him to call at the point that her exhaustion had peaked to explain that his boss had sprung for Jimmy John's. She thought about how he should have walked down to the lookout with her, and she thought about his reaction that morning on the road, telling her to punch it but later accusing her of overreacting. She was breathless now with fury, almost giddily anticipating the moment when she could thrust out her hand and say, witheringly, "Keys." Where was he? What had he been doing all this time? She imagined that he must have found the bathrooms unlocked after all and decided to go in and take his time, or maybe he'd walked to that gift shop just down the road, the one that advertised "coffee" and "country fudge," though Elise had always been too dubious to try it.

She realized, reaching out to try the doors to the visitors' center, that she was uneasy. She grabbed a handle, pushed, and was unsurprised when the door didn't budge. She rattled it for good measure, and Toby, startled, jumped back.

"Don't be so dramatic, dog," she said, her throat tight. She was still so damned angry—it was churning away inside of her—but the sensation was confused, despairing, as if her anger was at something other than her husband, at whatever emotion it was she was tamping down right now as she looked to see whether she could find his footprints leading away from the locked doors. There was nothing; the steady snow had erased any trace of him. She walked around the corner to the front of the building, and the parking lot spread out before her in perfect emptiness, the gift shop across the way dark and abandoned.

"Alan," she yelled, more loudly than before. Her voice fell flat in the hush.

She hunched down and buried her cold fingers into Toby's fur. "Where is he, boy?" she said, with false cheer that made his tail thump. She thought for just a second of unhooking the leash, seeing where the dog led, but she was irrationally afraid now to lose her connection with Toby. As long as he was with her, she wasn't alone.

They circled the building. Here was a service entrance, the door scuffed brown metal, the security light above it burning wanly in the gray morning. A bucket of sand was tucked against the back stoop, the ground around it littered with cigarette butts. There was an empty plastic Fanta bottle. A neon yellow sheet of paper with a shoe print pressed into it. Elise stared at each of these things as though they were artifacts from a culture she had only read about. She peered over a chain-link fence into the woods, hoping at any second to pick out the movement of Alan's gray coat, but the trees were bare and still. A loud crackle disturbed the silence, and Elise looked down to see that Toby had settled with the Fanta bottle between his paws, bearing his molars into the cap. "Give me that," she muttered, and when she pulled it away from him the indentations from his teeth were damp with pink saliva.

He panted at her, grinning, and she swallowed against what felt like a sob.

She had known this sensation before: loving panic, the sudden certainty of loss. Once, in the earliest days of her marriage to Alan, he had told her he was meeting a friend after work to watch a basketball game, and she had been tired, not listening closely enough, and had forgotten. She was worried by six, pacing the floor by seven, calling hospitals at nine. He wasn't answering his cell phone. Her texts to him were still flagged as unread. By the time he got home at eleven, she was hiccupping with tears. (And—this was so Alan—he'd put his phone on silent for a work meeting, then forgot.) A handful of episodes like that one—and didn't most couples have them? Those moments when she remembered with perfect clarity what she loved about her husband and promised herself that she would do better, would love better, if only he were all right. If only he were restored to her.

She promised it now. She pitched the plastic bottle into the bucket of sand and wiped her fingers against her jeans, and she and Toby headed back toward the front of the building. Alan would be waiting for her at the car, she told herself. They had been passing just out of one another's sight, like characters in a farce, and when they were reunited they would laugh in exasperated huffs and throw their hands up into the air, and they would argue about who lost whom, who should have stayed put. In this moment, as in all of those other moments of illogical, loving panic, she believed several truths at once. She was as convinced that he was around the corner as she was that he was lost to her, and she believed that there was time, still, for fate to be good—that nothing would be lost and nothing would be certain until she turned the corner.

She did not mistake the man with the cigarettes for her husband this time. He had emerged from the path to the lookout, and he was watching her and Toby as they returned to where they started. The snow had thickened again; it had already hidden the evidence of her path across the parking lot. It was as if Alan had never been here, as if she had never gone in search of him.

The man was still smoking, and he lifted his chin to paint a plume against the sky. They stared at each other for a pregnant moment.

"Need some help?" he called finally.

She wondered how to behave with a witness to her panic. She wondered what he would do if she ran. She imagined how Alan would laugh at her later, when the dangers were predictable again, and she tightened her grip on Toby's leash, nodding, getting ready to ask him if he had a cell phone, because that would be the sane thing to do, the polite thing. Where was his car? How did he get here? She thought for a second that she saw the Impala, but it was only her own car, now covered all over in white.

stars

The politician was a good public speaker, warm and spontaneous, and he was loath to stick to a stump speech as he toured the fellowship halls and multipurpose rooms and middle school gymnasiums of the 6th Congressional District—a cause for constant, low-level alarm among his small staff. But the stakes for this election were low, relatively; the district hadn't gone blue since the Carter administration, and no one expected that to change anytime soon.

No, this campaign was a testing of the waters. He was forty-two, handsome—actually handsome, not just politician handsome—charismatic, sharp. He'd amassed a respectable pile of money building a regional chain of outdoor supply stores, which gave him some credit with both the gun enthusiasts and the granola eaters, and he had a pretty wife and two young, blonde daughters who looked as if they'd been born to wear navy blue dresses in front of a billowing American flag. He was a rising star, scrutinized under a high-powered lens. He had a consultant, imported from DC, who was being paid, it was rumored, by Buffy Sherman, and it was this consultant who kept saying, "Give him some leash. The old rules don't apply anymore."

They gave him some leash. And so far, so good. No big gaffes, no embarrassing video uploads. He had a Bidenish tendency to affably slip up—get photographed making a funny face, mutter a mild curse loud enough for the hot mike to pick it up—but lacked the creepy uncle vibe. He was genuine. The consultant had muscled her way up the rungs of the DC political scene working under magnetic men, sociopaths, probably, who could fake sincerity well enough to fool most people. This politician, though, was different. No saint, but Americans didn't seem to expect saints anymore anyway. They wanted a man who believed what he was saying, even if what he was saying was complete bullshit, and the politician believed what he was saying, mostly.

Like tonight, at the library, when he trotted out the closest thing he had to a stump line or a refrain. "My grandmother had a saying," he told the folks gathered in the community room: about fifty people, capacity according to the fire code posted by the light switch, mostly sixty-something women balancing their polyester-clad bottoms on metal folding chairs. They leaned forward expectantly. They liked talk of grandmothers. "Every person you meet, they might be having the worst day of their life. I thought I might be late tonight because we got stuck behind a slow car out on Elam." (He always remembered the street names in the areas he visited, and he used them in the casual manner of a local.) "I won't kid you. He was making me crazy. Going ten, fifteen, maybe, in a twenty-five. I just about laid down on the horn. Then I realized we were passing the hospital. He was looking for a turn. And my hand was hovering above that horn, and I thought, maybe this guy's wife was in that hospital somewhere, dying. Or his child. Or maybe he was going in for a test and he was scared to death. And me, worst-case scenario, I might be one or two minutes late to this talk tonight. Those were the stakes. It's so easy to choose that satisfying outburst of anger over the more complicated act of empathy."

He ran a hand through his grayish-blond hair. "It scares me to think that, but it also inspires me. It's a choice. We have the power to make it. That's why I'm running for office. Because it seems to me that so many of the things wrong with our country right now can be traced back to failures of empathy."

If the politician had an obvious weakness, it was not knowing when to stop; he'd tire, lose some of his eloquence. He could feel the shift as it happened, the devolution of his sentences. Janette had chided him about this, had walked him through what she called "exit strategies," and he recognized their necessity but disliked their awkwardness, the tinny insincerity. After a few minutes of affable fumbling, he cleared his throat, took a sip of water. "Damn, I nearly forgot," he said, reaching into his jacket pocket. He produced a smart phone and wagged it in the air. "I want to take your picture. Is that okay?" Most of the people in the audience smiled self-consciously, nodding a little. The politician thumbed the screen, swiped up for the camera, and switched to the reverse camera, then leaned back against the podium and lifted the phone up high. "Say cheese, y'all. I've tried to be more creative than that, but you should see the faces people make when they say, 'Cunningham for Congress.'" The faces on his screen loosened into laughs, and he jabbed the shutter button a few times, rapidly. He glanced at the last photo. "Oh, good, you can't even see how thin I am on top in this one," he said, to more laughs. He pocketed the phone again.

"All right. Well. It's been a pleasure. Thanks for turning out tonight, folks, and for your support. I'll be over at the cheese now if anyone wants me." There was an eruption of enthusiastic applause, even some hoots, and the politician did a little waving jog over to the room's corner, where Janette and the younger of the two interns, Libby, awaited him, beaming. This was the worst part of the night—the awkward transition from performance to one-on-one, how he had to appear to go offstage when there wasn't even a stage, how he had to come up with some fake question for Janette, like, "And now we have about an hour for talking, right?" so as to not just stand there shuffling his feet until a line of audience members decided to form itself.

"Officially, it's another forty-five minutes," Janette says. "But it's straight to the hotel from here, so take your time."

"Great!" the politician said. The library employee was hovering nearby, uncertain—he had smelled her perfume, a suntan-oily musk, before he saw her—so he smiled extra wide and angled his shoulders to include her in the exchange. When he'd met her an hour ago at the circulation desk, he'd made a quick mnemonic to remember her name: *Sarah Sarah with the dye-job hair-a*, and it came back to him with a satisfying snap. Her hair, scoured of most of its color, had been raked back into an oddly severe half bun, tight enough that he could see a millimeter of brownish roots; the loose part hung, carefully waved, around her shoulders. She was youngish, midtwenties perhaps, and her face was bronzed and pinkened with makeup that shimmered strangely under the room's fluorescent lights, as if she had wandered in here by mistake from a 1980s cheerleading competition. She hadn't quite struck the politician as, well, librarianish, so without any indication to the contrary, he'd determined that she must be some sort of secretarial figure or part-time help to cover evening and weekend events like this one. He reached out and shook her hand firmly.

"This is a great space, Sarah," the politician said. "Thanks for all your help."

"Oh, it was a pleasure," Sarah said. "Was the sound okay?"

It took him a moment to grasp her meaning. "Oh. The mike? Yeah, perfect. Did it sound good to you?"

"Oh, I thought it was wonderful," Sarah said. Her face, ruddy with make-up, reddened even more, and a flush crept splotchily across her chest. The politician noticed she already had a plastic cup of white wine in her hand; she'd wasted no time. "Wait. You meant the sound. Yes, that too!" She giggled a little.

"Well, I'll take the compliment! Glad you liked it, Sarah."

"I have a son," she said. She bobbed her head a few times. "So, you know. A lot of what you said. About education. And the planet. It spoke to me."

"How old's your son, Sarah?" A line had formed behind her now—eight, ten women. Holding cups of wine, biting into hard little cookies with their eyeteeth.

"He's four," she said.

"What an age," the politician said. "Learning so much, parroting what they hear. And their brains are little steel traps."

Sarah giggled again. "Oh, yes. For sure."

He could never bring himself to close a conversation with the old "I hope to have your vote in November" bit, so he shook her hand again, patted it with his free hand, and said, "Well, again, thanks for all your good work here. I always feel at home in a library."

"That's great," Sarah said. "Can I get you something? Water or wine, or a plate of food?" She pointed to the folding table. "The Women's Club put together some local goodies. Benedictine sandwiches, mini pecan pies. Chips. I mean, just regular chips and regular dip. The kind from the store. But we have that too. Oh, and we have Cokes. I forgot to mention that before. And deviled eggs. That was me. I made them."

He'd smelled the eggs from the podium: the sulfur stench of yokes, bland tang of warming mayo. Like a promise, or a threat. But he nodded, smiled. "I'll take one of everything, Sarah, and two of the eggs. Thank you so much. What a treat this is."

"It was a pleasure," Sarah repeated. She smiled, bobbed her head, and backed away. A few minutes later, as the politician chitchatted with the next woman in line, she came briefly back to saddle him with a plate of food, and he thanked her again, and then he thanked her once more at the end of the evening as he, Janette, and Libby made their way, tiredly, toward the door. He knew this was only the tip of the iceberg, days like this. If he signed on for this life, there would be more long days, bigger rooms of people, more Sarahs with their vague need, their desire to see him, to be seen by him. More deviled eggs, and he'd have to pop them each into his mouth, whole, and chew and chew and smile as if he loved it. He wasn't a liar, but his grandmother had had another saying: *Grin and bear it.*

In another hour he was checked into the hotel. There was time to call Meg and the girls while Libby went to pick up Chipotle, and he ate his burrito bowl (chicken, no cheese or sour cream, no vinaigrette, one tablespoon—no more than that!—of guac) in bed watching an old *Forensic Files* episode. A beer would have been nice, but he knew better than to ask the intern to get him one. Sarah, after that last handshake of the evening, disappeared permanently from his thoughts.

He chewed the romaine, watched a detective discuss the significance of a missing light bulb in a lamp. He thought about how he needed to set his alarm early and hit the gym—too many 9:00 p.m. dinners lately, not enough trail runs. He thought about how thin his wife's voice had been on the phone, her constant talk of stress, of exhaustion—the girls' lessons and homework, their staggered pick-up and drop-off times, the questions they were asking about Dad and his job and why he was gone so much. And she talked, always, with a glum certitude, itself a kind of hope, that this would all be temporary. He'd run his unsuccessful run, dispatch with whatever sense of duty he'd felt (or succumb, at last, to the inevitable hubris), and resume their old life.

"I'm doing this for them," he said—he always said. It was true. He hadn't even wanted kids that much, that had been Meg's deal, but once they were here she'd focused her most intense anxiety on what Grady perceived to be trivialities: potential gluten allergies, charter school lotteries, the number of RSVPs they'd received for Amelia's fifth birthday party. In the meantime, he festered.

What kind of world are we leaving them? he'd ask her.

Oh, things always turn out okay, she'd say.

When has that ever been true?

If it's never been true, why are you worried about the future?

How can you not be?

I worry about what I can control, Meg would say.

So this campaign, maybe, was what he could control. He could know he'd fought the good fight. He'd changed a mind or two. And if the campaign took him away from his family, relieved him for four or five nights of the tremendous burden of his love, the tedium of the day to day—was that so bad? He had never once gone and knocked on Libby's hotel room door, though he'd sensed her receptiveness to such a scenario.

The woman on TV had been murdered by her husband. It was always, the politician thought with a complicated mixture of shame and defensiveness, the husband.

When Sarah got home, Jared was on the PlayStation. It was the cowboy game. What she knew about the game was basically this: it had cowboys and it cost sixty dollars. The day Jared brought it home from Walmart, he'd also come in with a bottle of Moscato and a bouquet of red roses, the grocery store kind that had a plastic sheet and a pouch of plant food rubber-banded around the stems.

Sarah sat on the couch and unzipped her boots. “Where’s Braden?”

“Upstairs,” Jared said, his eyes fixed to the TV screen. He wiggled a toggle on the controller with his thumb. “How’d it go?”

“Fine,” Sarah said. And fine it had gone, she supposed, but she’d driven home with her left leg jittering, the evening’s interactions, even the most trivial, circling her brain on repeat.

He shot her a look. “You sure?”

“Yeah. It went good. He said he liked the space. He liked the food. The ladies all seemed to like it. How about you? How was work?”

He shrugged. “Same old shit. I can’t complain.”

“Since when?”

He smiled. Onscreen, the cowboy swung off the back of a horse and started firing a gun at other cowboys. The animation was realistic but unsettlingly liquid, and Sarah found herself mesmerized by the gunfight. “Doug’s still a dumbass. Ashley’s still got a stick up her ass.” His tongue tip probed the corner of his mouth as he executed a play onscreen. “Lorrie ordered this cake thing for the break room, though. I almost brought you some. It was good.”

“That’s okay. There were pecan pies at the reception.” She checked her phone, did a quick scroll through Twitter, Instagram, and Facebook. Outrage and babies. Gloom and doom and a recipe for chocolate dump cake. Someone had tagged her in a Facebook photo—a picture of her talking with Grady Cunningham after his speech. She looked awful. Fat, shiny. Red-faced. The airy, loose-fitting blouse that had seemed so cute in the mirror this morning appeared baggy and cheap. She untagged herself angrily and closed the app. “How long’s he been asleep?”

Jared, despite his distraction, followed her pivot. “He’s probably asleep by now. He was in our bed watching *Bubble Guppies*.”

“Jeez, Jared. You just plunked him up there so you could play your game?”

He stopped, exhaled, and rolled his head toward her. “I didn’t *plunk him up there*. We had dinner. I gave him a bath. I asked him if he wanted books or to watch a little TV before bed, and he said TV."

"Well, of course he said TV. What else is he going to say if you give him the option?"

"Don't make this into something it's not, Sarah. He's fine. He's only been up there for thirty minutes, maybe."

She shook her head in disgust, stood. "Did you at least put him in his pajamas and brush his teeth first?"

He cleared his throat. "I forgot his teeth."

It was satisfying, in a way. Satisfying to leave Jared with his admission and his stupid game, satisfying to go to the kitchen for a glass of water and find on the countertop the grease-stained cardboard detritus from their McDonald's dinner, satisfying to decide, last minute, to instead pour a finger of Moscato into a jelly jar, then plod heavily up the grimy carpeted stairs. Satisfying in the same way it was to see that tagged photo of herself on Facebook—like, here's the worst possible version of me, the version I spend most of my day trying to believe isn't real. At least now I know.

When she was cleaning up after the reception, pacing the community room with a large black garbage bag and picking up the scattered wads of dirty napkins, the forks smeared with pecan pie goo, she'd found the plate of food she made for Grady Cunningham. She knew it was his; it was resting on the corner of the table next to where he'd stood for most of the evening, chatting with the people from the audience. A small bite was missing from one of the deviled eggs she'd made; the teeth marks, like everything else about him, were perfect, even. The other egg—and he'd asked for two specifically—was untouched. And it was stupid, but she'd felt, tossing the plate of good food into the trash, this sudden flush of anger and humiliation, not just at the uneaten food, at what it implied, but his smiling, bobbing . . . *damn it*, she couldn't even think of the word for it. Manner? Façade?

When she'd gotten the job at the library two years ago, she had been so proud and excited. It was good work, important work. Even fun work, like on the days when she got to change the seasonal bulletin board in the kids' room, or when the Women's Auxiliary reserved the community room for bunko and asked her to play with them, and sometimes she won one of the prizes—a china plate with a red bird on it, a set of tea towels. She loved to read. She read fifty books or more a year; she logged them dutifully into her journal. It was something people had noticed about her before she ever got the library job (*Girl, you always have your nose in a book!*), the reason Retta Lassiter, who had scanned Sarah's library card so many times, encouraged her to apply for the part-time circulation clerk position when it opened up. She loved bringing books home for Braden and reading to him too, and the teacher at his preschool was always saying how smart he was, how sweet and good, and whatever it is you're doing, Mom, keep doing it. How it warmed her heart to hear that!

She hadn't been anyone special in high school. She hadn't gotten a senior superlative, she hadn't gotten a college scholarship, she hadn't been an officer for one of the clubs or an athlete or a cheerleader or even one of the geeks or potheads or juvenile delinquents, notorious in their own right. She'd been the girl with the no-color, medium-length hair, slightly overweight, who made B minuses and Cs and whose senior section yearbook bio said, "DECA (1, 2), Home Ec, School Play Decorations (1)," and whose quote was from Katy Perry's "Firework": "Maybe a reason why all the doors are closed / So you can open one that leads you to the perfect road." She didn't remember submitting that quote. It must have been her; she had liked the song okay, like everyone else that year. But as with so many of her actions back then, or her inactions, the quote, now appended forever to her formal senior picture, the one with the velvet drape around her shoulders and the little gold wink of the cross pendant between her collarbones, seemed to have almost nothing to do with her. No one had suggested to Sarah then that there was a perfect road for her, that there were closed doors between her and her dreams, doors that she might one day open. No one, and that included Sarah herself, had operated under the assumption that Sarah *had* dreams, beyond marrying a steady, slightly overweight boy, as she'd done, and raising a few kids in a ranch house, where back-up two liters of off-brand Coke sat on the counter, awaiting their turn in the refrigerator. "Dream" was just a word—a word she'd painted in careful cursive on some graying pallet planks and hung above her bed, the way she'd seen on Pinterest.

Braden was lying under that DREAM sign now, awake but glassy-eyed in the bluish-purple light of his cartoon. "Oh, hey, Mama," he said. "You're here."

"Hey, buddy." She set her wine on the bedside table and snuggled under the covers beside him. He kept his eyes on the TV but wriggled sideways, positioning himself in the crook between her left arm and her breasts. The top of his head was still cool from the bath, and it smelled like soap. Sarah planted a kiss on his crown. "How was your day?"

"Good," he said. "Daddy got McDonald's for dinner."

"I heard that," Sarah said evenly. "What about school?"

"I had a gold day," Braden said. His preschool teacher awarded "medals" for behavior at the end of each day: gold, silver, and bronze. The real screwups got a frowny face note sent in the homework folder to the parents. Braden, thank goodness, had never earned one of those. Sarah would have been mortified.

"That's so great, buddy. What else happened?"

"I had a cheese quesadilla for lunch, but I didn't eat the peas because they were yucky. And I didn't like the crackers with the sweetness at the snack."

"Who did you play with?"

"I played freeze tag with Cooper."

"That sounds fun!" She squeezed him again and let her eyes flutter closed. It would be easy to fall asleep here, like this. Serve Jared right. She imagined him coming upstairs, finding Braden and Sarah unconscious and threaded together in the center of the bed. Turning around to go back downstairs and sleep on the couch. He'd probably just use it as an excuse to stay up playing more of the cowboy game, though.

"Buddy, it's time to turn your show off. We need to brush teeth and go to bed."

"But I want to finish this episode first."

"No, buddy," she said, churning again with that almost pleasurable anger at her husband. A note of defiance had crept into Braden's voice; he wouldn't consent to the show's being turned off without throwing a fit, especially since it was 9:30 now and he was well past overtired.

He screamed when she hit the power button on the remote, ran to his room, and slammed the door when she tried to corral him into the bathroom to get his teeth brushed. "Do you want me to come up?" Jared yelled from downstairs.

"Please don't," she yelled back down at him.

She thought about leaving it—just letting Braden tire himself out, alone, and eventually make his way to the bed or fall asleep on the floor among his Matchbox cars. It wouldn't kill him. Then she could get into her own bed with a book, finish a chapter before her eyelids sagged closed. But she felt, with her son more than she ever had with even Jared, that going to bed angry at each other was wrong. And, to be honest, she didn't really want to lie down alone yet, with the day and all it had churned up in her. Replaying the careful look on Grady Cunningham's face. You don't know me, she wanted to tell him. You don't know who I am. What's in my heart. She shed the baggy, uncute blouse and her leggings, shrugged on a T-shirt and a pair of Jared's boxers. She would let the toothbrushing go, she decided, pulling her hair down from its half bun and lining the bobby pins up on her dresser top. But she'd still go tuck Braden in.

It wasn't that Sarah had expected special treatment from the politician or that he'd been some kind of hero of hers—she wasn't even a Democrat. He hadn't done anything clearly wrong tonight. There would be no explaining it later to Jared, though he'd try hard to understand; he wouldn't tease her or belittle her. He'd try to say something supportive, like "He's just full of himself" or "What did you expect? They're all crooked." He wouldn't get it.

When she was pregnant with Braden, Jared had had to go away for a couple of days on a regional sales call, and she'd lain in bed one of the nights he was gone with her hand on her stomach and thought,

I'll never be alone again. She pictured, lovingly, the scenes she had heard other mothers complain about: hiding in the bathroom while the child hammered on the door demanding admission; the toddler screaming for her, hands extended, as she tried handing him off to a babysitter. It would be frustrating occasionally, she'd thought, but it would be worth it. To be needed like that. To be that little person's favorite person. What she hadn't guessed was that she'd not only continue to feel lonely after Braden's birth but that the nature of the loneliness would intensify, sometimes to levels she almost couldn't bear, and she wondered whether she was going crazy, if she should go *talk to someone*, though she wasn't even sure what *talking to someone* would entail. And sometimes, when Braden was asleep and Jared wasn't home, she would practice what she'd say to a doctor, if she ever saw one: I am terrified all the time. I don't know what kind of world I brought him into. I love him so much that I almost wish he didn't exist. And it feels like no one else feels this way. Jared doesn't. My mother doesn't. The women at work who are always asking me when we're going to have another. They don't. I feel like I'm either going out of my mind or I'm the only one who isn't. Does that make sense? What do you think?

She thought about Grady Cunningham, his easy smile, his earnest solutions, and the plate of food he'd left on the table for her to trash. He wasn't a bad man, and he was probably as good a man for the job as any of the rest of them. That was what scared her. Or rather, it was another thing that scared her.

Braden was splayed diagonally across his bed, playing with Optimus Prime under the full harsh glare of the overhead light. Sarah could tell from his loose shoulders, the softness of his mouth, that he'd already forgotten his anger. This meant that they would either start the whole showdown over again or move past it as if it had never happened.

"Buddy, it's bedtime," she said, keeping her voice pleasant. "I'm going to turn your nightlight on and the big light off."

He kept playing with the toy. "Okay," he said, and she sighed a little with relief.

When the overhead light was off and the glow-in-the-dark plastic stars on his wall and ceiling were emitting their dull, nuclear light, she took the Transformer gently from his hands, and he let her. She shifted his legs over, pulled him up by the armpits so that his head rested on his pillow.

"How about a story?" he whispered.

"I don't think I can come up with a story tonight, bud," she said. "I'm too tired. I don't have any good ideas."

"You can tell this story," Braden said. "Once upon a time, there was a boy with a dragon. The dragon could breathe fire, but he was also nice. They flew all over the world together and when the boy was hungry the dragon would make a fire for him to cook his food. And the dragon's name was Boo-lo-nee-fus. The end."

"That's a good story," Sarah said.

"Now you say it."

"What about a song instead?"

He thought about it. "Okay."

"Which one?"

"Farmer in the Dell," he said, and Sarah groaned, but at least it was better than the never-ending "Old MacDonald."

She made her way through the verses. When she was a kid it was just a song, like a dozen others the music teacher at school would plunk out on her piano, but now, like everything else, she'd overthought it, and it was ruined for her. The farmer takes a wife, she thought, singing it. Maybe I should change the verse sometimes. Maybe I should say, "The farmer takes a husband," so Braden knows that girls can be farmers too. (Or maybe he would think the farmer is gay? She hadn't been able to bring herself to explain homosexuality to Braden, and she could guess what Jared would have to say if she tried.) Why oh why couldn't she just sing her kid a song and not worry about every little thing?

The cheese stands alone, she finished. He always giggled at this part. "I'll eat that cheese," he said, pretending to snatch it from the air, and he went, "Yum yum yum yum yum."

"Was it good?" Sarah asked.

He nodded.

"Okay, buddy. I love you." She bent over to kiss his forehead.

"Wait. Where's French Fry?"

Sarah huffed and scanned the bed, turned back the covers. French Fry was a plush yellow cat he'd gotten at a Build-a-Bear birthday party: cheap, ugly, and not the thing Sarah would have chosen to become his lovey. What had been Sarah's choice, in fact—a beautifully made teddy bear with long arms and legs and amber eyes made of real glass—sat on the top of Braden's dresser, mostly untouched. "I don't see him," she said. "He's probably downstairs. I think you had him on the couch."

"You need to go get him," Braden said.

"Baby, just go to bed. French Fry's okay. You can see him in the morning."

"Get him," Braden said. "I need him."

"You can at least ask me nicely. You can at least say please."

"Pleeeeease?"

"Okay," she said. It was just a delaying tactic, but she would do it. She pushed to a stand. "Do you want anything else? Now's the time to tell me. Do you need to go potty? Do you want me to get you some water?"

"Just French Fry," Braden said.

"Okay, then."

The stairs creaked loudly with her descent. She'd told Jared once that she'd like to rip the carpet up—it was so ugly and stained, and no one had carpeted stairs anymore—and he'd said, "If we rip the carpet up there's no telling what's underneath." So each time she scaled or descended them, she thought of this. Of the logic. The stairs, held together by old carpet and their thin hopes, rotten through underneath.

"He down?" Jared asked.

"Just about," Sarah said. She crossed over to the couch, moved a cushion aside, a throw blanket. There. She snagged French Fry by the arm. "He wanted this."

"I would have brought it up to you."

"It's okay. It only took me a second." She looked at the stuffed cat and not at Jared. "I guess I'm turning in once I get back upstairs."

"I won't be much longer," he said. "I have to finish this mission before I can save."

"Good night."

"Good night."

"And today really was okay?" he said. "You sounded—" He paused to charge his cowboy, on horseback, into a herd of cattle. "—stressed," he finished. "Or something."

"It was really okay," she said.

Upstairs, she tucked French Fry under Braden's arm and kissed him again. "Love you, my boy."

"Love you, too."

"Dream nice dreams." Her throat was thick, and she blinked hard against tears she knew he couldn't see in the dark.

"I will," he said, and she envied him then. His casual certainty. His default contentment.

The wall stars never hold their light for very long. Each night at this time, when Mama closes the door for good and he knows he is truly alone until morning, he wonders why they can't just get wall stars that stay lit up. They could use batteries or electricity. And that way he wouldn't have to lie here tracking their dulling glow. The worst part is that they go dim without ever disappearing entirely. Sometimes, in the middle of the night, he'll wake up, throat parched, and see the faint, greenish impressions all around him. Like ghosts. I don't like the stars, he thinks. He wants to get out of bed, open the door, cross the hall to Mama and Daddy's room and tell them this. He grips French Fry and churns with indecision. It's important that he doesn't like the stars, and that his mama knows, but she will not think it's important. She will say, "Go to sleep, buddy," or, if she's mad, she will huff and say, "Braden, go to bed!" This is her yellow voice, and he doesn't like it. The yellow voice is "Braden, go to bed!" and "Dammit, Braden, hold your hands still before I hurt you!" when she's clipping his fingernails. Sometimes she has the yellow voice with Daddy, and then it is, “I wish I wasn’t the only person in this house who knew how to put a dish in the dishwasher!” Like that. When he asked for French Fry tonight, she almost used her yellow voice but then she stopped.

Braden is glad. He squeezes him and kisses the top of French Fry’s head rapidly, one-two-three. The Build-a-Bear birthday party was the greatest day ever. He didn’t know he was going to get a toy. He hadn’t liked Zoe very much, but then he liked her very much after he went to her party and got French Fry. Mama reminds him of this sometimes when he forgets. Sometimes, at daycare, Zoe tries to keep him from sliding and he gets mad. He tells Mama, “I hate Zoe,” and she says, “No you don’t, you like Zoe.” At first, this is hard to believe. His angry fists tell him he hates Zoe. But then Mama says, “Remember her birthday and how you got French Fry?” and then it’s oh, yeah, she is a nice girl after all.

Mama also has a purple voice, like tonight, when she said, “Love you, my boy.” The purple voice is somehow worse than yellow, even though it’s nicer. When she tells him goodnight with the purple voice, and then leaves him alone, he is gripped with terror, and he wonders why his mama loves him but lets him lie alone in the dark like this when they could just sleep side by side and everything would be all right.

Sometimes, he wonders what French Fry is thinking. He knows French Fry is a toy, and he knows *Toy Story* is just a movie and not real. He doesn’t think French Fry moves or talks when he isn’t looking. But when Braden hugs him, like *this*, French Fry likes it. And when French Fry gets left alone downstairs, Braden thinks, he is scared. He is wondering where Braden is. He is wondering if Braden doesn’t love him anymore. I love you I love you, he murmurs now to French Fry. The stars have almost disappeared. The night is long, and sleep seems like a far ways off.

fortress

The forecast called for rain, and the air all afternoon was pregnant with it, but Eldon Carlisle, who had a gift for ignoring the things that caused him discomfort and inconvenience, willed it away. Sweeping through his house in silk pajamas and slippers, running a finger along the tabletops and picture frames to check for dust, he landed in the front hall long enough to glance at the Covington Three Bells Clock (retail: $6,800) displayed on the living room mantelpiece. The Furniture Market showrooms closed at 5:30, and the last shuttles to the dying High Point Mall would be emptied of their freight of weary buyers and exhibitors by 6:00. He had another few minutes, at most, to hustle upstairs and hide out before making his usual late, and therefore more acutely anticipated, entrance.

One of the caterers paused between the kitchen and the back French doors, clutching a stack of plates. "Mr. Carlisle," she said—she had the North Carolina twang that made his last name sound as if it belonged to a gas station attendant on the *Andy Griffith Show*—"I'm worried about putting that platter outside. It'll ruin in the rain." *Roorn*, she pronounced it.

Eldon followed her to the patio. The table, banquet-sized, was black-and-white granite veined with gold, and the staff had already set out and lit three candelabras, which reflected prettily in its shiny surface. In the garden, where buds swelled almost wantonly on two large beds' worth of peonies, tissue-thin paper lanterns swung on shepherd's hooks. The patio's only shelter was an arbor snaked with vines; he loved the look of it, the gray-washed wood and the way starlight winked between rafters on a clear night, but it would not be protection in a thunderstorm.

"Negativity gives me the hives," Eldon said, enjoying her apparent bewilderment. "Go ahead and set up the way we talked about. If we have to regroup at some point, we'll regroup."

"Yessir," she said skeptically, and she hustled out the door.

He passed into the kitchen, where three more women ("forgotten Americans," no doubt, happy enough to take his money while lamenting the trajectory of his immortal soul) swung their bulk around the island and brushed hair out of their eyes with the backs of their wrists. "Ladies," he said jovially. "How are we doing?'

"We're good, Mr. Carlisle," the head caterer said. She was running her knife through a pile of marinated chicken breasts and dumping them by the double handful into a large stainless steel mixing bowl. The finger foods were simple, hearty fare that he knew he could get done well and on the cheap and serve at room temperature: chicken and veggie fajita wraps, fresh guacamole and salsa, pineapple shrimp skewers. One of the women mixed a large pitcher of margaritas, the only cocktail he'd be serving. The glasses were small (cute, people would say, all those little salted rims), and they weren't to come out until most everyone had started the evening with beer (Coronas for the first couple of hours, Bud Light when those ran out) or wine, of which there was a near-endless store of 1.5-liter bottles, Barefoot chardonnay and merlot. Eldon hated chardonnay and merlot, but he did not drink anymore, and wine had always been his weakness. The bad wine was a habit now, a ritual against long-vanquished demons—and he did get a kick out of watching his well-heeled friends drink it by the enthusiastic snootful.

"Tony will be around if you need anything," he told the head caterer. "I'll be stepping upstairs in a moment to change."

"Yessir, Mr. Carlisle."

Tony was on the front porch. He was forty-eight, nine years younger than Eldon, with wavy blonde hair that pushed back from a sun-browned forehead and bright blue eyes. He wore a Hawaiian shirt, linen trousers, and leather thong sandals; around his neck was a pink plastic lei. He was tipping back a Corona and looking down the front walk and long driveway, which was lined with luminarias. The sight of them, sweeping downhill in parallel ribbons, reminded Eldon of a long-ago night in Bangkok—had he even been thirty yet? —a warm breeze through a window, the tender touch of a lover. His tear ducts prickled, and he sighed.

"It's going to rain, you know," Tony said, because that was his job, the reason Eldon paid him: to worry about the things Eldon couldn't bother himself to worry about. "And not just some sprinkles, mind you. We'll be able to launch the ark."

"Launch the ark," Eldon muttered. "You sound like my meemaw. Meemaw is what the southern folks call their bubbie, by the way."

"I know what a meemaw is," Tony said.

Eldon gripped his shoulder and squeezed. "Of course you do, darling. Now listen. I want people in leis. Don't let them fight you. Tell them if they don't put one of those things around their necks, I'll strangle them with it."

Tony's lip curled. "They itch," he said. He gripped his lei and turned his head left and right.

"Of course they do," said Eldon. "And remember, VIPs in pink. I always get Lee DeSoto and Lee Wilke confused."

"Lee Wilketoast," Tony said dryly. "If you're talking to the most boring man in the room, you're talking to Lee Wilke."

"Every man here is the most boring man in the room," Eldon said. "I bought this house hocking paisley and plaid five-piece comforter sets. I'll have to worry if they suddenly get interesting." He used his shirt hem to wipe a condensation ring from the marble table Tony was leaning against. "Make sure Wilke has some Glenfidditch if he wants it. Carl Mercer and Armando Senes, too. I think Lauralie Wiley Whoosit is a martini drinker, so offer her one."

"What about the HomeTV guy," Tony said. "Barry Levin."

"Scotch if he comes, but he won't show," Eldon said. He tamped down irritation. It was like the rain: if he could just not care truly enough, maybe Levin would turn up.

"It's going to rain," Tony said.

"If it does, deal with it," Eldon said. "I'm going upstairs to change."

The house was relatively small in comparison with his other properties, and Eldon didn't want to be imposed on by overnight guests while Furniture Market was in swing, so he had converted most of the upstairs into his personal quarters, off-limits to anyone but the housekeeper: a large bedroom and adjacent sitting room; sumptuous walk-in closet with space in the middle for a round, tufted Louis XV–inspired bench upholstered in purple velvet; a full bath with a tiled steamer shower, a marble whirlpool tub, and brass fixtures; and a small personal office, where he did more internet surfing than actual business. His outfit for the evening was not that different from his pajamas: loose, silky black trousers, a long, button-down, black silk shirt, chosen for comfort and to hide the swell of stomach he'd been unable to work off in his middle age. He selected an orange scarf and draped it around his neck—no lei for him, of course—and slid his bare feet into a supple pair of leather loafers, which he'd bought almost twenty years ago in Florence. This was the time of the evening when he felt most acutely the absence of drink; ten years ago, he would have had a glass of wine or a bourbon in hand as he stood at the window and watched the arrival of his first guests, the ones who had driven right over from Market still wearing their gray suits and INDUSTRY badges. Ten years ago, when he still looked a bit like the man in the oil portrait down in his living room, he would have been waiting for that precise moment when the alcohol gave him courage—a loosening in his joints, a warm tingle in his chest—and when it came, he'd knock back the dregs of the drink, smooth his goatee into place, and descend the stairs with actual pleasure, actual anticipation for what the night might bring.

He sipped a room temperature mineral water. Sobriety wasn't unpleasant, exactly, now that he had gotten the hang of it, but neither was it natural. He wore it like a polite expression, worked at it the way he'd once worked at eradicating the Georgia drawl from his accent. Sobriety was like remembering the details of an elaborate lie or reciting the alphabet backwards. It took concentration and will.

He checked his reflection in the gilt mirror in the upstairs hallway. This morning, at the International Home Furnishings Center, he had seen the Sumner twins—glorified appraisers hocking shoddy reproduction furniture and calling it *revival*—and surgery had made them even more blandly similar, their smiling faces smoothed into planes, silver hair swooping back from spray-tanned foreheads as blameless as children's. They had bared their identical veneers at Eldon, looked him up and down as if to say, *Couldn't you at least make an effort?* Absurd, is what they were, and yet they had gotten their own show on public television, a spin-off of *Antiques in the Attic* called *Basement Booty*—*Basement Booty*, for god's sake!—in which they went into the homes of people desperate for cash, rummaged through their basements for items of value, and then auctioned the finds in a climactic sequence edited to produce nonexistent tension. So perhaps they knew something Eldon did not about the way the business worked today, what a man had to do to survive. If Eldon were to have his face stretched into a pleasant mask of anonymity, perhaps Barry Levin would come to his parties, and he'd be on one of those reality shows by now, judging amateur designers building a sofa out of popsicle sticks or sewing draperies out of corn husks.

It was 8:00. He could hear the murmur of cheerful voices downstairs, the murmur that meant his party was populated enough that he could respectably join it. The house, it seemed to him, swayed a little on nights like this one; the shuffling of feet on the hardwood floors, each board rasping against another, shivering the floor joists, the structural posts, the rafters, made the upstairs feel not quite solid, as if it could tip slightly and slide off the frame down into the peony beds. He gripped the handrail as he descended the stairs and reminded himself that it was always like this, the seasickness and uncertainty, but he had nothing to prove to these people, his guests—and in another moment he would be embraced, fawned over, and someone would say to him, as someone always did, "You have a beautiful home."

When his slippered foot took the last step, Tony appeared with a woman at his elbow. She was middle-aged, with brass-colored hair sculpted into waves, a long skirt with little metal accents that jingled as she swung her hips, and a protective cloud of perfume so strong that Eldon's eyes watered. She was wearing a pink lei.

"Eldon," Tony said, "this is Eva St. James. She's the new buyer for Belk."

"Mr. Carlisle," this woman said, her waxy lips pulling into a smile. "It is such a pleasure to meet you. What a lovely home you have."

Eldon kissed her hand. "Eva, Eva. My mother was named Eva. The pleasure is all mine."

His house—this house—was built after the Civil War, in the Southern Colonial style, though he had, to the chagrin of his architect and builders, insisted on certain adjustments: he wanted the Doric columns on the front colonnade replaced with Corinthian columns, the Georgian-style arched cornice over the door replaced with a Grecian-inspired frieze depicting women carrying jugs of water and baskets of fruit. The ceiling of the colonnade he painted a bright aqua to ward off bad spirits, and a crystal chandelier—delightfully oversized and gaudy—hung where a wrought iron lantern once had, illuminating the marble table where he displayed, as a joke that almost always went unnoticed, a bronze bust of Nero. The house was full of little jokes like this. The handsome leatherbound books on the built-in shelves around the fireplace included the Reader's Book Club Condensed Works of Great World Literature, a fifty-volume mail-order series from the 1960s, including *Condensed Moby Dick*, *Condensed Tristram Shandy*, and *Condensed Gone with the Wind*—that's how the titles were printed on the spines—which Eldon displayed near his Andy Warhol *Campbell's Soup Cans* print, one from the less iconic blue-and-purple series, but still worth a pretty penny. The cabinet hiding his fifty-inch OLED television had a picture of a cabinet television painted on it. The mosaic coffee table included, among the fragments of antique Italian and Spanish tile, Eldon's fifty-state magnet set, which he had been collecting from roadside gift shops since the '70s.

Even the oil portrait of himself, which he'd commissioned in the late '80s, when half of his money was going up his nose and people were still telling him he looked like George Michael—he'd once been completely earnest about it, and then he became embarrassed by it, and then the embarrassment turned to amusement, and he brought it to this house to display, all four feet by six feet of it framed in ornately carved mahogany and leaned up against a wall in the living room so that young Eldon seemed to be peeking at guests over the back of one of the leopard-print upholstered couches. When he had been interviewed a few years back by *Architectural Record*, he said, "I like to make fun of sincerity, to take design elements that are usually indicative of status or taste and twist them, but so subtly that the viewer may not recognize the twisting." The reporter had summed up the house as "eclectic and whimsical, a fortress of attitude." Eldon rather liked that phrase, "fortress of attitude," but he loathed the word *whimsy*. There wasn't any meanness in it, and therefore it missed the point.

It was practically obligatory that he grew up not in Georgian splendor but Georgia squalor, the youngest of four brothers, three of whom survived to adulthood, their childhood home a two-room farmhouse outside of Ashburn. His father, who worked on a peanut farm, died when Eldon was three. His mother, whose name was Loretta and not Eva, as he'd told the perfumed Belk buyer, worked sixty-hour weeks at a truck stop diner, brought home leftover catfish and chicken livers for supper, and scrubbed the dirt rings from her boys' necks each Sunday before dragging them to the Second Baptist Church. She kept a clean, Spartan house; her idea of home décor was dressing the kitchen table with a spray of coneflowers in a rinsed-out Coca-Cola bottle. Eldon, who at the age of nine was a sensitive, lisping boy named Eldon Carson, treated for free by the health department for rickets, drew a still life of the flowers, the bottle, and the table for a school contest, winning a blue ribbon and a five-dollar prize. Even now he could conjure a mental image of that drawing—the way he'd shaded to get the warble of light through the thickness of the glass—and feel a thrill of pride and excitement, and he could taste the tart penny candy his mother had let him buy with a portion of the prize money, and he could feel the rough weave of those five crisp dollar bills. He could also—and was this not obligatory, too?—remember the derision of his older brothers, Charlie and Lyle (Ned gone two years by this time, hit by a car walking home from baseball practice), how Charlie had called him a "fairy," no doubt just jealous and lashing out, and yet he'd touched something, sensed something, and that was the beginning of it all, Eldon knew now: the seed for his success and the reason he'd had to become another man to claim it.

Charlie, sixty-eight and still living in Ashburn, was a State Farm agent. A couple years ago, Eldon had accepted his Facebook friend request out of curiosity—he hadn't been in the same room with his brother in twenty years—and spent a long evening in his office, scanning through Charlie's photo albums of vacations (Hilton Head, Smoky Mountains) and church socials and meetings of the Rotary Club, noticing that Charlie and his wife, Pepper, had started to resemble one another in their older age, both broad and pale with bifocals and wispy graying hair. Charlie's status updates went like this: "Grillout with the fam, I am a Lucky man!!!!" Or "What is she hiding in the EMAILS, just like Slick Willie, LOCK HER UP!!!" Sensing the danger but unable to stop himself, Eldon had scrolled down to June 2015, and yep, Charlie had marked the legalization of gay marriage by musing, "Sad day for our great country, what is this world coming to." Fuck this, Eldon thought, and promptly unfriended him.

Lyle he still talked to occasionally. Lyle received a scholarship to Emory, graduated with a double major in biology and chemistry, then went on to get his PhD in horticulture at University of Georgia. Now he was, to the best of Eldon's understanding, on a research team studying the effects of climate change on Southeastern cash crops. He was fiercely intelligent and gentle spirited, but humorless; having a conversation with him was like talking to a very bright and awkward child, in that he only answered questions and never asked them, took almost everything Eldon said literally ("I'm having drinks tonight with a couple of old queens," Eldon said once, and Lyle replied with innocent wonder, "Really?"), and became easily distracted, once even interrupting Eldon midsentence to say, "Sorry, just had an idea" and hanging up.

Eldon sometimes forgot he had brothers. Someone would ask him, "Any siblings?" and he'd pause, momentarily bewildered, and reply, "My brother Ned died when I was very young," which was all the truth he felt like claiming.

His mother was still alive. Eldon had bought her a condominium in Sarasota, in a community called Lunar Estates, a name he liked because he could make the joke that he'd sent his mother to the moon, though Tony was the only person he'd ever made the joke to. He visited her twice a year, never on holidays, when he'd have to also contend with his brothers, and stayed each visit for a week, which was as long as they could stand one another. His mother had the infuriating habit of acting miserable for the entirety of Eldon's stay, complaining nonstop about the weather, the food at the expensive restaurants he took her to, Eldon's style of dress, the disrepair of the highways, the explicit nature of nighttime network television, the extravagant gifts he brought her from his travels to Europe and Asia—silk scarves, chocolates, fine bone china, Italian leather luggage—but then, each evening, sitting for hours in her living room talking on the phone to her cadre of elderly female friends, most of whom were also Lunar Estates residents, bragging insufferably and in excruciating detail about every moment of her and Eldon's day, down to what Eldon ate at each meal ("He had the pecan-crusted grouper with a lemon butter sauce and ate all but a bite"), and saying, "It was just real nice. Real, real nice."

"So you liked the restaurant, after all," Eldon said after one such call.

"It was all right," his mother said flatly.

He had run away from home at seventeen, not called her for eight months to let her know where he was or even that he was alive. He hadn't been trying purposefully to hurt her; he hadn't been thinking of her one way or the other. He'd just been living his life, first and briefly in Atlanta, then in New York, letting sixty-year-old businessmen snort lines off his stomach and suck him off, then sucking off the beautiful young men he wanted so much to be like, men in Valentino suits and Ferragamos who teased him about his twang and his lisp and made him pick up their dry cleaning, their Chinese takeout. He'd never had Chinese food before. He was clumsy with chopsticks, and he once dropped a wad of greasy lo mein noodles between his legs onto a white Silvio Garibaldi sofa, and the sofa's owner had screamed at him until Eldon fled the apartment in nothing but his underwear and a T-shirt. Eldon had understood—it was a beautiful sofa. He may have been a Georgia rube who didn't know a wonton from a bonbon, but he had an appreciation for beautiful things.

He finally called his mother because he had gotten a job, a real job in fashion, and he had no one else to share the news with. It was as a second assistant to the associate creative director at Halston, and he was still picking up dry-cleaning and Chinese takeout, but now he was getting paid $3.20 an hour, enough to rent a tiny room in a boarding house in the East Village. It wasn't until he heard her voice—her tired "Hello?"—that he wondered whether she would be anything but happy to hear from him, and he had paused a full beat before saying, suddenly full of fear, "Mama?"

She had started sobbing.

"Mama," he tried again. "Mama, calm down. I'm sorry." He wondered how long it would take before he could tell her his news, before they could cut through the dramatics and revel together in his success.

"Where are you?" she asked.

"New York City."

"And you're okay? You're not hurt?"

Eldon had laughed sharply. "Jesus, Mom, I'm fine. I'm great, actually."

"Don't call me again," she said, then hung up.

He was standing at a pay phone a block away from his apartment—his closet—and he returned the receiver to the hook with a shaking hand. *Of all the— the goddamn nerve of—* He started home, but it was only 5:30, and the airless room would be unbearably hot. He had eight dollars to last him until payday, not enough to spare for a movie or a beer or a meal in a restaurant, and though he knew on some level that he had no right to be angry at his mother, that he had been a bad and selfish son these last eight months, he was filled with a murderous rage. It was August, and the early evening air smelled of wet garbage and car exhaust. His stomach churned with hunger and nausea. He stalked down the sidewalk blindly and swung his fist at a wall, setting off an explosion in his hand that rang right up into his shoulder socket. An Asian woman eating in a sandwich shop stared at him through the plate glass, eyes wide with interest and fear, and Eldon saw her through a miasma of pain, and he staggered with light-headedness. It was 1977 in New York. No one came forward to check on him. His shredded knuckles oozed blood. Back at the boarding house, someone was locked up in the floor's one bathroom taking a crap, Eldon surmised from the smell, so he went to his room, wrapped his hand in a dirty dishtowel, and lowered himself gently to his pallet.

Fuck her, he thought, staring at the water-stained ceiling. *Fuck them all.*

He didn't speak to his mother again for six years. Even after the anger wore off and the guilt and longing replaced it—and perhaps especially after the guilt and longing replaced it—he held back, told himself he'd forgotten the number. In '81 he read an article in the *New York Times* about the Go-Go's, an all-girl band that had been getting a lot of radio play lately (though sneered at, mostly, by the New Wavers Eldon ran with), and he'd found himself pausing on the name of the lead singer, Belinda Carlisle; now *that*, Carlisle, was memorable, a name with some elegance and European mystique. He decided between sips of coffee to adopt it as his own.

There was no innate self, he had believed, no authentic core that a person either embraced or denied or displayed or obscured. A personality was a design, and the most powerful people were the ones who weren't afraid to immolate themselves, start fresh, throw out the bits that were no longer of use. "He's forgot what he come from," folks back home would say when a person escaped Ashburn to make a new life somewhere else, somewhere better. "He's done gotten above his raising." And what was wrong with that? Wasn't that the point?

Under the tab "About Eldon" on his website was this description:

> Eldon Carlisle came to New York City in 1976 and rose with startling speed among the ranks at Halston and later Anne Klein, where he gained a reputation for designing innovative accessories, especially leather handbags and footwear. In 1985 he traveled to Milan to study shoemaking with the masters but instead became so taken with the Memphis furniture design movement that he switched career tracks and has not looked back. After a decade of winning over high-end and celebrity clients with his distinct aesthetic, which combines traditional elements with tongue-in-cheek modernity, Eldon launched Eldon Carlisle Home, a furniture line specializing in versatile but stylish chairs, sofas, and sectionals. Today, Eldon Carlisle Home has expanded into the mainstream marketplace. EC Originals, which offers mix-and-match bedding, curtains, and rugs at affordable price points, is sold at Bed Bath and Beyond, Macy's, and Dillard's.

So much between the lines of that. So much left unsaid. Nothing about his mother, who finally spent her savings hiring a private detective to track him down, or his dead brother, or how he was fired by Anne Klein in what was called, diplomatically, a "managerial restructuring," which was why he'd fled to Italy. Nothing about an actor named John, whom he'd loved, and their eleven years together, or how John finally left him—sick, he'd said, of Eldon's thoughtlessness and falseness, his "disturbing lack of basic fucking empathy."

What he had always loved about designing the interior of a home, as opposed to designing a dress or a pair of shoes, was that there was never some perfect conclusion, some clear, final execution of his vision. A home was dynamic and ever changing. It had to evolve to suit its occupant. When his habits in a home became too rigid—when he'd worn a familiar groove between the sofa and the kitchen, and he could reach unconsciously for every pot, plate, and appliance, and the cedar trees had grown tall enough, finally, to obscure that unsavory little glimpse of the distant highway—when there were no more nooks to fill and problems to solve, and he'd found the exact right painting to hang over the mantle, the perfect cut glass doorknob for the downstairs bath—that was when he grew bored, not comfortable, and he knew that the time had come to move on. He had always taken pride in that restlessness, that lack of sentimental attachment.

The sky opened by 8:30, soaking the guests who had to park at the road and walk up the drive, extinguishing the paper lanterns and the candelabras, and ruining the tray of fajita wraps that had been sitting on the back patio. Eldon laughed in his light way, fetching towels himself from the hall closet. "Kick off those wet shoes, dear," he said to each of the women, who went around playfully in bare feet, leaving little oily smudges on the polished floors. The air wafting into the front door smelled luscious and green, and it was deliciously cool. No one seemed to mind the storm much.

"Welcome to my underwater luau," he greeted the latecomers.

There were a handful of guests in pink leis: the Belk buyer; Wilke, the chairman of the Furniture Market board of directors; a few others. No Barry Levin, but Tony whispered to him that there was apparently a dinner tonight, something sponsored by the local chapter of ASID, and perhaps Levin would show up later for a nightcap. Were there fewer VIPs this year than last? Fewer than five years ago? Eldon couldn't be sure.

Eldon was on the front porch, pressing a Jonathan Martin Fine Furnishings sales rep for dirt ("I was shocked, darling, just shocked to hear you're not displaying in the IHFC this season. Everything's copacetic, I hope?"), when a young man wearing a suit jacket—an awful, vintage-by-way-of-Goodwill thing—interrupted their conversation. "Can I take a picture with you?" he asked. Eldon glanced at his badge: STUDENT, it read. University of North Carolina at Greensboro. What was he even doing here?

Eldon smiled apologetically at the sales rep, who looked relieved to have escaped the grilling. "Of course," Eldon said to the student with steely politeness.

The young man was probably gay—most of the male design students were—but homely, cheeks crusted still with adolescent acne, narrow in the shoulders, wide, soft hips. Eldon didn't feel even a flicker of attraction, and he let his hand rest as lightly as possible on the shoulder of the young man's scratchy tweed suit jacket as the friend held up an iPhone and tapped the screen.

"Awesome," the young man said, examining the image. He typed something, his thumbs a blur, then jabbed the screen a last time with finality. It had been posted online somewhere, Eldon realized. He hadn't even been able to see the image first, to deem it acceptable or not.

"Well, then," Eldon said stiffly. "Enjoy yourself."

The young man quaffed a miniature margarita. "Yes, sir. I mean, we really are, sir. Thanks." He and the friend wandered to a platter of shrimp skewers and started loading up plates.

"Who the hell brought him here?" Eldon muttered to Tony, who was at his elbow—he was never very far from Eldon's elbow. "Jesus Christ, do I have to feed the college kids now?"

"That was the guy that won the Carlisle Prize this year," Tony said. "He had the idea for the flat-pack eco chair you liked."

"Oh, that's right," Eldon murmured. That had been a clever proposal, actually. The shipping materials were incorporated into the design, so there was almost no waste. But he was still annoyed about the picture, and it disappointed him that the young man had wanted his photograph because Eldon was the benefactor behind the contest, not because he was an industry celebrity. So he said, "Keep an eye on him and the friend. I don't want them getting drunk and causing a scene."

Tony shrugged easily and sipped his beer. "I'm sure they'll be fine," he said, and Eldon, filled suddenly with that same explosive anger from over thirty years ago, anger that made him want to drive his fist into something, snapped, "Just do as I say."

Tony put his hands in the air, as if he were surrendering, and backed away, his face betraying not so much as a flicker of annoyance. "Okay. I hear you. I'll watch them." He swung around, hands falling gently to his sides, and followed the young man and his friend back into the house, where they were undoubtedly hoping to find another passing tray of mini margaritas.

Eldon felt a tightening in his chest; it started in his sinuses and ended in his gut, like a hard string getting plucked. He looked, as he always did on nights like this, at one of the tables with the big galvanized bucket of ice and its bouquet of longnecks, then at the sweating bottle of chardonnay and the mostly full bottle of merlot plugged loosely with its plastic cork. When you felt like he was feeling now, almost anything would do, really. Maybe not the merlot, warm and puckery, a headache in a glass, but the cold chardonnay, sure: two big swallows and the taste didn't much matter. Even ten years after the last drop had hit his tongue, Eldon could nearly tremble with pleasure at the thought of wine. He'd loved every bit of the ritual of drinking it: grunting with the effort of pulling a stubborn cork, and the satisfying, soft *pop!* signaling success; a fine crystal glass with a wisp of a stem, and how his exhalation of breath over the rim made the faintest whistling sound. He loved the full, round flavor of the wine—*round* was the word, yes, the liquid like a pebble that his mouth moved around—and he loved that first flood of pleasure a few sips in, the creeping warmth from his neck to his cheeks, the sudden flush of confidence. He had loved, when he and John were still together, that first drink of early evening, the sun low and golden, the way, reunited after their workdays had separated them, there was always so much to say. A bad day, translated to a partner through a glass of wine, became bearable. It was worth having lived through his supervisor's stupidity or having missed the train. It was worth those times when his design got nixed, and he couldn't help but wonder, as he so frequently wondered, if this was ever going to happen for him, *success*. It was worth it for that sensation of drunkenly vibrating with passion and ambition, he and John confessing their grievances and dreams to one another before whipping themselves into tearful declarations of love, of plans for a glorious future together. I love you. I love *you*. It had been so easy, for a time, and so fine. And then it was not so easy. And then it was lost forever.

"They're gone," Tony said suddenly, and Eldon jolted, startled.

"Gone," he repeated. "Who's gone?"

"The contest winner and his buddy," Tony said. "I thought you'd be relieved to know."

Eldon's tongue felt dry and thick, and he swallowed. "Where?"

"Wherever they came from. They ate some shrimp and took off. I saw them get in their car."

Eldon processed this. "That's good," he said, but what he was thinking—too embarrassing to utter aloud, he knew—was *How dare they? Who do they think they are?* It occurred to him that the good parties were *supposed* to have young people at them, not a bunch of middle-aged men and women, gnarled toes and pasty legs exposed in their absurd Hawaiian shorts and flip-flops, worn without the faintest whiff of irony. One of the Italian designers he had apprenticed with so many years ago had a saying, which Eldon had been too young at the time to understand: *Il cinismo soffoca la creatività; sincerità uccide.* Cynicism stifles creativity; but sincerity kills it. He had thought himself impervious to sincerity, clever, hip; his was a life lived with an arched eyebrow. Yet here he was, in his sixties, and it seemed to him for the first time that his best was behind him. Barry Levin wasn't going to show up tonight. No one would be offering him a helping hand to the next tier of renown. And if he'd ever had any legitimate artistic integrity, he'd lost it by the time he OK'd the first batch of designs for EC Originals.

"Tony," he said. "I'm not myself. We need to wrap this up early tonight."

"You mean this party?" Tony looked, for the first Eldon could remember, uneasy, and he took a spiteful pleasure in having rattled him. Funny, how the thing that had made Tony indispensable to Eldon over the years was also the quality that most maddened him. To see some anger from the man, some passion—was that too much to ask?

"Yes. The party," Eldon said.

Tony leaned in so close that Eldon could practically taste the beer on his breath. "There are probably fifty people here. Including Charlie Haas. Eva St. James. Barry Levin's assistant promised me—"

"Fuck Barry Levin. Barry Levin doesn't get to skip my party. His invitation is rescinded."

"You can't *do* that, Eldon. You can't invite these people into your home and kick them out when they start to annoy you. You can't rescind Barry-fucking-Levin's invitation. I'm telling you that he might still show. I was just on the phone with Ally, and she's pushing him to put in an appearance."

"Pushing him," Eldon said.

"You've got to swallow your pride for once. There are people who depend on you, goddammit."

"Fuck them, too."

Tony was red-faced. "Go upstairs," he whispered with force. "I'll keep the party going, and then I'll say you felt unwell and had to retire early."

Eldon laughed. "Retire early. Like I'm an old man."

"You're acting like an old ninny."

Eldon passed the table of drinks on his way to the front door and ran his finger across the condensation on the large bottle of chardonnay. He had thought, after things fell apart with John, that getting sober might make some difference. That sobriety would reveal his best self, his suppressed core of goodness, and then the universe would reward him.

The indoors smelled of damp towels, sweat, onion, and cilantro. Eldon moved numbly among the laughing knots of his guests, unnoticed as they tilted their heads sideways over paper plates to take sloppy bites of the fajita wraps, as their drink levels fell and they reassured themselves by spotting the nearest restocked table of beverages. He remembered well that bright, buzzed panic. Is this my last drink? Please don't let it be my last drink.

He was almost to the stairs when he chanced to glance into the living room and saw a group of three people clustered conspiratorially behind the sofa, backs to the door, shoulders brushing. He crept quietly in behind them, his Italian slippers silent on the wood floors.

"He's watching us," the woman said with a comic whisper. Eldon spotted her pink lei before he identified her as the Belk buyer.

"*Darling*," said one of the men, the Jonathan Martin sales rep. "Darling, come closer. Speak into my ascot."

"You're not making any sense." She giggled like a teenager. Her wine sloshed a little as she hiccupped, and the third man made a show of blotting the spill from her bodice with a clean handkerchief.

"What a magnificent act of ego," this man said. Eldon didn't recognize him. "You almost have to admire the audacity of it."

"The delusion of it," said the Jonathan Martin sales rep. He waved a finger at the painted Eldon's unsmiling face. "I think he had George Michael sit for this."

The woman snorted.

"He did look like this once," the other man said. "He visited my class at Parsons. Early '90s, it would have been. He was quite glamorous, even with the accent. Our professor called him Scarlett O'Hara."

The Belk woman hiccupped again. "Oh, Jesus. You're killing me."

"Georgia Michael," the Jonathan Martin sales rep quipped.

"Dorian Gay," the Belk woman wheezed, her shoulders quaking.

"You didn't know Tara had so much leopard print, did you?"

He would have revealed himself if he didn't think it would ultimately please them, after they had gotten over their initial embarrassment and stumbled through their breathless, falsely stricken apologies. Instead, he made a silent retreat to the front hall and up the stairs. Without realizing how he'd done it, he found himself lying across his bed and staring up at the gathered center of the satin canopy. He knew every fold. He knew the way the lamplight gleamed this time of night on the polished bedpost. He knew the hanging gold thread that he had told himself so many times to cut the next time he had his hand on the cuticle scissors. The house swayed as another downpour echoed against the roof, his guests' laughter and good cheer washing up to him in waves.

Sometime after midnight, there was a knock on the bedroom door. Eldon, who had been dozing, gasped for breath and struggled to sit up. "Yes? Hello?"

"That's the last of them." It was Tony.

"All right, then," said Eldon. He swallowed hard. It seemed to him that there was a right thing he could say in this moment—words that would make Tony turn the knob of the door and look at him with something other than disgust. *You're the only friend I've got*, maybe. Or *I don't know why I'm like this*. But the words wouldn't come—his lips refused to form them. "Good night," he said finally, and the tone of his own voice dismayed him: the haughty impatience, the petulance.

"Goodbye, Eldon," Tony said. It wasn't very long at all before the sound of his car motor floated up to Eldon through the open window.

The rain had stopped. Eldon slipped downstairs, soft on his feet, as if there were someone in the house he might disturb—a beloved one, sleeping, warming the other half of the canopied bed. There was a stale smell in the air still, the lingering aroma of sweat and onion, but the plates and glasses and bottles had all been cleared away, the kitchen counters wiped to a shine. He checked the refrigerator, found three cellophane-wrapped trays of leftovers, a couple dozen beer bottles, and a half-full bottle of white wine. This last he grabbed, pulling the plastic cork roughly with his molars, and dumped down the sink. Tony usually did this for him, and Eldon wondered, sucking the faint sour tang off the end of the cork, what it meant that he had failed to.

On the patio, the marble dining table was beaded with water. His peonies were slumped flat, beaten by the downpour, and the paper lanterns, so briefly lovely, hung like wads of dough from the shepherd's hooks. He stood in the open doorway for a long time, staring out at them, and found that he was still holding the empty wine bottle, so he tossed it underhanded, like a softball player, and it exploded deliciously on the tabletop, sending a scatter of glass onto the lawn. The shards glittered like new rain.

At last he found himself in the living room, perched on one of the striped wingback chairs. Young Eldon regarded him seriously over the back of the leopard print sofa. The Covington Three Bells Clock marked the seconds between then and now. Someone had draped a pink lei over the mahogany frame, and it hung across the painted Eldon's forehead like a flower crown.

distancing

The roads of the subdivision were seared into a wooded tract back in the early '90s, and the homes constructed along them are spacious and spaciously placed—not a bad place to practice social distancing if distance you must. Jana told Brian, back when they were house hunting, that she wouldn't do a McMansion, but this is—let's get real—the McMansion's country cousin: four-bedroom, brick, with white pillars supporting a porch barely deep enough to accommodate a glider. They are in an excellent school district, though, not that it matters right now, with everything shut down.

Jana has been working at home for almost six years as a recruiter specializing in medical jobs at rural hospitals and clinics, and her business hasn't been affected yet—probably won't be unless times got even more desperate. Brian's is another story. Three weeks into the mandatory quarantine, he and his partners made the difficult decision to close the cosmetic half of their practice and to limit medical appointments to Tuesdays and Wednesdays. He has worked sixty- and seventy-hour weeks for as long as she has known him, and this new schedule of his is more surreal than the pandemic, than the world. Every day she wakes up and registers his presence in the bed beside her with a tremor of something she can't quite bring herself to acknowledge is disappointment.

He hasn't exactly been much help around the house. Jana spends the mornings trying to keep the boys, nine-year-old Shawn and eleven-year-old Trevor, on track with their schoolwork. Around 11:30, she goes to the kitchen to prepare a lunch—something out of the deep freeze, with a side of something else out of the deep freeze.

Then it's Brian's shift with the kids, which means Jana sequesters herself in the home office; the boys go to their bedrooms to stare at their tablets; and Brian, Jana supposes, does more of whatever he spent the morning doing: surfing the internet on his laptop, pacing the house, putting another forty minutes in on the treadmill. He makes excuses to go into the office on the days it's closed, and she suspects he accomplishes nothing there but watching porn on his office computer and, according to their Netflix history, sprinting through two seasons of *Rust Valley Restorers*. They are snippy in front of one another, even in front of—inevitably in front of—the boys. Jana's work has never been as lucrative as Brian's, not even close; she knows he views it as a step or two up from a hobby, something that barely mitigates their tax liability and won't sustain them if his practice goes belly-up. But it's income. And it's more productive than moping and masturbating.

When her compressed workday is done, she goes for a walk in the woods. Sometimes she can coax the boys into accompanying her. Once a week or so, Brian will tag along dutifully, edging around patches of mud in a pair of near-pristine trail shoes he bought two summers ago when they vacationed at Bar Harbor. But often Jana is alone, and more often than not she prefers it. She is drawn to the woods these days, which is odd, because she was never much of a nature person. Their appeal, during the house hunt, had been privacy—a buffer between their house, the highway, and the neighboring properties. During quarantine, however—at the age of forty-two—she has opened a door within herself that she'd thought was locked, to a room she didn't believe existed. It's a cool spring, and she can go out in long sleeves without being harassed by mosquitoes. The trees are in their most tender yellow-green leaf, and the last petals from the flowering trees—the redbuds and dogwoods that struggle toward light in the breaks between pines, oaks, and maples—dapple earth the color of brownie batter. It's the earth, the dirt, that most intrigues Jana. Again, strange—she has never been a gardener, doesn't even bother with a few herbs and tomato plants like most middle-class women her age. But when she's alone, she finds herself pausing, crouching, gripping fistfuls of soil and then opening her hands to reveal the impressions, faintly lined, her palms left behind. She brings the dirt to her nose, nostrils prickling at the richness, the faint, slightly allergic edge of mold or must. The word that comes to mind when she inhales is *delicious*—again, strange. And one day, with the casual unthinking reflex of a person pulling her hand out of a potato chip bag, she finds herself not just smelling the dirt but scooping a handful of it into her mouth.

When she was a little girl, she and her family drove across town two or three days a week to visit her granny. Granny smoked, and each room of her small house had an ashtray at the ready, heaped with spent filters. Jana's mother griped about the house, about the way the smoke smell oozed into their pores during even a short visit, but Jana had loved the cigarette stench, had put her face over the bowls of ashes and breathed deeply, getting a zing of pleasure that was probably, she thinks now, some kind of secondary nicotine hit. This is like that, a bit. The dirt doesn't taste like food, it isn't actually delicious, but it is something more than delicious. She takes one more bite before stopping herself, wipes her mouth with the back of her hand, runs her tongue along her teeth to try to clear the last of the grit from sight. She swallows, and the dirt hits her gut as comfortably as warm milk.

That night, after everyone else from the household is in bed, she Zooms with Mizha. Her friendship with Mizha is as unlikely as everything else in 2020; it began when Jana sought her out to interview for a surgical attending position at a regional hospital in rural Kentucky. Somehow, across a handful of Zoom meetings—most of which involved Jana trying to convince Mizha that Roma, Kentucky, was an up-and-coming bedroom community for Nashville and not a town of ten thousand where a small but ugly minority of people flew Rebel flags next to their UK banners—they made an honest connection. It's inexplicable. Mizha is thirty-three, Pakistani, stunningly beautiful. Her career was tainted early on by the bad luck of being named, as a resident, in a high-profile malpractice case out of Florida. She is in Kentucky now. It's not so bad, she assures Jana.

She gets to Nashville once a month, or at least she did before the pandemic. She is dating another doctor.

Jana tells her about the dirt eating, and Mizha surprises her by laughing.

"Jana," she says scoldingly. "You know what this is."

"I don't," Jana said. "I really don't."

"It is the change." Mizha wags her finger at the screen and across five hundred miles. "You are getting ready for the change."

"But I'm only forty-two."

"And when did you think the change happened?"

"My mother was fifty-one."

"Well, you may be fifty-one before it is final. It can take a while for some women."

"Jesus," Jana says. "Nine years! There is no way. My boys—what would they do?"

"The same thing the other sons of mothers do. They will wait and survive."

"They'll be men before it's over." She is remembering her mother's change. Jana was in her twenties already, at college. It hardly affected her at all.

"It almost certainly will not be that long. That is a worst-case scenario. And there is some research suggesting if you go to earth early, you get through it sooner."

"But they don't know for sure? That's a heck of risk."

Mizha shrugged. "It is women's health. No one is throwing money at it."

"Would you go to earth early? Is that what you'd do?"

"Yes," Mizha said without pause. "But I like to pretend I can control things beyond my powers."

"Crap," Jana said. The screen in front of her blurred. "I thought I had time."

"Everyone thinks that."

"You do. God. To be thirty-three again."

"My mother said it was her last great adventure," Mizha says. "What did your mother say?"

Jana thinks. She had asked her mother about it, awkwardly, because people mostly don't talk about the change. It is like that other little death—not a topic for polite conversation. A woman will go away for a while. Mostly, after a few months, she comes back and resumes a version of her life. Jana's father, when he told her about her mother's absence, had stammered, cleared his throat, and stumbled on in an embarrassed way: *She. You know.*

"She said it was like a nice nap." This had seemed, to twenty-one-year-old Jana, indescribably sad, and there had been a faraway look in her mother's eye that made Jana suspect that even this was putting a positive face on it.

"That is not so bad. See? That is not so bad at all. And when you wake up, maybe all this"—she motions at the screen, at herself, at the quarantined world—"will be over."

"Well, maybe. I'll think about it."

"Will I see you again?" Mizha asks. "Before?"

"I don't know," Jana said.

She is wide awake after they say goodbye and disconnect. She walks the downstairs of her house, examining the things that meant so much to her when she and Brian bought them or had them installed: the Stickley end tables and console; the marble kitchen countertops and farmhouse sink. The dinette set in the kitchen is littered with the boys' detritus. A bag of Doritos, left open to go stale. A couple of Eureka Math workbooks and two open laptops with dark screens. She has spent the last two months of mornings perched on a chair between them, chiding and redirecting them, praising them, occasionally losing her patience and nearly yelling, in voice she hopes will carry to Brian's study, "We could have been done with this an hour ago if you'd just stay on task!" In the brief moments the boys are both occupied, she looks at her phone, drinks cup after cup of coffee. If she isn't here, none of it will get done. Or maybe it will. She can't decide which troubles her more.

It is spattering rain when she steps outside, following the bobbing circle of her flashlight beam. She has never walked into the woods at night before—not in the twelve years she has lived in this house.

But she isn't scared. The night air is fresh and smells very green. The tree canopies form a protective roof above her, and she's able to pull down her hood and scan the ground for a bare patch, soft soil in which to burrow and invite the change. Maybe, she thinks, her mother's faraway look wasn't sadness. Maybe it was nostalgia or longing, the kind of longing a mother isn't supposed to feel for a time when she shut the rest of the world out.

This is a good spot. Jana drops to her knees and plunges her fingers into the ground. It is loose; it gives easily, as if it has been waiting for her, and clearing the oblong of earth is no work at all. Her pulse doesn't even rise. A sensation is sinking into her as she sinks into the depression she has made. It is like sleepiness, but not. This winter, she had a lingering cough so bad that the doctor prescribed a codeine cough syrup, and she took an extra-large dose one night, hoping to get some sleep, and there was a half hour, before she fell unconscious, when she lay in bed and stared at a band of light on the ceiling and felt a dreamy sense of rightness. Her limbs were perfectly placed; the sheet was smooth beneath her; even the lock of hair that had fallen across her cheekbone seemed like a soft touch rather than an irritant. This is like that half hour, but purer. She settles on her side into the ground's embrace, knees slightly bent, and the dirt starts to fall back onto her. She opens her mouth, puts out her tongue, and feels an electric ripple throughout her body. She is facing the lit wedge of her home that is visible through the dark slashes of tree trunks. When she rises again, months or years from now, the house will be the first thing she sees, and then she can decide whether she wants to go back to it.

axis

The hotel was thirty miles from the nearest beach, but the room décor was optimistically sea-themed. Scallop shells patterned the coverlets on the matching double beds. By the thermostat, set by housekeeping to sixty-eight, a bland watercolor print depicted a sand dune barbed by slumped fencing. Outside was humid, and the room, its air-conditioning unit chugging steadily, was clammy and smelled faintly of mold, more strongly of Febreze. The woman and her daughter lay stretched out, each to a bed, and stared at the water-stained popcorn ceiling. They'd driven in from two states west, almost nine hours on the road, and neither had bothered yet to open a bag, flip a light switch, or scroll through the basic cable offerings.

"You're probably anxious to get over there," the daughter said. "Should we go?"

The mother sighed. "In a little bit. I just want to lie here and rest a minute. It's probably going to be a long night." She rubbed her face and checked the digital clock on the nightstand. "Did you text her to tell her we made it?"

"Yeah. She said, 'Hurry up and get here.'"

The mother laughed. "Probably has her hands full."

"I doubt Nathan is helping much."

"Oh, he's all right." Down the hall, a door slammed. Kids' voices, pounding of feet. The swimming pool beckoned. "Don't be so hard on him. It's going to be a long week if you two start bickering."

"No one's going to bicker," the daughter said. She grabbed the phone she'd just set down, jabbed the home button, and started scrolling. "She already has, like, fifty pictures posted."

"You would, too. Why are you so negative?"

"I'm not negative. But, and okay, this is the last thing I'm going to say. Calliope? I mean, why?"

"It's cute," the mother said. "And they're calling her Callie."

"They should have just named her Callie, then."

"Are you done?"

"Um, probably. For now."

"Any comments about the baby? Maybe she should lose some weight? Maybe her taste in music is bad?"

"Nope. Baby's perfect. Except for her name."

"You can give her a nickname, then."

"I have: Lil Shit."

"But that's my nickname for you."

"Littler Shit, then."

"That's Laura."

"Littlest Shit."

"Perfect."

The mother stretched, flexed her toes. They popped audibly. She had done most of the driving so her daughter could log some hours in on a work project, and her wrists and hands were numb from the vibration in the steering wheel.

"Did I ever tell you about the first time I felt you move, when I was pregnant?" she asked. "It was in a hotel room just like this one. I was traveling for a book festival or something. Some work thing. I don't recall all the details, just that it was a bad chain hotel in a city full of strip malls, and I couldn't drink alcohol, and I'd already called your father to say goodnight. I was lying in bed trying to read, but I couldn't concentrate. I tried to watch TV. Nothing worked. I just felt bone lonely. I wanted to be home. And that's when I felt you move. It was like a guitar string getting plucked down in my belly. It was the first time I'd actually felt pregnant and not just sick. It was the first time I knew I had another person inside me." The mother's eyes, a watery pale blue, blinked rapidly. "And I thought, 'I'll never be alone again. My baby is with me.' "

The daughter rolled onto her side and propped her head up on her palm. "Now wait a minute. That's from your first book. The story about the maid."

"Is it?"

"Remember? She's cleaning a room between guests, and she's tired so she climbs into the bed. Then she feels the baby move."

"Well." The mother's cheeks pinkened visibly, even in the gloom of the room. "I use little details from my life all the time."

"But Mom"—the daughter's mouth had drawn, twisted into a half smile—"you published that book two years before I was born."

The mother thought about it, trying to arrange the events in her mind in a way that would prove her daughter had it wrong. Her first book, the story collection, was published the year she turned thirty. Easy to remember—she'd been sore she hadn't managed it in her twenties, had felt that she was behind where she was supposed to be in her career, no longer golden. Silly. And she'd met the girls' father that same year, in another race against time. "I want kids," she'd told him flatly, perhaps a month into dating. "I just want to be clear about where this is going." He'd shrugged. "Sure," he'd said. And this time, she'd managed it: Lil Shit and Littler Shit, both before she turned thirty-five.

She barely remembered the maid story now, hadn't gone back to look at it in—Christ—decades probably. But yes, there'd been a maid, lying down on the bed she'd just made, pregnant. She'd felt the baby move for the first time.

"And the part about never being alone again?" the mother asked. "That was there?"

"I'm positive it was. Want me to check?" The daughter held up her phone.

"Dear god, no. What about the guitar string? That wasn't in it. There's no way."

The daughter was jabbing her phone, scrolling. "I don't remember. Hold on. Just let me check."

"This is mortifying," the mother said. "If you love me at all, you won't put me through this."

The daughter had rolled onto her stomach and put her feet in the air. She started kicking them cheerfully, the way she'd done when she was a girl lying on the living room floor and watching *Sesame Street*. The kids had watched so much TV in those days, the mother thought, still faintly ashamed, though her daughters had turned out just fine, their brains unrotten, more or less. She'd wanted time. Needed it. Time to read a book, to scribble sentences across the lines of a legal pad, to hide in the kitchen with a cigarette, exhaling into the stove's exhaust fan. Time to pull the phone receiver by its cord into the downstairs bathroom, whisper plans that would never come to fruition, weep, curse, and then declare, always, her hopeless, pointless love. Time to wash her face. Reapply her eyeliner. Wait for the girls' father to get home. *Sesame Street*, *Sabrina the Teenage Witch*, *Gilmore Girls*, the shows strung across the years, her girls glassy-eyed before them while the mother hid in the corners of her own house, seeking out the solitude she'd once found so terrifying.

"Piano chord," the daughter said.

"What?"

"Piano chord." Her voice lowered. *"That was when she felt it. The baby. It was not the flutter she'd read about in the baby books or the cramp that could be mistaken for gas. It was like a piano chord echoing in an empty sanctuary, a perfect—"*

"Stop, stop, Jesus. Point made. You've proven that I'm a shitty mother and a shittier writer. Just quit while you're ahead."

"You're not a shitty writer," the daughter said.

"Wow." The mother laughed. "Put that in the dictionary under 'faint praise.'"

"You're a good writer. And a fully adequate mother."

"Well, I tried. Some days more than others."

"I'm kidding. You're good."

"It's okay. Let's drop it." The mother sat up decisively and swung her legs around to hang off the side of the bed. She was a tiny woman, a full six inches shorter than her older daughter, and her feet barely grazed the nubby carpet. "I honestly didn't realize I was plagiarizing myself. That memory felt real. Feels real. Christ, that's embarrassing."

"I'm sorry I even said anything. It's not a big deal. You're just tired."

"I'm old. I can't even tell fact from fiction anymore."

"Maybe you're psychic. You predicted the future."

"Oh, close it."

"No, really, I'm serious." The daughter rolled onto her side and snuggled a pillow between her cheek and the crook of her arm. "I don't mean literally psychic. But a good enough student of human nature that you made a guess and got it right. Or you made a guess and got it close enough that, when the time came, you remembered your own metaphor."

"Simile," the mother said, and the daughter made as if to toss her pillow at her.

"Here I am, trying to make you feel better," the daughter said.

"Okay. Please continue."

"It's kind of like when—" She stopped. "Um. No. Never mind."

"What?"

"It's going to be really awkward, Mom."

"Any worse than it is already?"

"Oh, much worse. Don't say I didn't warn you."

"Consider me warned."

"So, your first novel. I read it when I was fifteen."

The mother processed this. "Okay."

"There's the part about the woman, you know, god. Oh, man, I can't believe I started this conversation. Getting off for the first time. With her husband's friend."

"Right," the mother said. She tried to neutralize her voice, keep the wariness out of it. "I know the part."

"The way you wrote about that. I didn't understand it then because I'd only ever kissed a guy. And I still didn't understand it later with Ethan because it never happened for me. With him. But then, with Carrie. Okay. Then I got it. And the image you wrote was what I thought of. The moment when you ride a bike for the first time, and the wobble stops, and your two wheels are humming quietly along the cement. And then the beautiful shock of the crash. You think you've figured out what you're doing, you hit a rhythm, then you hit the ground. That's what it was like with Carrie. And I remembered that part in your book later on as I was trying to figure out what the hell had just happened to me. What it all meant about me. It helped. It was like you wrote something, you knew something, that I had to live through to appreciate, and once I lived through it, I was glad someone else had put words to it."

This was as close as the daughter had ever come to pouring her heart out. She'd never been like Laura, so quick to scream "I hate you!" but equally quick to curl up on the mother's lap, even as a teenager, and weep sweetly into the crook of her neck. The older daughter was steady, wry. Occasionally furtive, though that had made sense later to the mother when Carrie came on the scene, and her furtiveness was validated when her father balked, cursed, accused her of being immature and contrary, not a lesbian. And even then, when things soured between the two of them, the daughter's tactic was never shouting, never theatrics. It was silence. She withdrew. The mother attempted occasionally over the years to encourage a reconciliation between them, though she and her ex hardly spoke themselves, and the daughter may not have been so quick to take the mother's side had she not been nursing her own grievances.

"I'm glad you told me," the mother said finally. "Even though it was embarrassing for you. It's a big compliment. It means a lot."

The daughter nodded, eyes distant, and then, just as the mother assumed the danger had passed, said: "You cheated on Dad, didn't you? With what's-his-name. The guy from his work. James?"

"Joseph," the mother said. "Yes."

"I always figured," the daughter said. "The book's not exactly subtle."

"It hadn't happened yet," the mother said. "When I wrote that."

"So you *are* psychic. Or something."

"Or something," the mother agreed.

"Does Laura know?"

"I don't know. Does she?"

"It's not the kind of thing we'd talk about," the daughter said. "I won't tell her, if you're worried."

"I guess the thought hadn't crossed my mind yet. But it's not a secret I'm asking you to keep. Those were my actions. My responsibility. I have to live with the fallout."

"I doubt it'll come up. Her hands are full right now."

"Yes. They are," the mother said.

The mother fluffed a pillow, positioned it against the headboard, and leaned back. They rested in silence for a couple of moments, listening to the chug of the AC, the vibration of a television in the neighboring room.

"I don't even think I want kids," the daughter said. "But it still seems weird that Laura's doing it first."

"You don't want kids?"

"Do you blame me? Look at the world."

The mother shrugged. "Laura's always wanted this. You know that."

"She's not even thirty."

"My, how times have changed," the mother said. "I was an old hag when I had Laura at thirty-four."

"You had a career. It all worked out."

Had it? The mother had thought often, over the years, about the choices she made leading up to the birth of her daughters, the choices she made later on. The existence of a child had a way of validating itself. Unless you were a monster. The girls wouldn't be the girls they were if they hadn't been conceived in the precise moments they were conceived, if a different man had been their father. But she and her ex had spent eleven years making each other miserable. Eleven years was a long time. And her career, oh, her career, she had it, yes. And the act of writing had always been life-bringing to her. But was she better off now because she burned through her twenties chasing a brass ring? She could barely remember that first book now. Didn't even know, apparently, when she was stealing memories from it.

"What's Carrie say?"

“She’s about like me. Neutral-to-negative. Doesn’t want to be pregnant, doesn’t think we have the energy or money to try to adopt. And it’s not like an accident’s going to happen.”

“No,” the mother laughed. “That’s true.”

“This is going to sound stupid,” the daughter said. “But I sort of wish we had that chaos element. Like, this thing that might be out of our hands. I mean, it’s not that I want to get pregnant. Truly. I just wish sometimes, in a way, like—ugh. I don’t know what I’m trying to say.”

“You’d like the option of an accident,” the mother said.

“Yeah. Sort of.”

“I get it.”

“Not that it matters,” the daughter said, “but will you be disappointed if we don’t?”

“Not that it matters,” the mother echoed sarcastically, “but no. Of course not.”

“Because Laura gave you a grandbaby,” the daughter said.

“She didn’t give me anything. I’ll be lucky if I see this baby four or five times a year.”

“But you know what I mean.”

The mother considered her feelings. She had always tried, whatever else her failures and weaknesses, to do that for her children. To take them seriously, to tell them the truth. To tell them when she didn’t know what the truth even was. She was looking forward to seeing the baby, holding it. Remembering what it was like to press that precious weight against her chest, to feel the velvet fontanel against her lips. She was looking forward to seeing Laura’s joy and satisfaction, to being needed, even temporarily, by Laura. Hold the baby. How do you burp her? What’s wrong with her latch? Can you get me some water? Where did I put the wipes? Are these bumps on her cheeks normal? Mom, did I cry this much when you brought me home? Mom, can you get me a Percocet? The mother—grandmother now—would happily spend the week running and fetching, sending a grateful Nathan on trips to Target and Harris Teeter, taking the baby on long strolls through the old neighborhood where Laura and

Nathan lived, with its peeling bungalows and towering willow oaks. But a vein of sadness cut through her thoughts. Worry, sure. About Laura, Callie, the world. Some dread, because she was almost sixty-five, and she had lingering nerve pain from a long-ago running injury, so the week would be work as well as joy, and yet she'd have to pretend this wasn't the case. She'd have to power through the exhaustion.

"I'm glad to have Callie to get to know," the mother said finally. "I'm glad I get to find out what being a grandmother is like. I look forward to seeing Laura be a mom. I think she'll be a good one. But if you had a baby, I'd feel all those things all over again. Laura's having a baby doesn't affect that, really. No more than having Laura changed the amount of love I felt for you."

"So you lied, then. You would be disappointed."

"You just said it doesn't matter."

"It matters a little."

"I didn't lie. Disappointment isn't what I feel. Maybe unsatisfied curiosity. Maybe that's closer. But there are gains, too. For me, selfishly."

"Like what?"

"When I had you girls, I respected my parents more, I appreciated them more, but I loved them less. They went from being the most sacred love of my life to you two. I bet that's already true for Laura. She's going to be glad to see me and glad to have my help, and she still loves me, but she loves me less. Maybe you never will love me less."

On the nightstand, the daughter's phone rattled and chimed. The daughter leaned over to see the screen. "When are you getting here?" she read. "In all caps with about ten exclamation points."

"Tell her fifteen minutes," the mother said.

The daughter jabbed at the screen with her thumbs and the phone emitted its *whoosh* send sound. Instead of lying back down, she stood, crossed the couple of feet separating the beds, and jabbed at the mother's shoulder. It was supposed to be a playful jab, the mother thought, but it hurt a little, and the look on her daughter's face, too, was mildly pained—the look of a person about to get a pimple on her back popped or assessing the weight of a piece of furniture before attempting to lift it. "Scooch over."

"Why?" She moved over a few inches though, just because of the authority in her daughter's voice.

"I was thinking on the drive over about hug 'n' roll. Do you remember that?"

"Yeah. What about it?"

"Let's do it."

"You want to hug 'n' roll with me?"

"Sure," the daughter said. "Come on. It'll be fun."

"I can barely even get a regular hug out of you, and you want to roll around on this bed with me?"

"Just shove over, Mom. Jeez. You overthink everything."

The mother shoved over, and the daughter stretched out beside her. The last time they'd done this, the daughter had been six or seven. The mother would wrap her arms around her, and the daughter's cheek would end up settling comfortably between the mother's breasts, and they'd roll, giggling, from one side of the bed to the other, bound to the same invisible axis. It had been a way for the mother to get affection from the child, this child who didn't reciprocate hugs so much as surrender to them—by turning the embrace into a ride.

Now, lying side by side, the two assessed each other, tried putting their arms out, collided, switched, and ended up with the daughter's arms on top, the mother's woven around beneath the daughter's armpits, the mother's head tucked under the daughter's chin. Whether this was humiliating or poignant, the mother could not say. She could smell where the daughter had dabbed perfume on her collarbones. She could smell the sour roast of gas station coffee on her daughter's breath. She could see, this close, the earliest hint of the crepe-textured skin that had plagued her own passage from youth to middle age. They squeezed each other, their hearts thudding against each other's chests, and the daughter said what had always been the mother's line: "Ready, Freddy?"

“Ready,” the mother said.

The bed was a queen, and they managed, grunting, one full rotation to the right, then another back to start position, their knees and ribcages knocking uncomfortably into one another. Even that little bit of activity shortened the mother’s breath, but when the daughter asked, “Again?” the mother said, “Yes,” thinking this was a kind of gift or perhaps a punishment, and whatever it was, she wouldn’t rebuff it. Was this moment, too, in a story she had written? It seemed like something she would have come up with back then, when her bitterness was academic, her sense of sentimentality shameful but keen.

“What do you think,” the daughter said, panting. “Again?”

“Yes,” the mother said.

visitation

In the end, Neil packed only the necessities: his desktop and two monitors, his laptop, the Switch, the PlayStation, the Xbox. All the clothes and shoes he owned fit into two suitcases. He was able to dismantle his desk and gaming chair and cram them into the car's hatch once he'd laid the backseat down, so he didn't even have to make two trips, which was good, because gas was cheap right now, but money was tight. The rest of the furniture—his bed and mattress, the sofa, the coffee table, the tiny dinette set he never used—he just left. If his landlady decided to evict him, well, first of all, fuck her—but second of all, if she did, she could deal with it all. Put the stuff out on the street or up her rotten snatch for all he cared. He'd gotten half of it for free on Craigslist, anyway.

His mother had said on the phone, in one long, weary exhalation, "Well, I guess you'd better move back in with us and ride this thing out." "Yeah, I guess I better," Neil had replied, and that was that. His adult life was surprisingly easy to dismantle. He bought an ounce off JT. Emptied the fridge into a trash bag and tossed it with a crisp clatter into the dumpster behind his building. Shut off the thermostat. Sent a few texts. It occurred to him that he probably ought to let Angie know, but if he called, things could get quickly awkward. So he pulled up Messages and thumbed:

Decided to stay awhile at my Moms and Dads place. You going to be ok?

He wasn't the type, normally, to sit and stare at the phone, waiting to see if a reply would come in, but his gut churned, and he just wanted this to be done. It wasn't as if Angie could expect him to invite her to come with him, right? They'd had sex a dozen times, twice in the backroom of 1Up Video Games when they shared a slow shift, and this was not, by any reasonable measure, grounds for moving in together.

Angie's reply, though, like the girl herself, was prompt and straightforward:

> **yeah I'm OK. Picking up hours at Total**
> **Wine. Have fun**

A second later, a thumbs-up emoji appeared.

Great. Cool. Why had he worried? He always got worked up over things that turned out to be nothing.

The lines at the ABC were bad and extended around the side of the building, but he took his place in one anyway and handed over half an hour of his life in service of procuring three plastic jugs of Smirnoff and a handle of Ancient Age. A few people were wearing masks; Neil regarded them with a mixture of contempt and panic. He could see, looking from his place in line out across the parking lot, the figure of a tall, broad man, oddly still, his face—swaddled strangely in some kind of thick brown scarf despite the mild weather—as featureless as a dinner plate. The image gave Neil a chill, which annoyed him, so he grunted and looked down at his phone to do an unconscious little thumb tap dance between social media apps. When he looked up again, the blank-faced man was gone.

Half an hour later, he pulled out of the ABC lot, not once referring to his rearview mirror and its sobering preapocalyptic view of masked zombies shuffling in a line toward cheap booze. There was a subreddit he frequented called ABoringDystopia—and boy, was it ever. He'd always sort of hoped for a capital *E*, capital *T* End Times, with the promised bands of roving survivor camps, new political structures, and hot, unlikely sexual liaisons between people who never would have had the time of day for one another in the current reality. Well—give it time. He took the I-40 on-ramp and sped up to merge, scrolling, with half an eye on his phone's playlist, for something to get his blood moving while he drove. He landed on the Strokes, *Is This It*, and it was either the best choice or the worst, because some cymbals, tom, and a couple of chords later and he was back in high school, a time for which he never, ever would have believed he'd feel nostalgia. He and his best friend, Brad, would listen to the Strokes' album or *Yankee Hotel Foxtrot* and play *Grand Theft Auto III* and talk about how bullshit their lives were. But nestled within their anger and cynicism, Neil realized now, was the hope—no, the certainty—that better things awaited them. Their future selves, slimmer and cooler, their intellects stimulated, their ambitions nurtured, would leave Hickory forever and be rewarded in some profound way, some magical way, for their specialness. You had to laugh!

His dad stood in the doorway of Neil's childhood bedroom, arms crossed over his broad belly, and watched as Neil unpacked his electronics.

"What is this," he asked, "the Situation Room?"

He was trying to say it in a joking way to mask the real insult, and Neil, as a thirty-four-year-old man, was now mature enough to bite back his first and second and third retorts and to respond, with similar fake humor, "Heh, heh, yeah. Situation Room. I guess it's a lot of stuff."

"You play games on all that?"

"Well, Dad, it's my job. I have to know the technology."

His dad leaned into the door jamb. "You think the job'll still be there when all this is done?"

"People are going to want games more than ever," Neil said. He got down on his hands and knees and crawled under his desk to connect the monitor cord to a USB outlet in his desktop tower.

"Can't they just buy it all on Amazon? Or, you know, download it?"

Neil sat back up on his heels, huffed, and let his eyes widen but not quite roll. He'd been home for less than two hours. He'd entered his old room, long ago stripped of most evidence of his former occupancy, to find the bed made up fresh and a stack of matching peach-colored towels positioned at its foot. His mother had fashioned a nest-looking thing out of a hand towel and arranged a few peppermints and travel-size toiletries in its center like eggs. He'd stared for a full minute at this strangeness, wondering whether he should interpret it as a gesture of love or benign pleasantness, something an overeager Airbnb host would do.

"I guess I don't know, Dad. Maybe they will and my store will never reopen and I'm screwed. Is that what you want to hear?"

"I'm just saying this might be a good time, while you're here and you've got nothing going on, to think about a next step."

"Okay, Dad. I'll do that."

"You're so smart. That's all I'm saying. I bet you could design those games and not just play them. You've got a mind for that sort of thing." He waved his big, thick-fingered hand in a searching circle. "You know, you think of good stories, and you could always draw pretty good. Remember all those notebooks you filled up when you were little? All those comic things you did?"

Neil remembered. He remembered being small, just starting to read and write words on his own, and showing one of his "books" to his dad. Something about the book had upset his father, had made him snap at Neil, then hiss with exasperation or disappointment. Neil could remember the tone now but not the words, and if he were to ask his father about the moment, his father would deny it. One of the great frustrations of Neil's life was not getting to be the authority on his own childhood. His parents took his memories, his impressions, his pent-up bad feelings, and dismissed them. They told stories about a happy, well-adjusted Neil who seemed mythological to him now—Bigfoot, captured briefly in blurry snapshots.

"But you also know computers," his father continued. "That's where the money is these days. I told you that the company offered me that computer course in the '80s, didn't I? I always regret I didn't take it. You kids were babies, and your mother didn't want me going off for a whole month. But it woulda been worth it. Oh, well. We did all right."

He'd heard this story—and its lesson of half-hearted gratitude—many times.

"Sure. I remember you telling me that. I'll think about it. I'll come up with something."

"All right, then. You need help with any of this?"

"No, I got it. Thanks, though."

"Your mom won't admit it, but she's tickled you're back here. I know that probably don't mean much when you've just lost your job and had to move back home, but I figured I'd tell you."

"I'm glad," Neil said, and he was, sort of. Annoyed glad, if that was a thing. "Someone should be happy."

"I'm glad you're here, too," his dad said.

Neil found himself blinking against an unexpected swell of emotion, which he attributed to the stress of the transition and the overall fucked-up-ness of the world.

"Mom's cooking chili," his dad said. "And we were thinking about renting a movie through the TV. Maybe that *1917* movie. Does that interest you?"

Neil wanted to watch a serious war epic about as much as he wanted a case of COVID-19, but he said, "Sure, that'll work."

"We'll get through it," his dad said. It was the same tone of voice, decisive and a little stern, he'd always used to insist his will would be word in Neil's world. When Neil fell and skinned his knee: *You're fine. It don't even hurt that bad.* When Neil was rejected by the girl he asked out to his first middle school dance: *She ain't worth a count, anyway.* When Mom had the ovarian cancer scare while Neil was still away at college: *She'll do the chemo and be good as new.*

"And clean the dinner dishes up after, would you? Even if you never do it again the whole time you're here, do it tonight for Mom. It'll mean something to her."

Neil was insulted his father thought he had to say this, but he also realized that the idea would have never occurred to him. "Fine, Dad, okay, but can I have a little alone time for now?"

"Oh. Yeah, a' course," his dad said. He pulled the door to behind him.

The little slide lock Neil had installed in high school was gone now; he inspected the door and could see the faint impressions where his mother had spackled the screw holes. His parents wouldn't just barge in on him now, probably, but all the same: he'd have to make an Amazon order.

He spent the next two months doing exactly what his father had suggested, subtly, he shouldn't do: playing videogames. He'd get up at 9:30 or 10, wander into the kitchen, and fill his travel mug with tepid coffee for a trip back to his bedroom. Sometimes there were breakfast leftovers on a plate on the island; sometimes he'd fill the smallest metal mixing bowl with corn flakes and whole milk. He'd go to his desk, balance the food in front of his keyboard, and log in a few hours on *League of Legends* or *RuneScape* because with those games, it could be like punching the clock—in a good way. He'd socialize a little with the other players, watercooler talk about toilet paper shortages and curfews and the podcasts they were listening to, then emerge at lunchtime having herded a group of wild horses into a pen or solved a six-part cryptograph, feeling almost accomplished, like a man who'd done an honest and difficult day's work. After lunch ("There's ham and turkey slices in the meat drawer and the mayo's on the door," his mother said every single day, a kind of incantation), he'd unload the dishwasher and put in his crumb-dotted plate, his milk-dotted bowl, then he'd return to his room, where he'd cue up a movie or TV show on one monitor while playing something upbeat and brainless, like *Mario Kart*, on the other. Late afternoon, he showered, mostly to have a private place to jerk off, and then he added a pair of cargo shorts to his morning uniform of T-shirt and boxers.

After dinner and an obligatory hour or two in his parents' company—usually spent in front of their TV watching *NCIS* or *The Masked Singer*—he'd say he was going to go out for a walk, which was when he'd slip down the street to the river, stake out a shadowed spot on the bank, maybe look at his phone a little, and take a couple of hits off his pipe. He always felt during these excursions, especially once he was at the river, as if he were being watched, and he caught on the breeze an occasional whiff of something foul, like the stench of a long-unwashed body. Maybe someone slept out here. Maybe he ought to be more careful. But once he'd toed a hole in the dirt and buried his pipe ash, he felt pretty good—better than good—and he'd walk slowly back home, savoring the softness of the spring air, the almost coconut sweetness of blooming trees, the buzz of the streetlights, the calm tableaus visible through the neighbors' picture windows. Back at his parents' place, he'd get a coke or a glass of juice from the kitchen, return to his room, and add a healthy slug of vodka or whiskey to the glass. This was when he liked cuing up the shooter games and horror games: *Doom Eternal, Resident Evil 3*. He'd turn off all the lights in his room, put on his headphones, and set the volume up a few notches. He wanted to be terrified, and then he wanted to clamp his hands around the pulsing tendoned leg of a mantis-shaped demon, twist the leg off with a dry snap, and plunge it into the demon's single yellow viscous eye. Or obliterate the zombie's head under his bootheel or thrust his rifle's bayonet under the shelf of the zombie's jawline so that black blood sprayed across the inside of his monitor's screen and the zombie's wail vibrated through his headphones and chair. He'd gulp from his cup in celebration, feel an echo of the night's earlier high, and, for a few seconds, all was well.

It was immediately in the wake of one of these kills that he saw the figure for the first time. Well, he noticed it for the first time; later, that distinction would seem significant.

He had just blown a blood punch through the center of a Hell Knight. The demons rushed at you unrelentingly on Ultra-Nightmare mode, so there weren't a lot of opportunities to take a rest and look at the scenery, and the background graphics weren't the point of *Doom* anyway. Neil generally noted what was rushing right at him and registered peripheral movement only so he'd know which direction to pivot after completing the kill. But he'd cleared the building's basement, so he had a breath, a beat, before he opened the door into the stairwell and began the next rally. He swung the first-person view around, double-checking, and there it was. In the room's corner, sitting—nothing *sat* in this game—on an old office desk.

"Huh, weird," Neil murmured out loud. The sitting thing seemed to be covered all over in fur, and its proportions were odd (not that odd proportions were odd in the *Doom* universe). It was long and capsule-shaped, so that the length from its feet to the place where it folded to sit was perhaps a third of its body. The torso extended into what Neil assumed was its head, without a narrowing to indicate where one began and the other left off, and he saw a flicker of a long, shaggy face—well, less than a face. An expression. Mournful, or maybe merely bored. It seemed uninterested in him; it certainly didn't jump up to attack him.

Almost unconsciously, he jabbed Ctrl and PrtScr. If he had a thought at this moment, it was that this was some kind of glitch or maybe an Easter egg dropped by a programmer, and he'd check online later to see what others had to say about it. But then the stairwell door opened, a zombie came stumbling out toward him, and he was back to making brains explode. He forgot about the figure and his intentions to investigate it. When two a.m. came he finally crawled into bed with his phone, and only when his grainy eyeballs were throbbing with the discomfort of keeping his eyelids open did he toss the phone on his nightstand and surrender to his usual poor, stressful, half-drunk night's sleep.

A couple of weeks later, it was sunny and warm, so it seemed like a good time to open his bedroom window, air out some of the bachelor funk that had accumulated (despite his mother's occasional sieges with the Febreze bottle), and play something lighthearted. He turned on the Switch, loaded *Mario Odyssey*, and resumed gameplay where he'd left off before the pandemic, collecting the Power Moons he'd missed in Wooded Kingdom. The game gave him a mild case of motion sickness, oddly—few videogames affected him like that—so he tended to play in bursts, until the pressure behind his sinuses became too much for him to tolerate, and then abandon the game for others that took a less physical toll. Now, though, feeling good and even clearheaded, he started Mario down the forest path, remembering the swell of joy a Mario game could give you, the sense that some greater harmoniousness could be achieved through a series of perfectly timed jumps. He executed such a triple jump up onto a rock outcropping, where a stash of purple nut coins was hidden, and then he saw from this new vantage point a shape that triggered in him something hovering between déjà vu and outright recognition. He toggled the camera view more fully toward it.

"No fucking way," he muttered.

It looked like the odd shaggy figure he'd seen in the basement on *Doom Eternal*. Just like it. Neil hopped Mario down from the rock ledge and navigated him toward the thing, telling himself as the figure drew closer and closer that he was seeing some trick of the graphics, that his view was about to warble apart into something else entirely —a tree, a mound of dirt, a Goomba. Then, as he approached the figure, and it was unmistakably the capsule-shaped beast of his memory, though rendered graphically in the Mario style, he decided the thing from *Doom* must have been something different. His memory couldn't be trusted. Neil brought Mario closer to the beast, which was sitting this time on a squared-off tier of ground leading up to another area of gameplay, but he held back a bit, worried that entering its radius would trigger the figure into action or maybe even make it disappear. *Modern Mario* was a very different sort of gamespace from *Doom*; you were supposed to stop, look around, discover the nooks and crannies. So Neil was able to calmly swing the camera view around to consider the figure from multiple angles. He rolled his desk chair over to his keyboard, woke up his PC, and went to his screenshots folder, heart starting to pound in a way that he found vaguely embarrassing, as if someone were watching him get all jacked up over nothing. He double-clicked the icon for the image file from two weeks ago.

It was the same figure. Exactly the same. And his recognition seemed deeper, somehow, than the side-by-side comparison of these two images; Neil felt certain he had seen the creature somewhere else. He *knew* it. The thought nagged at him, tickled unpleasantly like a hair caught in the back of his throat. Where else had he seen this thing?

He sat back and sighed. Okay, he thought, working a knuckle against his eye tooth. Maybe Nintendo owned *Doom* now, somehow, the way they said media companies could all be traced back to a few big evil behemoths? Or maybe there was a rogue programmer out there, putting this weird dude into all the games he worked on like some kind of an electronic Banksy. If that was the case, someone else had to have noticed it. He hit Capture on his controller, paused the game, and brought up his browser. He searched Reddit, some gamer forums. He did a few different Google searches:

same figure on mario doom eternal
monster on mario doom eternal
programmers on mario doom eternal

He couldn't find anything. He watermarked and uploaded his screenshots to Imgur, wrote up a query, and posted it to NeoGAF, r/TrueGaming, a few others:

Ok this one's weird but bear with me. Playing DOOM eternal and saw this guy in the lower level of Arc Complex. Not a demon, didn't attack or move. Then, saw him again behind the sphinx in Mario Odyssey. Can't find any other reports of this. Anyone seen this guy or know of a connection between the games to explain it?

It wasn't long before his in-box started pinging with replies.

Whoa, that's wild. Just played that level on Eternal and didn't see Harry and the Hendersons. Following for the update.

This is some extremely weird photoshop karma-whoring, but you do you.

Looks like a dong.

And so on. Neil closed out his browser with an irritated huff. Waste of goddamn time.

He'd never shut down *Mario Odyssey*, so he picked up the controller, did a few more screengrabs from different angles, and then figured he may as well go up to the beast and see what, if anything, might happen. He moved Mario forward, and the A-button icon appeared, indicating that the character would speak to him. His heart began to skitter. He hadn't been this excited in—he couldn't remember. Maybe he should delete his forum posts, gather some more information, and then put the whole story on social media in some way; maybe he'd stumbled into some kind of grand digital scavenger hunt funded by Elon Musk or Zuckerberg or someone like that, and he owed his discovery to his own open-minded nature, his determination *not* to specialize and obsess, his pure gamer's heart. It was golden ticket time. He jabbed A.

I'll find you at the river.

He frowned and pressed the button again. The dialogue box disappeared, which meant that the figure had nothing else to say, but he hit A again anyway, only for that same cryptic line to reappear. *I'll find you at the river.*

A river in this game? That had to be what it meant, but the image that popped into Neil's mind was the Catawba just down the road from his parents' house—site of his nightly smoke, site of his occasional (frequent), shivery sense of being watched. When he was a child, the river—or, more specifically, the park beside it—had been his hideout, a place to play his mostly solitary games of pretend—precursors to *RuneScape* and *Doom*, games where he got to be a hero felling bad guys under the edge of his magical elf-forged sword. Thinking about that time made him think of his notebooks and his father's sneer of disapproval. What had been so bad about them? Why had that image of his father's anger fully eclipsed in his memory the notebooks' actual contents?

The euphoria he was feeling mere seconds ago, a kind of bright cone of light in his middle, turned to cold sludge.

Neil powered the Switch off and tossed the controller on his desk instead of docking it. He was getting a case of cabin fever, that was it. Playing too many games, not getting out enough, drinking too much. He probably needed an exercise routine and to eat something other than ham sandwiches every day and to lay off the depressants for a little while. A couple of days. Tonight, at least. He needed a good night's sleep and a conversation with someone other than his parents. Maybe he should shoot Angie an email or see if Brad was planning to be back in town anytime soon. He could call JT—he was due a re-up, anyway. JT was good for a laugh, and because of the nature of his business, he could pick back up with you after months of radio silence with no awkwardness at all. Neil sprawled out across his bed and pulled the contact up, hovering his thumb over the phone icon. Then he lost his courage and hit Message instead.

Hey my dude. How you holding up. Thinking about coming in to the G tomorrow or next day. You around?

JT replied right away.

Hey man. You fixing to protest? We're going to elm tomorrow nite but I won't have anything on my for the obvious reasons. Could connect w you afetnoon before or maybe Sunday.

Neil stopped himself a half second before replying, "Protest what?" Shit, that would have been embarrassing. He just hadn't been that tuned into the news lately, given how miserable it always was and his total inability to do anything about it, but he'd heard about Michigan, or was it Minnesota? He knew the gist. And now he had to wrap his mind around the vision of JT, a skinny, forty-something white weed dealer with a tattoo of Totoro on his bicep, going into the streets to protest police brutality and racial injustice. This said less about JT and anything Neil thought he knew about the guy he bought an ounce off of once a month or so and more about Neil and what he had assumed to be true about the world and the people in his immediate circle and what they might be capable of. Maybe he *ought* to go, he thought. It would be something to do, and he could see whether he'd been locked out of his apartment yet, maybe call up Angie and try to wrangle from her an invitation to come over. Quarantine (god, it felt melodramatic even calling it that) had been long and rough; no wonder he was going a little nuts. Stuff was reopening—maybe not 1Up, but he could probably get on at one of the GameStops or in the electronics department at Target or Walmart. If he hadn't been evicted, if his apartment key still turned the lock, what was there to stop him from resuming a version of his old life?

He mulled, then typed: **Maybe. Not sure. Text you if I make it in.**

It was only a little after 11 and his room was starting to get uncomfortably hot. He sat up and rubbed his bare feet against the carpeted floor, sending an almost luxurious shiver up his spine. What now. He could pack. He could play another game. He could do some other fucking thing, though who knew what. Get on Monster and upload his thoroughly unimpressive resume with its 14-point Tahoma font and its bullet point about how he'd reorganized 1Up's inventory system, which in reality amounted to the creation of an Excel spreadsheet? Man, it was steamy in here. He pictured what the weekend's protests would be like, a bunch of sweaty, angry people elbow-to-elbow downtown, nowhere to take a leak unless you wanted a cop nailing you for indecent exposure, and the idea of the trip to Greensboro started to lose some of its charm. But for the first time in a long time, he couldn't think of a game he wanted to play, either. Within him—he could admit it—was the niggling worry that he'd see the beast again, and he didn't want to think right now about what that might mean.

He found his mother in the living room. She was in his father's rocker-recliner with a paperback novel open across a thigh and her glasses perched on her nose, but the TV was also on and tuned to a talk show, one of the ones with a panel of screechy women discussing the news. This time the screechy women were corralled into their own little boxes, broadcasting from home. His mom's eyes flickered from the book to the screen to Neil, and then she folded the book over her index finger. "Hey," she said, a little too eagerly. "What are you up to?"

He fell back onto the couch. Shrugged. A plump blonde woman was waving her arms and saying something, in a frequency he could barely register, about looters. Thankfully, his mother hit MUTE. "Nothing. Just bored."

He could sense her desire to step into this opening he'd offered. When he was a kid and complained of boredom, she'd snap, "Well, go clean up your pigsty!" or "Ride your bike!" or "Read a book!" Boredom was only ever evidence of laziness. And she surely still believed that, sitting here and multitasking her mystery novel and talk show, something already simmering away for dinner in the Crock-Pot—smelled like a roast. But she didn't dare say it to him. What odd, near useless power he had now, thirty-four years old and living with his parents.

"Well, yeah. I've been going a little stir-crazy myself. We could go to a park and take a walk or go to Walmart. I'm running low on groceries, anyway."

"Eh," Neil said. "I don't know. Maybe another day. To be honest, I'm wondering whether I should move back to Greensboro and look for another job. I can't just stay here forever."

"You could go back," she said evenly, but he could see her displeasure in the set of her mouth. She started bobbing the rocker, making the springs wince. "Do you have somewhere to live?"

"I need to check," Neil said. "It might've been, like, illegal for Lila to evict me. I'm not sure. It's not like she's going to have a line of people wanting to come in and start a lease right now, probably."

She exhaled and traced the raised lettering of her book's title with a pink-polished thumbnail. "Well, if you're going to go, you might as well go on and do it. I think things are probably what they are through the summer, and then it'll go to hell again in the fall. But it's not like you can wait it out indefinitely."

She was like this: if she experienced something as a slight, even something that had nothing to do with her, she put up her hackles. Two and a half years into college, when Neil had come home for Christmas break on academic probation and floated the idea of taking some time off to think things through, she'd said, "Well, we'd been holding off on buying your sister a car, but if I know your tuition money isn't going out of the account, I guess we can go ahead and move on one." She had wanted Neil to back down, confess that he was wrong, but Neil wouldn't do that, not ever. And here they both were.

"I guess not," Neil said. "I guess you're right." To twist the knife a little, he added, "I was thinking about driving over to go to a protest with some friends."

She scoffed and rolled her eyes. "You couldn't pay me to insert myself into that mess."

He thought there was probably a good insult he could level at her about boomers, but he knew the effort would be wasted, and he wasn't up enough on the nuances of the situation to feel ready to debate her. Instead, he shrugged again. "So I guess I might drive over tomorrow and see what's up."

"Sounds good," she said, and she unmuted the TV. Screeching resumed.

"Mom?" he said.

She looked away from the screen. "Yep?" she said coolly.

"Do you still have, like, any of my old drawings from when I was a kid? Those notebooks I drew in?"

"I kept all that stuff. You mean Mister Gone-Gone?"

"Gone gone?"

"Or Gun-Gun, I don't know. You were still talking funny. I mean that monster you always drew."

Neil swallowed hard against a sudden rise of nausea. "I guess that's it. I don't remember much about it."

"Hold on. I'll get your tub out." This hadn't been his intention, but she seemed to have accepted his curiosity about the drawings as a kind of peace offering, and her tone softened.

She resurfaced a few minutes later from the basement, bumping a twenty-gallon plastic storage bin against her bony hips. She dropped it to the kitchen floor with a loud huff. "You'll have to get it from here. I forgot how heavy this was."

"That's because my rock collection's in it," Neil said. Until a moment ago, he'd forgotten entirely about this store of his childhood mementos, but the sight of it—that dark purple Rubbermaid tub, his name slashed across its lid in Magic Marker—brought its motley freight of contents right back with a snap.

"And all the yearbooks," his mom added breathlessly, wiping dust across her jean-clad thighs.

Neil moved the tub to the dining room table. Its lid removed, it omitted the not-wholly-unpleasant smell, to Neil at least, of decaying papers and mildew. Unless his mom ever went to the basement to look through her children's old things—and it was possible she had—this had last been opened maybe fourteen years ago, when Neil was still in college. He could vaguely recollect coming home one weekend and mining it for evidence of his earlier, better self, that Neil-with-so-much-promise who made the A honor roll and won spelling bees and got accepted to the Governor's School. But his excavation then hadn't taken him all the way down to his single-digit efforts. Kid stuff—drawings, certificates of participation, smeared handprints, even his own—hadn't much interested him.

Here was his prom boutonniere, a yellow carnation his mother had pressed between sheets of wax paper. A little lower down was a grainy newspaper photo of Neil and Brad dissecting a fetal pig in Anatomy and Physiology, such a grim scene, presented in the paper with so much cheerful banality that Neil laughed out loud. Here was his eighth-grade graduation program; a red Field Day ribbon; a story, written in loping cursive on blue-lined spiral paper, titled, "The Alien Police Squad," which he seemed to recall was a pretty blatant plagiarism of *Men in Black*. Down the pile he dug, handing his mother sixth-grade mementos, fifth; a cassette tape of his Fourth Grade Farewell that looked too warped to play now; pencil sketch, clearly some kind of school assignment, of the family's old dog, Annie, a yappy terrier that was old by thc time Neil was born and decrepit by the time she died eight years later. He had felt absolutely no love for that dog—only disgust and a little fear—and Neil couldn't recall why he ever would have drawn her.

"Hey, there's one of them," his mom said excitedly, pointing to a composition book. "I think that's one of the last you did."

He peeled back its moisture-warped cover. The first page, he noticed with relief, was nothing dark or weird—just some colored pencil sketches of Woody and Buzz from *Toy Story*. He flipped forward, and here were more cartoon renditions: Scrooge McDuck, The Mask, a version of Superman with muscles that looked like sausage links under his blue tights. Then some poems—Neil hurried past these with superstitious pain, not wanting his eyes to land on a phrase that would mock him later—and some comic book panels that seemed to always peter out a few pages in or rush in the last panel or two to a sudden, unearned conclusion. An old stress came back to him: he'd wanted so much then to make things—write things, draw things, create things—but he'd never known how to finish any of them. He didn't want to work on them; he wanted them to already have been done, perhaps by some bizarro Neil who actually enjoyed patient, painstaking effort and always knew what the next step was supposed to be.

At the end of one of these aborted comic strips Neil had drawn, with what seemed to be angry, careless slashes, a familiar figure: torpedo-shaped, shaggy, mouth-downturned. THE END, he'd written beneath it, in block letters. Its appearance in these pages was inevitable; unthinkable.

"Whoo," his mom said with a laugh. "I forgot how creepy that guy was."

"And you say I drew it a lot?"

"Don't you remember? I don't see how you could've forgot." She dug in the tub and pulled out, close to the bottom, a red folder labeled neatly with his name—that unmistakable feminine bubble print of an elementary school teacher. "They sent this one home from kindergarten at the parent-teacher conference. Your teacher got such a kick out of you. She thought you were so creative."

He started flipping through the yellowed pages.

MI FREN MSTR GUNGUN, the first drawing declared. Here was Neil's beast, recognizable even in a five-year-old's drawing. And why not? It was just a hot dog with arms and legs and scrawled fur. This time, though, the mouth looped up into a grin.

"I feel like Dad hated this stuff," Neil said.

"What?" Her voice went up several octaves. "Your dad's always been proud of you."

"But I can remember him getting on me about it," Neil said. The pages of another notebook purred as he fanned them, letting the images flicker past in a blur, occasionally pausing for a closer look. It wasn't all Mstr Gungun (or Mister Gone-Gone). There were stick figures and dogs and houses and dragons, trees, mountains, Rube Goldberg–style machine designs. The beast always popped up though. Smiling, mostly, and sometimes frowning a terrifying frown. Sometimes waving, sometimes stretching an arm from its unnatural height to grasp a small stick-Neil's hand. "He gave me the distinct impression I was doing something wrong. So eventually I didn't do it anymore."

"It wasn't the drawings," his mom said, and that word, *it*, took Neil by surprise. There was an "it." She was acknowledging its existence.

"So what, then?"

"He just thought you were a little too obsessed with the monster guy. I told him it was an imaginary friend and to leave it alone, but you've got to understand what parenting's like. You don't get to see into the future. You don't know if your kid's going to turn out okay. So if your little boy's saying his best friend's a monster, and if the phase lasts as long as Mister Gone-Gone did, you worry something's wrong. I mean, you were talking about this guy for a while. All through kindergarten and into first grade. Then you lost interest, and it turned out all the worrying was for nothing."

Neil stared at the last image of the monster, trying to remember drawing it, calling Mister Gone-Gone his best friend. He recognized the general truth of his mother's history without being able to assign any specific memories to it, though even in this crude child's drawing he felt a visceral pull, a physical sensation in his sinuses and gut. He didn't remember Mister Gone-Gone, but he remembered believing what the movies had promised him: that he'd be rewarded for his specialness with a magical encounter of some kind, a trip to Narnia or Oz, a visitation from E.T. or Totoro (at that, JT's poorly drawn tattoo sprang into his mind). Mister Gone-Gone was probably just a manifestation of all that wishful thinking.

"And in the end I turned out just peachy," Neil said.

"You did," his mother said, missing his sarcasm. Or maybe she did catch it, because the next thing she said was, "Are you taking this tub with you back to Greensboro? We could use the space downstairs."

"I guess I can. If I decide to go."

"All right, then." She returned to her recliner. "There's bologna in the meat drawer this time if you want a sandwich."

He'd sleep on it, he figured, see how tomorrow looked. He felt no special urgency in one direction or the other: he didn't feel like packing; he didn't feel like playing a game. He didn't even feel much like lunch, but he made a bologna-and-mustard sandwich anyway and ate it with a handful of Lay's potato chips and a tall glass of whole milk, just like he would have as a boy. Add a can of Campbell's for a really balanced lunch, he thought, but Mom was the one who always did that: dumped the can in the scarred little pot, refilled the can with water and dumped that too, stirred the soup to boiling with a metal spoon. Then she'd serve it to him with an ice cube floating in it.

The balance of the day passed with agonizing slowness. His father mowed the lawn, and Neil thought about going outside and offering to weed-eat, but he was afraid of getting pulled into a conversation about whether or not he was leaving, since his mother had undoubtedly passed along the maybe-news. He killed the rest of the day by rewatching *Rick and Morty* episodes, but even those, whose rhythms felt like home to him, alleviated none of his restlessness. As he streamed the show, he Googled some news stories in an attempt to feel something—anything. He read about the protests and the black people who had been killed and tried to work himself up into a productive rage. It was like trying to believe in God; he wanted to, but he couldn't turn the desire into authentic feeling.

He ended up closing the browser, shutting off *Rick and Morty*, and lying down. The room was still hot; he'd forgotten to ask his mom to put on the AC. Soon, it seemed as if the only thing left to do was sleep, so he did, and it was nighttime before he awakened to his dad's tentative knock on the door. The roast was ready if he was hungry.

Eating again was something to do, so he said yes.

After a movie with his parents (*Dolittle*, which made him wish desperately he was already high), he murmured noncommittally in response to their questions about his plans for the next day, then said he was going to take his walk. He stopped by his bedroom first, pulled out the balled pair of athletic socks in the back right corner, and went ahead and grabbed what was left of the last ounce and his pipe. He'd sort of, kind of, promised himself not to smoke tonight, but there was so little left that it would be stupid to save it, and he'd almost certainly not mix himself drinks later.

The long, cool spring seemed to have officially and decisively ended. The air smelled sweetly of the grass his father had cut today, and a greasy sheen coated his skin before he'd made it to the end of his parents' block. As a boy, he'd ridden his bike more times than he could count along this same path, pedaling pell-mell until he reached the river's edge, where he'd skid to an incomplete stop and spring off his bike frame in one fluid motion, leaving it on its side, barely out of the road, like a shed skin. The river had seemed special to him then. His.

He sat on the riverbank and started packing his bowl with the dregs of the ounce. He had settled in the tacky, rocky soil near the water, edging around the poison ivy and trying to get some distance between himself and the nearest deposit of beer cans and cigarette butts, a half-full plastic Gatorade bottle. Fuckers. People were nasty. Hopeless. A tree limb bobbed jauntily in the moonlit water, and a sound like a snort or a clotted sigh rumbled somewhere behind him and to the right. Focused on the pipe, he both noticed the sound and didn't. So he finished packing the bowl, mouthed the stem, and flicked his lighter a few times until it sprouted flame. It wasn't until he was getting ready to tip the flame down and inhale that the sighing finally registered, and that was when Neil turned around and saw the creature.

As it had been in both videogames, the beast was sitting. It was a little higher up the slope of the riverbank, in the opposite direction from the way Neil had come, so he supposed that was how he'd missed it, though the creature wasn't easy to miss, even in such low light: seven or eight feet tall, at least, and Neil could possibly span its torpedo-shaped torso if he tried to put his arms around it (as if he'd want to), but barely. Its hair was long, dark brown or gray, and matted into the kind of clumps the old family dog, Annie, used to get on her belly and in her leg pits. It emitted an odor of such profundity that Neil wondered how he'd possibly sat all this time not noticing it—a stench like wet dog and the almost fungal edge of very bad body odor, the kind of body odor you encountered on homeless people. The face was hard to make out—too shadowed, too obscured by the long fur—but deep-set eyes gleamed greenish-yellow like a cat's. It noticed Neil noticing it—Neil registered this awareness as a shift in the thing's strange posture. It leaned a little to the right, placed a huge, fur-napped mitt on the ground, and adjusted its weight, reminding Neil of an older person with a bad hip or lower back. The thing nodded at him. This too was strange, because there were no shoulders or neck that Neil could see, just a large, oblong mass, with arms extending from both sides slightly below the suggestion of a face, fused to a bottom and set of long legs. So when it nodded, what it really did was bob from the waist, and the top of the torso swayed slightly, like a cattail.

The thing raised its mitt now. Neil, reluctant, raised his hand. And then the thing pushed itself awkwardly (and, it seemed, painfully) to a stand to trudge downhill, in a few long strides, and close the ten or so feet between them. With just as much difficulty, it sat again. This close, Neil could make out another detail that reminded him of Annie: her chest, sides, and back had bulged in her old age with fatty tumors, and rippling beneath this beast's fur were flashes of pale skin that sagged with firm round masses. The smell, this close, was eye-watering. Noxious. Its clogged breathing, as if the thing's trachea were plugged with mud, was painful to even hear. Nothing about its body was natural, to this world or any other. Nothing about it seemed designed properly to a purpose: to walking, sitting, waving, nodding, respirating. It looked like a study in suffering—ugly and inchoate, a misfire.

His mouth tacky with dryness, Neil managed to mutter: "Mr. Gone-Gone?"

The thing's top half swayed forward again, confirming.

"Can you talk?"

It stared at him mutely. It didn't have a head to shake. Figured, Neil thought bitterly, that this was what he ended up with, *this* was his magical friend: a mangy, crippled, mutt of a monster. But still, it was here, in Neil's lowest (surely!) moment, right as the world had stopped making sense, and that had to mean something didn't it? The creature might be ugly and smelly and poorly made, but it was supernatural, and it was his. His beast. Neil knew from the way his skin prickled, a kind of primal electric charge, that this was true: the thing was his; it belonged to him.

"Are you here to help me?" Neil asked. "Are you here to tell me what to do?"

Another mute stare.

"Well, are you? What do you want from me? Why have you been following me?"

The beast's only reply was the clotted sound of its respiration. It shifted position a little, and a dim ribbon of moonlight picked out its wide-set eyes, making them glow faintly in the tangle of filthy fur. It was those eyes, the warmth of their reflected light, that stoked a sudden memory: Neil's ear pressed against silken fur while a heartbeat lulled him to a steady sleep. Mister Gone-Gone: never impatient, never angry, never disappointed or peevish. Just mass and heat and the steady rhythmic churn of strong lungs.

"Look, just leave me alone, okay." Neil was trembling, close to tears. "I don't remember you. I don't need you. You can go back where you came from."

Mr. Gone-Gone waited a beat. Then he lifted his mitts, as if offering an embrace, and Neil scrambled back on his bottom in a panic, heels digging earth. The thought of it touching him, *hugging* him—no, no-no-no-no-no. "Don't fucking touch me!" he stammered in a breathless squeak. "Go away! I don't want you!"

The thing got slowly back to its feet. Neil's heart hammered harder for a moment as the beast towered over him, its rancid dander thick in his nostrils. But then it took a step back. And another. Neil's breath calmed. The calm allowed him to feel a flicker of remorse, but mostly, he was relieved.

Mr. Gone-Gone swayed very slightly in place. Neil sensed in him the pride of an old man in a nursing home; he jittered on his long limbs, and his labored breathing had become clipped and raspy with the effort it had taken to stand. He conveyed a kind of tragic dignity, like in those grainy old photos you saw of Abraham Lincoln.

The thing gave him a last took, turned, and started off down the riverbank, the top of its body tipping alarmingly as it tried to dodge tree branches. It stayed in sight for several excruciating minutes, and Neil could hear its labored progress for a few minutes even after that, and then, finally, the beast was gone. Hands shaking, Neil sparked the bowl and inhaled so deeply he had a coughing fit, but the effect was immediate and comforting—the warmest, safest of embraces, the only magic an adult life needed.

Later, walking home, a thought occurred to him, the kind of philosophical thought he often got while high, but this one had a ring of truth to it. Wouldn't it be funny, he thought, if that thing wasn't my monster, but I was *its?* Like, maybe it thought Neil was this powerful creature who could help it, fix it, the one he'd been waiting his whole life to rediscover. Maybe it had wanted Neil to comfort it this time. And Neil told it to get lost.

He began to plan the drink he would mix himself once he'd gotten back to his room. Just a small one. To help him sleep. And maybe some *Doom* to calm his nerves, because he was certain now that Mister Gone-Gone was—well—gone, and wouldn't be infiltrating his videogames or dreams or thoughts any longer.

ark

We had all sensed, when Lauren sent the sudden Evite out about the get-together at her house, that we were going to be on the receiving end of a sales pitch. Lauren liked having Church folks over to her beautiful home, but usually only on the holidays. This sudden Evite went out in late July to only some of the church's adult women and—so far as we could tell—no one from the Empty Nesters class. And it followed weeks of vague Facebook posts—mostly hot pink-on-white inspirational quotes, like I'M GOING TO MAKE THE REST OF MY LIFE THE BEST OF MY LIFE and ANYTHING WORTH DOING IS A RISK. So, you know, we knew. But Lauren is a force, and no one wanted to get on her bad side. As for me, I guess I was desperate enough for a night out that I even found myself sort of looking forward to it.

The other weird thing about this get-together, once we arrive, is that Lauren is offering us all wine. Now, there are people in our congregation who drink a bit, and the big scandal last year was when it came out in the papers that David Pemberley had gotten a DUI out on the road to his farm, but drinking is something you do, if you do it, entirely away from Church folks. I mean, I don't feel too bad when my husband talks me into getting a daiquiri at our monthly Outback date night, but if someone from Church were to happen over to our table and spot it, I'd probably die. So when she holds up the green bottle with the weird foreign-sounding name and asks if she can pour me a taste, I am about as shocked as I would be if her usually pristine house were a mess or if she'd come to the door wearing a sweatsuit and a baseball cap. It's a tricky situation, because

I don't know what would be worse here: accepting the drink and what that implies about me or turning the drink down and insinuating something about Lauren. So I say, laughing uncomfortably, "Oh, just a taste," and Megan, who drove us both over, says, "Me, too." When Lauren hands us the Solo cups, there's a full three inches of golden liquid in each of them. I think I'll take a tiny sip and then just pour the rest out when I can get to a sink, but I'm surprised by how delicious the wine is. This isn't the stuff I tried a long time ago on my honeymoon, which was more like vinegar than grape juice. It is sweet and alive-tasting, like the tiny bead of nectar you get when you pinch the string out of a honeysuckle flower.

When Lauren hurries off to welcome another guest, I turn to Megan and say, "Oh, this is dangerous."

She bugs her eyes out at me and nods. "If I drink this whole cup, I'm gonna be flat on my back. We'll have to call Cal to pick us up."

"Jeremy wouldn't let me live it down," I say. We go where Lauren had indicated: to her formal sitting room, the one with all the couches and chairs with wooden legs and claw-feet and little embroidered doilies draped across the seat backs. She didn't tell us to put our purses in the guest room, like she usually does, so Megan and I choose chairs next to each other, near the fireplace, and tuck our bags behind our legs. I find myself feeling a little sophisticated, holding my wine, perched on the edge of an antique chair in a beautiful room with a genuine fireplace, not just a little electric faux fireplace like I have, and a view, through the big bay window, of the yellow-green bounty of Lauren's husband's soybean crop. It's too hot, of course, for Lauren to have a fire going (how beautiful it was at Christmas, though—big enough and deep enough you could hang a kettle over it!), but she has lit a row of linen-scented Yankee candles, and they flicker prettily across the scrubbed bricks of the hearth. She even has one of those little talking speaker things, and it's softly playing a playlist of Christian Contemporary but also some mainstream stuff that takes me back to my middle and high school days, like Collective Soul and "Drops of Jupiter," and I know that Jeremy would be impressed by the sound quality.

I love my dear little family more than anything, and motherhood has been the greatest blessing of my life, but there are times, now and again, when I see what the women on television are doing—having coffee dates, meeting for cocktails, "hitting the gym" in leggings and smart-looking zip-up jackets—and I think, I don't know, that a little of that might be fun, now and again. In my mind, as Megan chatters about Louise's swim meet, I go back over the invitation list I'd viewed on Evite, and I scan the room to see who from Church showed up, and who the mystery women on the email list might be, and I allow myself to wonder whether maybe this party is kind of exclusive, maybe even a sign that Lauren would like to be not just someone who goes to church with me but my friend. Socially.

The group of us gathering in Lauren's sitting room, arranging ourselves around the coffee table and its spread of little triangle pimento cheese sandwiches and salted cashews and Pepperidge Farm Milano cookies, are mostly thirty- or forty-something, though there are also a couple of the younger women from our Parents class: Cassidy, who's twenty-five and has four kids between the ages of six and one; and Mary Beth, a bit closer to thirty, who reached something of a tragic heroine status in our church because of her series of miscarriages, though this last pregnancy, at five months, looks like it might finally be the answer to her (and our) prayers. Cassidy is sipping what I assume is a glass of wine, just like the rest of us, and her ruddy cheeks are even pinker than usual. Mary Beth has a sweaty plastic cup of iced coffee, green straw tucked into the corner of her pink mouth. Everyone is talking softly, and we're sort of turning our bodies instinctively toward the gap in the circle of chairs, where we know Lauren will eventually place herself and make her pitch.

Driving over, Megan and I speculated on what we were getting ourselves into. Thirty-One would be an obvious fit, but another woman at church sold their bags already, and we wondered whether Lauren would have the audacity to undercut her. Megan and I ended up making a friendly wager: essential oils and Megan must buy me lunch; powdered diet drinks or vitamins and I have to buy lunch for her. We agreed that there was no way we'd do more than buy the smallest, cheapest product Lauren had on offer, and we bit our tongues before we could express bitterness about doing even that much. The thing is, Lauren is doing really, really well. There's her house, of course, but there's also the agrobots her husband has been able to purchase for their farm—rumor has it that each one cost as much as a hundred thousand, and he bought three of them at once. Every now and then, one trundles into view through the frame of the bay window. It's a strange view if you grew up in the country like I did: not a man on a weather-beaten tractor or harvester but a streamlined white-and-silver spiderlike thing that expands and contracts itself along each row in a weird dance—especially creepy, as is the case in this moment, when the background tune is the Goo Goo Dolls' "Iris." My point is that Megan and I both have little '80s ranch houses on the edge of town, with postage-stamp yards, and our minivans are about ten years old, and maybe we'd like to put our spending money toward something besides Lauren's new hobby.

All this is swirling around inside me—resentment at Lauren, desperation to be liked by Lauren—when Lauren herself finally enters the room. "Alexa, stop the music," she says to the tin-can speaker, and the speaker, like everyone else, obeys her. She grins. She is carrying, awkwardly, one of those kids' art easels, the kind with a chalkboard on one side and a wiper board on the other. She places it in front of the fireplace, and we can see that she has done one of her beautiful, elaborate lettering jobs on the chalkboard side. It reads: **Are YOU *ready* for what is *COMING*?** The *O* of the **YOU** is a little smiling sunshine, its rays stretching to the edge of the chalkboard, and raindrops are falling from ***COMING***, which is bubble-lettered to look kind of like a cloud. It's cheerful but still ominous, in the way those big signs on the interstate that say JESUS IS COMING! are. I mean, I for one welcome Jesus's return, but when you put it that way, in big block letters with an exclamation point, you're making it seem like something to be afraid of. So I stare at Lauren's chalkboard and wonder, What's *what*? And *am* I ready? How can I be ready if I don't even know for sure what *what* is?

Megan and I exchange quick looks. We're not so sure if anyone is getting a free lunch this time.

"Ladies," Lauren says, "I want you to look around at each other. Besides the obvious fact that we're all women here, what do you think you have in common?"

Smiling shyly, we swivel our heads, scanning the group. I'd already been wondering this, but still, having some mystery point of connection binding us all—having Lauren point it out—is both exciting and alarming. Here are me and Megan: midthirties, richer than poor but poorer than well-off, mothers each to pairs of children who are now in middle school, though mine are boy-girl and Megan's are both girls. There's Cassidy and Mary Beth in their almost matching pastel Lily Pulitzer dresses and sandals, smiles tight, looking (I'm probably reading too much into this) like they're a bit offended getting lumped in with the rest of us. From Church are eight other women. The oldest of them, Imogene, is in her early fifties, though her youngest, who has Down syndrome, still lives at home—and always will, I suppose. I don't know four of the women, who have secured a love seat and pair of armchairs together in the corner nearest the door, but I think they're from the bank where Lauren works part-time as a teller. Most of us have the slightly thickened middles of mothers, dimpled biceps that are freckled from too much sun, little flashes of gold jewelry that were probably Christmas gifts from our hardworking husbands. What *don't* we have in common? I think of asking, but Lauren would probably see that as a dig.

"Are we all moms?" Imogene asks. "Or moms-to-be?" she adds, smiling at Mary Beth.

Everyone starts nodding. Lauren points at Imogene and says, "Bingo," and I wish I'd thought to speak up. I forget sometimes that the obvious answer is also the right one.

"You've got it," Lauren says. "But there are some other things y'all have in common. You're women of faith. Faith is important to all of us here. And because your kids still live at home, you've all had to figure out ways to help support your household while also making your children the center of your world. Am I right?"

My nodding is probably a little less enthusiastic this time, just because I don't think I can accept credit for that amount of self-sacrifice. To me, "center of my world" means I love my kids better than anything and would throw myself in front of a train to save them. Which is the truth. But for Lauren, I'm betting, it means all those things plus more, like making them little chore charts with her beautiful chalkboard lettering and reading Bible stories to them every night and putting them in coordinating outfits for professional photographs. So that's why my nod is a half nod.

"Okay, I want to do a little exercise," Lauren says. No one groans out loud, but there's a sort of collective sigh, like we're all at the bottom of a big staircase and readying ourselves to scale it. Lauren hands a stack of rough-cut half sheets of paper to Megan. "Take one of those and pass it around," she says, and then she circles the group in the opposite direction, handing out little half-size pencils like you find in a Boggle game. It occurs to me that everything in this party is half size—papers, pencils, sandwiches—except the wine, and it further occurs to me that this is a wine-induced thought. So I put the wine down under my chair beside my purse and spread the sheet of paper across my thigh. It feels like the beginning of one of those getting-to-know you games we always had to do at church camp, Two Truths and a Lie or the one where you write something unique about yourself, and then the papers get shuffled and you have to go around the room and try to match your interesting fact with the person who wrote it.

"Okay, here's what I want you to do," Lauren said. "Write down where you see yourself and your family in thirty years."

One of the women from Lauren's work put up her hand. "Is this supposed to be our fantasy or what we actually think will happen?"

Lauren laughed. "Go for optimistic but realistic. What you hope will happen if everything goes according to plan."

According to plan. It is so very Lauren to have a plan for thirty years down the pike—to assume most people have one. I guess Jeremy and I have planned to the extent that he has a retirement account at the plant, and he puts an extra fifty dollars a month toward it now that

I'm working part-time, because his contributions are matched. We talked about starting college funds for the kids, but neither of us went to college ourselves, and we don't want to tie up lots of money we don't have in something that we didn't need ourselves and don't fully trust. We figure, if the kids end up being the college types—and Sarah Lynn might, she's bookish—they'll get scholarships and take out loans to make up the difference.

But beyond that? I have no idea.

Sixty-six years old. I try to imagine it. Luke talked me into putting this app on my phone that shows you what you'll look like when you're old, and boy, was that scary. I hit the filter button and boom, there was Granny, my daddy's momma, and I wasn't one of those darling old women or elegant old women you hope to become, either, but scrawny and hollow-eyed, like something that pops up, cackling, behind the plexiglass in a carnival funhouse. I started slathering on the moisturizer after that, you can be sure. So I'm sitting here, optimistically picturing a moisturized version of little-old-lady-me. Jeremy is seventy. Sarah Lynn is forty-three and Luke is forty-one, and goodness, that's about more than my heart can take. But a picture forms in my head and I start to scribble, having to make my marks faint because the pencil point keeps jabbing through the paper:

> Jeremy is retired. Me too but I volunteer part time somewhere, maybe I crochet hats for the newborns at the hospital. I have grandbabies. Sarah Lynn's are probably in high school but maybe Luke's are still little. The kids still live close by, maybe Bowling Green or Nashville at furthest. Jeremy and me live somewhere bigger with plenty of room for the kids and grandkids to visit and maybe also a pool. (above ground okay)

I think, but can't bring myself to write, that I'd like the house to be something like this one, Lauren's, or maybe a place in Hillvue, which is the neighborhood in town where our pastor lives, along with some of the other more well-to-do folks from Church. Reading it over, though, it all sounds so superficial, so I add:

> We will all still be very active in Church and strong in our faith.

My leg is bouncing under the paper, and I make a conscious effort to stop it, then fold the paper in half and hide it under my sweaty palm. It's like I'm back in high school again, terrified the teacher is going to call on me.

"Okay," Lauren says, "it looks like we've all finished up. Would someone volunteer to share theirs?"

Cassidy holds up her paper. "I'll go."

Lauren beams at her. "Go ahead, Cassidy."

Cassidy takes a sip of her wine and then sets it on the coffee table. She clears her throat. "I'll be fifty-five-years old," she says. "Tristan and I will have two more children, so six total. We'll probably have several grandchildren because Braylan will be thirty-six by then. We'll have the house paid off. When the kids are all in school I will focus on my design business, which will be a success."

"Sounds great, Cass," Lauren says. "Who's next?"

We all end up taking a turn. Here, too, are more similarities than differences, and I don't know whether that speaks to a boring sameness among us or just "the human condition." In thirty years, there are middle-aged children, grandchildren, debts paid down, houses paid off or upgraded, retirements earned.

Imogene's stands out—so much so that I wonder, as she reads it, whether Lauren regrets this activity now or if she regrets inviting Imogene, because how else could hers turn out, if the imperative is to lodge it in any measure of reality?

"In thirty years, I'll be eighty-three," Imogene says. "I hope I'll still have Wyatt by then, but with his heart problems, it's hard to depend on. All I can do is pray and try to get him to watch what he eats and exercise. Lonnie—" She pauses, throat thick, and swallows. "We are saving for him. We don't want him to be a burden on his brothers and their families. He'll be forty-two. He will have a lot of life left. I want him to be with someone that loves him and will take him to church. In my dream he'd have some independence but also people to rely on. There's a place in Nashville we're looking into, but it's very expensive." She stopped here, her voice thick. "I'm sorry, Lauren. That's what I've got."

“That’s perfect,” Lauren says, and her voice is husky now too. It’s kind of moving, and I find my own eyes getting damp. The wine, I guess. Another good reason not to drink, as if I need one: I turn into a sniveling crybaby.

Lauren is back in front of her easel. “Most of the businesses you hear about on Facebook make promises to help you earn extra money to put toward things like your kids’ college funds, retirement, swimming pools”—she smiles pointedly at me, and I’m a little embarrassed about that, as I’m the only one who mentioned it—“or even just your weekly groceries. That’s fine. It’s great, even.

“But think about the products themselves. Are the products themselves going to make a difference to you in thirty years? Is that makeup palette or handbag or package of fingernail transfers even going to last you a year?”

Well, no, I thought. I was struck by how profound this statement was—and sad—but also: *And?* Here is Lauren, dressed in the famous Draper James Chambray Ruffle Shift Dress, which is $115 (I looked it up), and I’m sure, by next summer, Reese Witherspoon or Jennifer Garner or whoever will make some other dress *the* essential look, and this dress will then appear at the church’s charity shop, but I won’t buy it; even if it fit (it wouldn’t), she’d know.

“What do y’all know about MLMs?” Lauren asks.

“It’s like Amway,” Nancy Turner from Church says.

“That’s a big one,” Lauren says. “What else?”

“They’re pyramid schemes,” Imogene says, and I swear, there is an electric crackle in the air. We can’t believe she said it. But we also know she is the only woman in here who *could* say it—because she is older, because she has Lonnie, and because she just got choked up talking about Lonnie, and that was Lauren’s fault.

“You know what, Imogene? A lot of them are,” Lauren says. She lifts the easel and turns it around to the markerboard side, and there it is, drawn carefully in three different colors: a triangle-shaped diagram with little percentages labeling each tier. “Take Amway, for example. It’s not a sustainable model, and that’s why most of the people doing it never make money. There’s nothing exclusive about the products, so the sellers are pressured to keep pulling more and more sellers in below them. That's called 'the downline.'" She points to the bottom of the pyramid. "Eventually, you end up with thousands of people trying to peddle overpriced toilet paper to their friends and family, and eventually they give up. The model's designed for that. Get as much out of people as you can, then throw them away. Just like toilet paper. But imagine if the products being sold *were* exclusive and desirable? And imagine if this shape"—she traces the triangle with her index finger—"was the ideal way to connect those products to the people who most desire them? More than that—the people you'd *want* to have them?"

She picks up a sheaf of papers from the mantel—I hadn't noticed they were sitting there—and begins to hand them out to each of us, as if they are too precious to simply pass around. As she reaches me, I'm hit with her perfume, a light, citrusy-herby scent that reminds me of a marinade I sometimes use on chicken cutlets. This is the power of Lauren: she can make a chicken cutlet marinade seem fancy.

"At the risk of sounding weird, I'm going to have to collect these back at the end," Lauren says.

That does seem a bit strange. I look at what she has given me: a little stapled-together booklet, nothing fancy: the cover is printed in color on thicker paper, but the inside pages look like regular sheets out of a laser printer. The cover says ARC in big letters and under it, like the tagline for an action movie, *Make Sure You're On Board*. There's a picture of a family, a perfect family: a mother and father, both of them sandy-haired, big smiles, white teeth, and three tow-headed children, two boys and a girl, all of them under ten, probably. They look like they might be camping; they wear parkas with hoods and complicated sets of zippers, and they're seated around a little electric cookstove, holding graniteware cups beneath their chins so that the steam off the hot liquid blurs their faces slightly.

Camping? That's what this was all about? I flip the booklet open. Megan, who has done the same, casts a troubled look at me, and then we both stare at the page again, wondering whether this is a joke or maybe some kind of party game.

Apocalypse
Readiness
Club

Make Sure You're On Board

ARC is a different kind of business opportunity. Specializing in innovative disaster preparation products, ARC exists not only to help members prepare for the 21st Century's greatest challenges but to create a like-minded, faith-based network of leaders for the new America.

Join ARC, and you and your loved ones will survive the next Great Flood.

"I can see in your faces that you've all read the first page," Lauren says with a light laugh. "Go ahead and have another sip of wine, y'all. I won't judge." We titter uncomfortably. Lauren's influence is strong, and I'd warrant that she could have accosted us with any number of sales pitches todays—heck, maybe even that one that sells the sex toys—and we'd be good-naturedly taking out our checkbooks. But this, this is a bit much. I start flipping deeper into the booklet, looking at page after page of grainy pictures and product descriptions and complicated tiered pricing: water purifiers, portable solar cells, shelf-stable bulk food items, books of waterproof matches, thermal raincoats, utility knives, and on and on it goes. My heart starts to hammer, and I can feel the wine I've drunk boiling behind my cheeks.

"I know this isn't what you expected to see today," Lauren says. "And I wouldn't blame you if you thought I was crazy right now, but I beg you to hold your horses and hear me out."

In the back of the catalog are pages of guns and boxes of ammunition rounds. Jeremy would know what to call them all, but my sense is vaguer: I see handguns, hunting rifles, semiautomatic rifles. I know just enough about the law to wonder how it could possibly be legal to order a gun as if you're getting lipstick from the Avon lady.

"ARC isn't just a side hustle for me," Lauren says. "Travis and I put months of research and prayer into this, and we made the commitment because we know change is coming, and we want to be ready for it. We want to protect our children, and we want to protect as many of our loved ones as we possibly can. That's you," she said, swiveling her head around, honey-colored hair swinging around her slim shoulders.

"But Lauren," Imogene says, "you're not getting pulled into this global warming panic, are you? I'd have given you more credit than that." Another unspoken electric crackle passes among us, and we all shift, seats suddenly uncomfortable, skirts and slacks wrinkling unpleasantly beneath our thighs.

Lauren laughs lightly, but it is a brittle tinkling.

"Do I think Florida's going to be underwater in a decade? No. Do I think the government should be stepping in and telling us how to run our businesses and what kind of cars we can drive and how much money we all get to make? Definitely not, and that's one of the biggest threats of this whole business, but I'm getting ahead of myself.

"Travis's a farmer. As long as I've known him, he's kept a copy of the *Farmer's Almanac* and a ledger in that secretary over there"—she motioned to a beautiful antique positioned next to the door to the dining room—"and he keeps a detailed record of the weather and the yields. We didn't get the agrobots because we're lazy or to show off, even though we know those are the comments going around town. We got them because the weather's gotten unpredictable enough that the old machinery doesn't do the job well enough. So *something* is happening. Do I know what that something is, exactly? No, I do not, and neither does Travis. Do I think that this is caused by humans? I've seen no evidence to convince me this is the case. And like I said, we don't want the government mixing itself up in it or trying to stifle a free market. That's what's so great about ARC." She wagged a copy of the pamphlet she'd distributed, a little testily, and I could sense a slight disturbance in her cool. "It's a free-market response that addresses what's coming as both a challenge and an investment opportunity."

"What do you think is coming, Lauren?" Lily Rhea, from Church, said.

“More unpredictability for farmers, certainly, and not all of them have the resources Travis and I have to troubleshoot the uncertainties. That’s an economic problem, but also a food supply problem, which is why ARC offers so many healthy and delicious shelf-stable meal options. Honestly, probably more natural disasters, though we’re blessed to live far enough inland that most of those don’t touch us here. But the hurricanes are going to drive people toward us, so immigration is going to be a worse and worse problem, and that’s going to come to a head, eventually, even if we get our Wall, and I pray every night we do.”

Cassidy looked terrified. “What do you mean, come to a head?”

“Civil war. The liberals want to take our guns away. Why do you think they’re so bent on doing that? Why do you think they would want, given what they claim is true about rising oceans and hotter temperatures, to put out a red carpet for every person in the world who’s falling on hard times? Because they’re more decent people than us? You know better than that. These people don’t have God, and they certainly don’t care about the fate of some Mexican they’ve never met. They want the race wars. They want to destroy this country and start all over with the government saying who gets what and how much and when they get it. The way Travis sees it, conservatives are making a mistake by saying there is no problem. The worse things get, the more the liberals control the narrative, the more they get to say, ‘See, we told you so, so we’re right about the rest of it, too.’ But they’re not. And that’s the real threat here. That’s what we’ve got to prepare ourselves and our children for, and that’s why I’m here today telling you that ARC is the greatest hope we have for a faith-based tomorrow.”

I reach to the floor, trembling, and grab my cup of wine. There’s an inch of liquid left, and I down it in a gulp, afraid, if I stop, I’ll spill what’s left on Lauren’s blush-colored Berber carpet.

Megan says, hesitantly, “Buying the stuff here”—she flips the catalog’s pages with her thumb—“that’s the answer? We all need bunkers, or whatever?”

“The products are part of a three-tiered platform,” Lauren says. “When you buy the products, you’re not just setting aside a survival kit for tomorrow's uncertainties, you're supporting the faith-based businesses who produce every item in that booklet, you're supporting the farmers like Travis who grow the beans and oats and soy. That strengthens our economic foundations.

"Tier two is the network itself. I told you that pyramids aren't bad things when they're directed to the right purpose. Picture God at the top of our pyramid. Beneath God are the founders of ARC, and you can go Google them tonight. They're three godly men, and two of them are ordained ministers. Beneath the founders are women like me, women of faith, with families and a way of life to protect, and we're using our Church communities to reach out to other women we love and trust, other women with families to protect, and the idea is, who do you want on the ark when the Great Flood comes? What's *our* vision for the America of thirty years from now?"

"Shouldn't the men be doing this?" Marnie McIntosh asked. "This feels to me like the province of our husbands, of the church elders. I couldn't make a decision about this without my husband, anyway, and I certainly wouldn't trust myself to buy the right things." She ran her pale index finger across the grainy pictures of guns in the back of the catalog.

"Our husbands will be integral to this, but believe it or not, the ARC founders knew what they were doing when they conceived this business as one that grows through women. Women are the communicators, the community builders. It's through our friendships and relationships that we'll grow this pyramid into an army, relying on the guidance and support of our husbands along the way, and our husbands will be the ones to take up arms if it comes to that. I pray it doesn't, and that's another good thing about this system. Amassing the resources gives you power even if you never have to use them."

"What's the third tier?" I find myself asking.

"The most important one of all," Lauren says, favoring me with her most brilliant smile. "The ark itself. And I mean A-R-K now, not A-R-C. What I'm talking about is a two-thousand-acre compound in the Ozarks southern Missouri. Apocalypse Readiness Club already owns this parcel of land, and a portion of each of your sales will go toward construction of an exclusive gated community complete with luxury condominiums, resort amenities, a fully equipped armory, a water treatment plant, its own power grid, and its own medical center. I've seen the plans for this place, and it's about as close to heaven as we'll get while we're still on this planet."

"And we'd all get to go to it?" Mary Beth asks.

"Not exactly," Lauren says. "If you come on right now as an Elite-tier seller—so that means, instead of just buying some products from me, you join my team and reach out to your own networks of friends and family—you get a vestment in a property on the compound. If you hit your sales and recruitment goals, by 2050 you'll own it outright. You can sell it, will it to your children, whatever you want. But that's not even the best part. You'll have access to it by completion of construction in 2026, so that means you can use the condo for vacations, or you can retreat to it in the event of another pandemic lockdown, electrical outages, whatever. How many of you go on a yearly vacation?"

Most of us raise our hands, including me, though our "vacation" is usually a three-day weekend at the Smoky Mountains, not a week in Orlando or something, or one of those vacation-mission trips to exotic countries that Lauren and her family always seem to be taking.

"You know how much those add up, even if you get a place with a kitchen and try to be frugal. Everyone goes out to Joe's Crab Shack for dinner one night and you're out a hundred bucks, easy. Hotel for seven nights is going to be in the thousands. Souvenirs, tickets to the theme park, and before it's done, you've spent your sales quota for ARC and then some."

This time, when Megan looks at me, she's lifting her brows, shrugging a little, as if to say, "Huh, hadn't thought of it that way." My own face is hot, and I put my cold fingertips against my cheeks and forehead, taking deep breaths to slow the rate of my heart.

"The ark's going to be built with access to Table Rock Lake," Lauren said. "It's a thirty-minute drive to Branson, where I know at least some of you like to go on trips anyway, and it's about six-and-half-hour's drive from here. You wouldn't have to fly there, which is good for your wallet and also good if the planes are grounded. You could make it from here on a full tank of gas too, depending on your vehicle and the conditions."

"And everyone here today could be Elite sellers if we want?" Megan asks.

"Not quite," Lauren says. "I've been granted permission to take on five elite sellers. You have to pay in fifteen hundred dollars, but that gets you your first shipment of goods, and the markup you can charge on your stock is 35 percent, so you're going to get that investment back as soon as you sell a little over half of it. Or you could do what Travis and I have done and sit on it for your own purposes."

"What does the fifteen hundred get you?" one of the women from the bank asks.

Lauren points at the catalog. "We bought in on the Founders package, but you can find an example of an Elite package shipment on the third page."

I turn to 3.

ELITE SALES KIT

(Actual package will vary depending on availability; ARC may substitute these items with products of similar value.)

* Five gallon drum dried beans (3)
* Five gallon drum long grain white rice (3)
* Five gallon drum rolled oats (3)
* Sanctity 1000-gallon water purifier with 5 replacement filters (2)
* Medical Grade First Aid Kit (5)
* *The Readiness Bible: A Faith-Based Guide for Surviving the Next Great Flood* (hardcover, 5)

This doesn't look like much for $1,500. The water purifier seems useful, and I'm not entirely sure where I'd go buy that in real life (though I make a note to myself to check the prices tonight on Amazon), but forty-five gallons of dried beans, rice, and oats? Who would I sell that to? Where in my house would I even store it? My breath is tight in my chest because I feel the urgency of Lauren's offer. There are fourteen of us in this room, besides her. She can take on five Elite sellers, and those are the only ones who can get a vestment at the compound in Missouri. But the stress is two-headed, because at the same time I'm processing the stakes, that I'm recognizing this might be *the* turning point in my life, the moment I look back on later with anguish and fury, because I'd had my shot at protecting my children and missed it, I'm also wondering how in the hell Jeremy and I could free up fifteen hundred dollars, and who would we sell this stuff to even if we managed it? Momma and Daddy? My sister? And say I get them scared enough about what's coming to buy from me; how do I tell Krista that hey, sorry, the condo is only for me and Jeremy and *our* kids? That she has to stick to stashing away gallons of food and hope for the best?

Beneath the Elite Sales Kit, I notice, is another list of products: Premium Sales Kit. It has most of the same items as the Elite kit in smaller quantities, and the books are listed as paperback rather than hardcover. "What's this?" I say, pointing. "What's a Premium Seller?"

"Well, that's one of the best all-around deals ARC can make. Premium Sellers get a slightly smaller starter kit, but their commissions, incentives, and discounts on products are all the same, for a cost of five hundred dollars. Now that doesn't get you a dedicated unit in the compound, but it does set you up for a kind of time-share structure in the project's second phase. So, assuming you meet your sales and recruitment goals, by 2028 you'll be able to schedule two weeks' worth of vacation a year at the Ark, and you'll be eligible for a lottery in the event of a crisis situation."

"A lottery?" Imogene asks. "For what?"

"For use of a unit. Not everyone could descend on the time-share units at once, of course, because the infrastructure wouldn't support it. But all the Premium Sellers would be part of a randomized lottery, giving their families a shot at secure, off-the-grid housing if times get really hard."

I am about to ask what everyone else in that scenario is left with—a basement full of dried beans and rice?—when Megan says, "How many Premium Sellers can you take on?"

"That's the good news," Lauren says. "I can take on as many Premium Sellers as I wish. And you can recruit an unlimited number of Premium Sellers under me. At some point the company will phase out adding in new Elite and Premium Sellers entirely, but for now, this is like getting in on the ground floor of Google or Facebook. And the company also trusts this faith-based model to really shape the growth in the right sorts of ways. They don't expect a free-for-all or want it. They want you to recruit knowing that the people you ask on board might be your neighbors when disaster strikes."

I sneak looks around, wondering if the mix of emotions I'm feeling is showing on anyone else's face. It's a strange moment. The sun is setting, gloriously framed by the bay window, and the room is suddenly dark, or maybe I've just noticed the darkness; it's that sliver of time before someone realizes that they ought to switch on a lamp. I feel a passionate longing for home, for Jeremy and the kids, but I wish I could be transported to them at a point before this evening took place or maybe to an alternate reality in which I'd never attended. I am furious at Lauren but also wondering if I should just blurt out, "I want to be an Elite Seller." I am picturing our checking account, our meager savings, and what would be left of it if I subtracted fifteen hundred dollars. I am thinking about that last thing Lauren said—who I'd want to be neighbors with if disaster struck—and wondering: What if it were Cassidy and Mary Beth? Are those the ones I'd choose? Would I choose Lauren? I don't know the women on the loveseat, from the bank. I don't really even know the women from Church, beyond superficial pleasantries and idle gossip. The only person here I love is Megan. Megan was the maid of honor at my wedding, and I was the third person, after Megan herself and Cal, to hold each of their sweet newborns. Megan was the one who brought me back to life after my miscarriage—Jeremy had been stumbling, bewildered—and the one who quietly gifted me two hundred dollars of her own money that time when Jeremy was laid off from the factory. I would stand with Megan at the frontlines of any war, but everyone else here?

"I'd like an Elite spot," Megan says in a rush, and then she giggles a little, self-consciously, and adds, "if this is the time to say so." She flashes a bright, nervous smile at me, the smile my son wore the first time he went wobbling down the sidewalk on two unsupported bike wheels. That same manic glee, the same dazed shock. Or maybe it is another kind of smile. When Sarah Lynn was a toddler, she developed the habit of shouting, "I love you!" and grinning every time we walked up on her doing something she wasn't supposed to be doing: pooping her underwear, pulling one of my porcelain figurines off a shelf. Maybe this is Megan's "I love you!" smile, the smile that assaults you with affection, attempting to distract you from her moment of sneakiness.

"It certainly is the right time," Lauren said. "I'm thrilled for you, Megan."

Mary Beth's hand shot in the air. "And me too."

My failure to raise my hand, to call out for a spot, is not a decision. It's paralysis. In seconds, two more Elite spots have been claimed, and then two hands go up simultaneously for the fifth. One of the women from Lauren's work is red-faced, close to tears, and I wonder for a moment whether I'm about to witness a physical fight for the first time in my life, but then Lisa Mahoney says, "It's all right, hon, I'll just go in at Premium," and everyone in the room seems to sigh at once. Lisa looks as exhausted as I feel.

"I should add," Lauren said, "that if an Elite member leaves the club, the Premium members have first dibs at moving up."

The near frenzy has died down at this point. There's less urgency around those unlimited Premium slots, our blood is starting to settle, and those of us who missed out on Elite vestments are, I'd wager, starting to feel a trickle of relief along with our disappointment, because $1,500 is a lot of money, and it's really not the sort of decision you should make without talking to your husband first. Lauren moves around the room, switching on lamps, and a fresh green bottle of wine is suddenly in her hands, and she's offering everyone a celebratory pour. "Because today is good news. Today's about hope, and it's about opportunity and prosperity. You should think of today as the start to something very, very good."

I don't accept the offer of wine, but I don't have the voice to deny it either, and Lauren slops some into my cup. Megan has retrieved her purse from under her seat, and she has her wallet folded open, pen poised above her checkbook. "Do I make this out to you or to ARC?" she asks Lauren, and Lauren says, loudly enough for everyone to hear, "Please make your checks out to ARC Partners LLC and make sure you put your phone number in the memo section." When Lauren moves away, I lean toward Megan and whisper, "Are you sure about this? What's Cal going to say?"

She flashes a look at me. It isn't exactly warm. "This is my money from Gram's estate. Cal told me it was mine and to spend it how I want. This is what I want."

"Are you going to be able to sell that stuff? You told me—" I don't have the words. I'm trying to remember what she'd said on the ride over, how it went exactly, and all I can come up with is a general sense of our conversation, how we'd agreed that these network marketing businesses were a big waste of money and we were surprised Lauren had gotten suckered in. "You told me it was silly," I finish lamely. Maybe I was the one who'd said silly.

"You know this isn't the same thing," Megan says. She swallows the fresh pour of wine Lauren gave her, rips the check out with a shaking hand, and stands. "I'll be right back."

And then she is by Lauren's side, handing her check over alongside perhaps half the party's attendees. They're a lively faction, but those of us left behind are silent. Cassidy has her phone out and is jabbing furiously with her thumbs, so I assume she's messaging her husband, trying to convince him to spend the money. The three other women from Lauren's work seem shellshocked; one of them has her slip of paper and half-size pencil back out, and she's scribbling figures, making slashes through them, using her free hand to tap out numbers against her knee. Imogene, I notice, is using her cell phone to take pictures of the pamphlet Lauren distributed. I glance quickly Lauren's way, to see if there's any risk of her catching Imogene in the act, but Lauren is occupied with collecting checks and filling out receipts. When I look back at Imogene, her eyes meet mine.

"I don't do anything in a hurry," she says.

“Are you interested?” I ask. Of all the people here, she surprises me the most. I could see myself joining ARC before Imogene, who once told me she didn’t have a single credit card and would no sooner spend money on the internet than she would set her life savings out in front of her house in a cardboard box marked HAVE SOME.

“Probably not,” she says. “But you see how people jumped on this. If it’s a scam, it’s a gosh darn good one.”

I put my cup to my mouth out of reflex, but as soon as the wine hits my tongue, my stomach turns. I let the liquid roll back out and rub my tongue across the roof of my mouth, sneering against the sour taste. Megan is talking intensely with Lauren and the other “Elites,” scribbling notes down in the little spiral notepad she always carries in her purse—the pad, I know, where she jots down her shopping lists, book recommendations, little notes to her kids that she tucks into their lunches. I don’t know how long she will be, but more than that, I don’t know whether I can stand the fifteen-minute ride with her back into town, so I get out my own phone, pull up Messages, and text Jeremy:

Megan got suckered lol so she might be here awhile. Can you come get me

A few seconds later: **Yeah there in a sec**

It’s probably rude of me or melodramatic, but I don’t care; I set my wine on an end table and slip out without saying goodbye to anyone, without telling Megan that I’ve called Jeremy. She’ll figure it out. The sun’s absence has taken the painful scorch out of the air, but it’s still hot and muggy out, and the relief of October seems a long, long way off. I can smell a distant whiff of the stench from a pig farm, and a petty part of me thinks that Lauren’s house isn’t so perfect after all. On a hot evening like this, if she and her family go out on that pretty deck with a pitcher of lemonade or sweet tea and the breeze moves a certain way, it can’t be long before their noses wrinkle, and the kids whine, and the burgers (or steaks, probably) on the grill start to seem unappetizing.

Twenty minutes later, I see the familiar wideset round headlights of Jeremy’s pickup truck. He must have left the kids at home. I can picture it as if I'd witnessed it firsthand: Jeremy gathering his wallet, keys, and phone from the little table in the entryway and yelling, "Kids! Wanna come with me and get Mom?" And their chorus, intoned from their spots on each end of the sectional: "Noooooo." A few years ago, ice cream would have been enough to change their minds, but ice cream no longer holds a candle to whatever pleasures they're always finding on the internet, even the parental-controlled version of the internet we allow them.

The truck stops beside me and Jeremy cranks down his window. "Hey, pretty lady. Want a ride?"

"Yes, please," I say, trying to laugh along with him. I jam my thumb into the handle and pull the heavy door open, then slide across the bench seat and belt myself in right beside him. This truck is an '82 model, a long-term project of Jeremy's, and the air-conditioning is a sluggish trickle from a single set of vents in the middle of the dashboard.

He kisses my cheek. "Have fun?"

"It was okay," I say.

"So what was she peddling?" Jeremy asks.

I'm torn between wanting to tell him all of it—the wine and the pamphlets and Lauren's dark vision of the future—and wanting to bury it all deep inside me, obliterate it. Jeremy might think it's all a big joke, or he might be interested. He might encourage me to go back inside and secure one of those Premium slots, even though that five hundred dollars would be a big hit to us, and Lord knows he wouldn't be much help to me actually unloading the products. On the other hand, he might be angry. He can be bitter when the subject of Lauren and Travis comes up; he and Travis went to high school together at County, and Travis was, he tells me, an asshole—I always flinch at that word—and Travis wouldn't have this farm and house and "robot slaves," Jeremy says, if he hadn't had it all handed to him on platter by his rich daddy.

"It was a bit weird," I say after a pause. "Kind of a disaster prepper thing. Water purifiers and MREs and stuff like that."

"Huh. That's a new one. You have to buy anything?"

"Nope. I slipped out."

"Good for you. But Megan fell for it?"

"She seems to've." We've done a three-point turn and are rumbling back along Lauren's long gravel drive. The agrobots are still at work, I see—one of them is only thirty or forty feet to my right, a hulking shadow punctuated with white lights, scissoring down a row. "I don't know. Maybe she's the smart one and I'm the dumb one." What I'm actually thinking is that I might have lost my oldest friend, or at least I might have lost her in the only way that matters—some deep trust between us has been shattered, and all it took was Lauren and a few scary predictions about the future.

"You're no dummy," Jeremy says.

I pull his hand from the steering wheel and squeeze it, and he tucks it between my legs and grazes my knee with his thumb. It takes me back to the days when we were dating, driving the half hour to Bowling Green for a movie, or maybe walking around the Greenwood Mall for an hour and then eating dinner at Garfield's.

"Don't suppose you'd want to pull off somewhere and—" He squeezes my knee twice. It's the same funny voice he used when he first drove up and greeted me, asked me if I wanted a ride, and I know that he expects me to laugh him off, as I always do. So when I say, "okay," and he practically jolts in his seat in surprise and delight, it's the one nice thing to happen all day.

It's still country out here, the roads narrow and undivided, with winding gravel tributaries leading off to farms and firebreaks and family sinkholes burping up seventy-year-old steel appliances. Jeremy slows, looking, and turns off his headlights. We take an unmarked dirt road, rolling quietly down it until it bends behind some trees and the highway is out of sight. He silences the engine, and we crank down the windows. The air is hot and close, the seat vinyl creaking beneath us, and each time I close my eyes I see the undulations of the agrobots, ancient-seeming beasts in a never-ending sea of soy.

shelter

She pulled her bathing suit off the shower curtain bar and stepped into it, rolling the damp cloth over her belly and shouldering the thick straps with a grunt. The neckline sagged, exposing her newly heavy breasts, and she smeared sunblock over as many exposed spots as she could reach, the motion only reexciting the itch of the mosquito bites that stippled her from stem to stern. It had been a bad summer for them—worse because the rental house, which she had reserved in a last-minute pang of nostalgia, was on the sound side instead of oceanside. Worse, too, because she had been trying to stick to the DEET-free insect repellent, and the organic stuff just didn't work.

The trip had been a miscalculation. She had imagined a pleasant last hurrah with her husband and their two closest friends, lots of time spent reading and napping under an umbrella, a restorative before her October due date, when she and Jimmy would begin the next, more grown-up phase of their lives. But she had not thought about the misery of walking across Highway 12 and down the long, rutted path to the beach, sand grinding between her swollen toes, stumbling to keep her center of gravity on that steep final climb over the dunes. She had not thought about making that same long trip back once, twice, a third time to use to the toilet, so at last she had just called Jimmy on his cell phone to say that she was done with the beach for the day, to have fun with Charles and Rhonda, stay as long as he wanted, that she needed a nap and some time out of the sun and a cool drink. She had not realized the extent to which the fun of their previous beach vacations, seven years' worth now, had depended on alcohol, and she found herself at a loss when all she had in front of her was a book and the eternal crashing of waves, and the rest of them were as pink-cheeked and blearily cheerful as they'd ever been, their Coronas sweating into the cup holders on their folding chairs. "Just have one," Rhonda had said, but no—Jen wouldn't have been able to enjoy it, bracing herself for the dirty looks people would give her, any more than she could heed her husband's encouragement to "just go in the water" when the press of her bladder became excruciating.

"Look at the cutie-pie," Jen had tried to say to Jimmy that afternoon, pointing at a toddler in a pink bathing suit with ruffles across the bottom. The little girl was digging in the sand with a plastic shovel, blond hair glinting white, limbs plump and golden.

"Yep," Jimmy had said. He tilted his bottle and not his head so that his lower lip jutted out, apelike. "Cute."

Now she was back at the house. She had changed into her pajamas, watched television for an hour, and napped for a while on the wicker sofa in the living room, where the ceiling fan could blow on her. The cushions on it kept shifting around, jostling her before she could sleep deeply enough to dream, and her lower back twinged in almost every way she positioned it. The bedroom, hers and Jimmy's, was small and gloomy, the bed hard, the door perpendicular to the flow of the house's one air-conditioning unit. So she stayed on the couch until she could not take it anymore, and then she decided that she could at least get up and go wade in the sound until the rest of the group came home. She didn't like the sound much, really. The shoreline was the dirty gray of cat litter, the water greenish and lukewarm, and it had always disturbed her how you could walk thirty or forty feet out and still only be wading hip deep. But it was something to do.

She scrawled a quick note and pinned it to the refrigerator with a magnet. Then she packed a tote bag with a clean towel, a bottle of water, the suspense novel she had been trying to read, and a tube of sunblock, donned her sun hat and shades, and scooted into her flip-flops. She squatted and grabbed her beach chair from the floor of the utility room, which was sticky with damp sand and smelled like a drained fish tank. A mosquito whined near her ear, but she kept missing when she slapped at it, and she felt a sudden pulse of crawling heat on her neck.

The water at the sound was flat and dull, so the noise of the gathered swimmers, mostly children and young mothers, was loud. There were no waves to drown out the shrieks or the splashing or scoldings; staying focused on her book was impossible. Jen stowed her chair and bag at the shore and waded out, grimacing at the muddy give of the ground, the way her toes kept snagging on slippery strands of algae. A kayak glided by on the horizon. Two boys fought over an inner tube, splashing Jen in their struggle. "Sorry," the older boy said with deadpan disinterest, and the younger boy quickly echoed him: "Sorry." Jen didn't reply, and neither of them seemed to notice.

She trudged until she reached a quiet spot and turned and looked back toward the island. Hatteras extended long and lean before curving toward the coastline, the Buxton lighthouse just visible in the bend. The sky to the south was cloudy and smeared charcoal, making the light over here, which was still bright, eerie in contrast, almost green. The weather forecasters had been breathlessly tracking the progress of a storm system, upgrading its category, tracing its trajectories along different prediction models. The usual. Turn on CNN, no doubt, and you'd see the footage of bent-in-half palm trees on some onetime island paradise. Hatteras would miss the worst of it this time, or at least that was the belief. No evacuations. Shelter in place.

Her gaze dropped. She could see a young couple, late teens or early twenties, kissing intently, the water up to their chests, and she thought about those eager days of her own youth, the pleasure of kissing—just kissing—her first boyfriend. But then she saw (and it was subtle) the boy shift and hike up the girl, and there was something too familiar about the way the girl settled her hips, about the sway of her shoulders so that her breasts kept grazing his collarbone. The girl turned out of the kiss to tuck her chin into the boy's shoulder, and it might have looked like just an intense hug from farther away, but Jen knew better.

Under the water, she rubbed her stomach. The baby was moving, roused by the sensation of water, maybe, and Jen imagined that she was an aquarium with an eel slithering around inside her, and in her mind's eye her womb was green-tinged with algae, the eel a small, slick thing with plenty of room to swim and curl and hide. She didn't know what time it was or when her husband and their friends would be back at the rental house. She wondered whether they had even registered her absence. The couple grappled and grunted, the suppressed sounds of their coupling traveling efficiently over the glassy water, and Jen kept watching until they locked onto each other tightly, trembled, and stopped. They disentangled, sheepish, pleased with themselves, and Jen did not pretend to look away when they checked her direction for witnesses. She simply stood and stared.

Jimmy, Rhonda, and Charles were back at the house by the time she returned, and she could tell from the moment she opened the screen door—just from the way Jimmy's overloud laughter cut across the house to her—that they were all drunk. Jen was hungry, and she stopped at the kitchen counter to munch a few pretzels and check the contents of the refrigerator. There was a package of hamburger meat, which Jimmy had promised that morning to grill out, but it was well after six now, and he hadn't yet started the charcoal. She grabbed another handful of pretzels and chewed them slowly, trying to settle her stomach before greeting the group. She was starving and grumpy, and she wasn't looking forward to a second night of watching Jimmy and Charles line up beer bottles on the windowsill or Rhonda try to sneak through the kitchen on her way back from a bathroom break so that she could dump more gin and tonic water into her tumbler. This time last year, Jen and Rhonda were passing back and forth the Beefeater, or Jen was pulling the cork on a fresh bottle of white wine and topping off both their glasses whenever the levels fell to half, and at some point one or both of them would go to the kitchen, wobbling on the journey but suddenly graceful and confident once there, and they'd dress the tilefish or the red drum fillets simply with butter, garlic, and lemon, and they'd boil new potatoes and use the back of a wooden spoon to smash them in sea salt, and Rhonda would put together one of her good salads, like the one with fennel and orange slices, and they'd all eat up on the deck where they could see the ocean. But Jen couldn't eat the tilefish this year because of the mercury, and she was nervous about all the other fish too, even those on the OK list her doctor had given her. This rental house didn't have a deck—just a graveled patch of yard with a picnic table on it, and a neighboring house blocked the view of the sound.

This was their second night at the beach, with five to go.

When she was certain that she had settled her stomach enough not to snap at Jimmy in front of their friends, she poured herself some mineral water and lime and joined them in the living room. Charles and Rhonda were perched on the edge of the wicker sofa, cards fanned out in front of them. Jimmy was on the other side of the glass coffee table, sitting on the floor with his legs crossed. "Jen!" they called together, and she smiled, feeling wanted, and pulled up a chair.

Rhonda looked at her hand and put a couple of cards face down on a pile. "Two kings," she said, and she reached to a side table, Jen noted, and quietly ground out what looked like a fresh cigarette.

"Hmm," Jimmy said. He plucked a card and added it to the pile. "One ace."

"Bullshit!" Charles yelled, slamming his palm over the pile. He flipped Jimmy's card over, revealing an ace of spades, and Jimmy wheezed laughter.

"Goddammit!" Charles said, collecting the pile. He was a big man, bearded and muscled like a lumberjack, and the fingers organizing his cards were as broad and blunt as rolls of quarters. "Shit ass fucker. This game's never going to end." He put down three cards. "Twos."

Rhonda threw down a card and stood. "One three. I've got to hit the baño." She took her glass.

"Are you guys hungry yet?" Jen said quickly. "I'm fading, Jimmy. You might want to go on and stoke up the grill."

Jimmy leaned against her chair and reached up to pat her thigh. "Well, we were just talking about that. That storm's coming in. Guy at the beach told us that they're calling for gale-force winds." Jen watched him put down an eight of hearts. "So this might not be the night to cook out."

Charles grunted. "I know that's not a goddamn four, but I don't care at this point."

"Call it like you see it, my friend."

Charles shook his head and lay down a couple of cards.

"Well, what then?" She chewed her thumbnail. "Babe, I need something on my stomach other than pretzels. I don't care much what it is."

Rhonda came back with her glass refreshed. "We could go down to the Captain's Wharf."

"What about the storm?" Jen asked.

Rhonda sat on the couch and pulled her bare feet under her hip. She had always been lean, could look scrawny depending on her clothes. Her collarbone jutted out of the stretched neck of her T-shirt, sculptural as a dune. "We heard that's where the locals go to hunker down and listen to the CB."

"Because it's sound side," Jimmy said. Jen could tell that they had discussed this plan already, had practically settled on it. "It's on the interior of the bend, honey." He was twisted around to look up at her, his eyes, which were guileless and blue, framed by his most reassuring expression. "It's weathered the last three major hurricanes without major damage. Plus, like, it's a tradition around here, almost. Everybody kind of huddles together."

"Like a party," Jen said.

"Yeah, exactly."

"Babe, look at me." She grabbed her stomach. "I'm thirty weeks along. I want a meal, not a party. I'm sorry, but I don't have it in me to stay up all hours and watch you three get drunk with the townies."

"We don't have to stay long," Rhonda said. "Jen, you could drive us and just take off when you're tired."

"Fuck that," Jen said. She felt, despite her attempts to quell her anxiety with pretzels, her sinuses grow suddenly heavy and sore, her throat tight. Jimmy and Charles exchanged looks. "I'm sorry to be a killjoy, guys. I really am." She couldn't control the warble in her voice. "But I'm not your damn DD. If y'all want to go, walk. Do it with my blessing. But I'm staying here. I'm getting in the shower, and then I'm frying myself a hamburger."

"Oh, Jen, we didn't mean—"

She stalked to the bathroom.

In the shower she scrubbed herself roughly with a washcloth, tears leaking down her face. She was so twisted up with embarrassment and fury that her breathing was constricted, and she imagined, with a whistling exhalation, trying to climb out of the bathroom window to avoid the awkward, inevitable reunion with Jimmy and their friends. She hated them right now, all three, and she missed them terribly and wished she were one of them again. Not that it had ever been easy, these friendships. Jimmy would sometimes grumble with resentment when Charles bragged about installing kitchen cabinets in his and Rhonda's house or when he ribbed Jimmy about wasting money on oil changes when it "didn't take a genius" to just do it yourself at home, and they'd once nearly come to blows over the outcome of a Duke–UNC game, and Jen had sensed Jimmy's panic over that—had known, though Jimmy wouldn't have ever admitted it to her, that he didn't think he could hold his own against Charles. (She would never have admitted it to Jimmy, but she didn't think he could either.) And Rhonda, who taught math at the community college, had a tendency to get smug and superior when the subject of work came up, so that Jen, who had dropped out of college, would grow quiet, sullen, and never speak of her job as office manager at Triad LASIK, though she was happy there.

And there was that time, a while back, when Charles had kissed Jen. But they were all really drunk that night, Jimmy passed out and Rhonda making a run to the Safeway for more cigarettes, and Jen didn't think that Charles even remembered the next day that it had happened. He never mentioned it, at least.

But Charles and Rhonda were the only couple she and Jimmy had ever been able to more or less agree on and equally enjoy, the only couple who had known them since their early twenties, when Jimmy and Charles worked a summer together on a construction crew and none of them was married yet, and spontaneity was the rule of their lives rather than the exception. Even that kiss, that inappropriate kiss—there was a part of Jen that felt warm toward the memory, nostalgic for it. For years, the kiss represented for her something unacknowledged and unformed, a seed—dormant maybe, but no less real—for major change if she found she ever needed it. But yesterday, just after their arrival at Hatteras, Jen had realized that the unacknowledged and unformed thing had become a dead thing, a thing that didn't exist. It was when she had emerged from her and Jimmy's bedroom for the first time in her swimsuit, round belly preceding her, and Charles had cleared his throat and quickly shifted his gaze, as though the sight of her embarrassed him. And her dismay at this turn between them had nothing to do with desire for Charles, who had only interested her because she knew that she interested him. It was witnessing the disappearance of that interest. Poof, gone.

When she shut off the water and stepped out of the shower, she could smell burgers cooking, and the baby kicked. She put on sweatpants and a T-shirt, combed the knots out of her hair, which was too short to tangle much, and checked her face carefully in the mirror. Her eyes were a little red, but not too bad. Her nose had started to broaden in the last few weeks, confirming her mother's assertion that Leone women get "pregnancy face," and "you may as well resign yourself to it." Her mother had also told Jen to expect her blonde hair to fall out at an alarming rate, only to grow back brownish and coarse, and that her feet would expand at least a shoe size. Her mother made pregnancy sound like a virus in a horror movie.

Everyone was in the kitchen when she emerged from the shower: Jimmy turning burgers in a nonstick skillet, Rhonda chopping a red onion on the scarred plastic cutting board, Charles leaning against the refrigerator door with a fresh beer. "Jen!" they called as they had before, meekly this time, and Jimmy left the stove to come around the bar and herd her into a seat at the dinette, where he, or someone, had already laid out plates, silverware, and napkins. She let him pull her out a chair and refill her glass with mineral water, and she didn't argue when Rhonda came over to top the glass off with a dollop of white wine. "You can at least have a spritzer, right?" she said.

Jen nodded, still mute with humiliation.

"Honey, I know we've been insensitive," Rhonda said, resting her hand on top of Jen's. "We weren't thinking. We're just keeping at it like it's old times."

"I want it to be old times," Jen said hoarsely. She could see how the rest of the week would unfold, with the others tiptoeing around her, trying not to drink or smoke, and resenting her for it. Or drinking on the sly like teenagers. Encouraging her to go to bed early. *Hon, you look tired. Why don't you lie down?* And what did Jen want from them, anyway? What could they do to make this vacation play out exactly as she'd hoped it would? She tried, hand twitching under Rhonda's hot palm, to imagine a scenario. Drew a blank.

"But it's not old times, sweetie pie. And that's a good thing! Right, Jimmy?"

"Right!" he called from behind her, now back to manning the crackling skillet.

Rhonda slid into the chair by Jen's. "We're too old for old times. I mean, shit! Charles will be thirty-four next year."

Charles snorted humorlessly.

"And next year, you'll have this sweet baby that we're all going to love so much." She leaned across the table to give Jen a hug and to smack her cheek with an enthusiastic kiss, and what was left of Jen's angry resolve trickled away. She had never loved or trusted Rhonda the way she did the friends of her childhood and teens. Such friendships didn't exist in adulthood, she had come to believe, or perhaps they were the province of single women without husbands to rely on. But it was something she inexplicably longed for, that kind of closeness—something she had hesitantly sought from Rhonda over the years, with little success.

"I'm so humiliated," she confessed. She dug her fingernails into the tabletop, as if the despair she was feeling were a tangible thing, a wave she could get carried off on. What was wrong with her? Was there such a thing as prepartum depression?

"You'll feel better when you eat," Jimmy said, sliding a burger onto her plate. The bun top shone with grease or steam. She grabbed at it like a raft.

She did feel better, in a way. Like she'd gotten tethered, at least. For several minutes the four sat silently, contemplating the decimated meal in front of them and sighing. Rhonda's fingers twitched around her fork. Jimmy and Charles nursed longnecks. Jen had not argued when someone topped off her glass again with wine, and she felt a little warm in the cheeks now, pleasantly tired. It had grown darker out, the little light remaining a dingy yellow, and cool wind blew through the window screens, ruffling the paper towels they had used as napkins. The first soft patter of rain roused them all, as if they'd been awaiting a signal.

"I guess we should close the windows and track down the flashlights," Charles said.

Rhonda stood quickly. "I'll go look in the utility room."

Jen rose to help and Jimmy waved her off. "Sit," he said, motioning toward the wicker sofa. "It'll only take us a minute."

She tucked herself into a seat corner, using the thin bolster to cushion her lower back, and pressed her palm firmly against the skin where her belly met her pubis. The thickness of her hand gave her a little relief from the cutting elastic waistband of her sweatpants, and the pressure seemed to ease the baby, who was aggravated by either the red meat or the storm or her anxiety at the storm's approach. Windows started to slam shut around her, then three almost at the same time, as if choreographed. The rain grew steadier, so that individual drops turned into a charge, a coordinated assault. She wondered whether she had been stupid to balk at the Captain's Wharf plan, whether they would have been safer there. Jimmy turned a lock on the window, grunting as the rusted metal cut into the meat of his thumb. His expression of calm industriousness was the one he wore when he scraped ice off the windshield of the car or changed the battery in the smoke detector.

"Is it going to be all right?" she asked him.

He squinted. "Is what going to be all right?"

"The storm," she said. "Being here."

He struggled with another window. "Course it is."

They gathered around the coffee table and resumed their silent contemplation from a few moments before. Rhonda's findings from the utility room and under the kitchen sink were scattered across its surface: two flashlights, a nearly full box of white candles, two tarnished brass candleholders with looped handles. A box of matches. The electric lights flickered, then held, and Charles said, "Play some hearts?"

"Eh," Rhonda said. "I'm sick of cards."

"TV still works," Jimmy said. "For now."

No one moved to turn it on. Their boredom and resentment baked off them. They might have been children sent to their rooms after supper.

A banging sounded at the back door and they all jumped. Jen's instantaneous first thought was that the wind had blown something against the house or that the storm door had pulled loose from the latch, but the banging continued—three quick raps, a pause, three more—and she realized it had to be a person.

"Who on earth—" she started.

"Maybe they're evacuating the island after all," Rhonda said.

The door opened before they could mobilize themselves to act, and Jen found herself grabbing Jimmy's hand and clutching it with absurd ferocity. A swirl of water and wind blew into the utility room, knocking a roll of paper towels onto the floor, and a person entered, a girl or a woman, and pressed her back against the wooden door to drive it shut. The air smelled sour and green, like a dressed salad.

"I'm sorry," she sputtered breathlessly, her chest heaving. She ran her hands over her face and across the crown of her head, smoothing water away, and turned toward Jen and the others with wide, frightened eyes. "I got caught out there. I didn't know what to do."

They all stood dumb for a few seconds, casting hesitant glances back and forth. Then Rhonda said, "Let me get you a towel." The person—more woman than girl, Jen decided, but not by much—shakily nodded her gratitude.

She was probably barely out of her teens. Even sopping wet, her hair had evident streaks of white blonde, and her exposed shoulders, stomach, and legs, all lean and taut, were the smooth, buttery gold of a person who swam throughout the summer, not just over a week's vacation. When Rhonda returned with towels, the young woman smiled brightly, teeth bleached and square and charmingly spaced just a bit too far apart, and gave herself a brisk rubdown from head to foot, leaning over to get the ends of her hair, the back of her neck. Her feet were bare, Jen realized. And then she realized that they had all been staring stupidly at her toweling off, and her face grew hot.

"What were you doing out there?" she asked.

The girl dropped the wet towel on the floor and wrapped the second, dry towel around her shoulders. "I was at the Captain's Wharf right as the rain started, and me and my boyfriend got in some stupid fight. I thought I had time to get to our house before the bottom fell out. But the wind was really bad, and I got turned around, and now I don't even know which side of the highway I'm on."

"Sound side," Charles said. His voice was rich with something—a texture of interest. Jen wondered whether Rhonda noticed.

The girl laughed, bright and sharp. "Well, that's good. Maybe I'm close."

"You'll want to sit with us and wait it out," Jen said reluctantly. She couldn't send her back out there in good conscience. "Would you like something to drink? A Coke?"

"Sure," the girl said. Then, with an almost childlike lack of politeness: "You got vodka?"

"We got gin," Jimmy said, grinning.

"*You've* got Jen," Jen told him. When everyone looked at her strangely, she rubbed her stomach—she did it defensively, as if to remind them that its contents trumped their disdain—and she said, "Joke. That's my name. Jen."

The girl laughed again, in a way that made Jen feel like she was getting made fun of. "That's awesome. Wow. Well, I'm Kat."

The others introduced themselves, and Jen could sense them becoming easy with one another, as if the girl hadn't just barreled into their house without permission. Jimmy went behind the kitchen peninsula, pulled a tumbler from a cabinet, and rinsed it out under the tap. "You like it with tonic?" Jen flashed him an angry look, which he missed, or pretended to miss.

"I don't think I've tried it that way before," Kat said.

"You haven't had a G and T?" Charles hunched over the peninsula, cracking his knuckles and regarding Kat as if she were a really good basketball game. "God, you must be even younger than you look."

She held up the three middle fingers of her right hand, and a long-forgotten memory pinged for Jen: the Girl Scout salute. "I swear I'm legal."

"Make me one too," Rhonda said. "Lots of lime."

There was a new energy in the room, as if Kat had shown up with some of the missed excitement of the Captain's Wharf. "It was lame," she assured them, leaning back in one of the cushioned wicker chairs and curling her toes over the lip of the coffee table. "Old drunks, mostly, and foreigners. Russians or something. And the drinks were expensive." She bent over and peeled a large, dirty-looking bandage off her right knee. Jen caught a whiff of it, tang and musk and something vaguely medicinal, and tried to surreptitiously cover her nostrils.

"Christ," Jimmy said. "What happened?"

"Just poison ivy." She blotted the bumpy red patch with the bandage, folded the square into halves a few times, and set the little wad on the table. "Sorry, but it got wet and gross out there. It was about to fall off."

"Did that happen here at the beach?" Rhonda asked.

Kat bent and extended her pretty brown leg. The rash, bumpy and shiny-damp and oozing an iodine-colored trail, was oddly striking against the obvious facts of her youth and her beauty. "Nah, we were in the Smokies last week. Got it hiking a trail."

"How's that drink treating you?" Jimmy asked.

"Good!" she said, gulping. "I like it. It'd be good with some 7UP, too."

"You mean instead of the tonic or with the tonic?" Charles was grinning at Jimmy. If the girl were eighteen, he'd be practically twice her age. And though Jen had thought of him as young—of all of them as young—he looked haggard and lecherous next to Kat, bags under his eyes, gray peppering his hairline.

"I mean, whatever, I don't know." Kat polished off the rest of the drink and rolled an ice cube around her mouth. "Just something to sweeten it up some," she said around the ice.

"We don't have any 7UP," Rhonda said, "but I can fix you another. I'm having one myself."

"That'd be great," said Kat.

"Anything for you, Jen?" Rhonda had paused with her and Kat's empty tumblers. "Another spritzer?"

Jen shook her head. She couldn't seem to make the hard line of her mouth loosen.

The wind outside revved, sounding a newly high and desperate note. Jen walked to a window and peered around a curtain, cupping her eyes to get a better look into the rain-drenched dark. There wasn't much to see from this side of the house: just the nearest rental and the shadow of another across the street, a couple of scraggly pine trees curved into scythe shapes by the wind. Then the security lights cut out, and there was nothing but haze. She backed up uncertainly. The loss of electricity had cut the conversation short, and Jen's ears felt muffled and cottony, as if darkness were tangible enough to affect her sense of hearing, too.

"Hang tight, y'all," Jimmy said. A flashlight beam splashed suddenly across Kat's face, making her blink, and Jen recognized her.

"You were at the sound earlier today," she said. "You and your boyfriend." She remembered their grappling in the water and couldn't keep a note of accusation out of her voice. "I saw the two of you."

Kat laughed in a vague way, as if she'd missed the punchline of a joke. "You might have. We were there for a while."

Jimmy knocked sharply on Jen's knee with a knuckle and shot her a look of embarrassed warning.

"You seemed to be having fun," Jen said to Kat anyway. "Out in the water."

Kat's expression sharpened, or maybe it was a trick of the flashlight. "We always have fun. Except when we're pissing each other off."

"Hey," Rhonda called from the kitchen. "Some light over here."

The beam of the flashlight swung away from Kat, toward Rhonda, who had fresh gin and tonics in each hand. "I'm lucky I can do this in my sleep," she said.

"Get me one?" Charles said.

Rhonda lifted the glasses. "Hands are full."

He staggered to his feet from where he'd been sitting on the floor and swayed a little, having to reach out and grasp the back of Kat's chair for balance. "Steady there," Kat said laughingly, and he took another couple of halting steps to a structural post, leaned against it for a second, then a few more steps to the kitchen peninsula. He walked with his legs bowed and his toes curled up, as if across hot sand. Only Jen was watching him now, in the little bit of light thrown from the two candles Jimmy had lit, and she realized before Charles did that the bottle of gin he was tipping into a glass was empty. He shook the bottle, then turned and held it to the wan candlelight for confirmation. "You girls drank the gin up," he said, thick tongued.

"I thought you were doing beer," Rhonda said.

"Dammit," said Charles. "There was half a bottle last time I looked."

"Hey, hey, hey." Kat had lifted a hip off her chair and was digging in the pocket of her denim cutoffs. "Don't be mad. See what I got?" She tweezed a Ziploc bag between her finger and thumb and dangled it in Jimmy's flashlight beam. Jen made out a pill bottle and a small, candy-colored glass pipe.

"What is that?" Jen blurted, and then her cheeks prickled with heat at Charles's drunken laughter.

"It's pot, honey," Jimmy said. "Remember pot?"

"But the bottle," she said vaguely. She had seen the pipe and the medicine bottle and thought—well—pills, or *pills*, and then she'd thought crack, and then crystal meth. It had been a long time since she'd smoked marijuana, and she'd never liked it enough the first time around to miss it.

"That's just where I keep my bud," Kat said. She had already wriggled out of her chair and was sitting cross-legged on the floor in front of the coffee table. She emptied the bag, unscrewed the cap on the bottle—Advil, Jen saw, and felt a measure of arbitrary reassurance—and tapped the bottle twice with her index finger, spilling the pot into a harmless-looking pile. "Give me some light," she directed Jimmy, and he complied. She packed the bowl with brisk efficiency, surveyed her work, seemed to deem it good. She held up the pipe. "Who's first?"

"Jesus, guys," Jen said. "Are you really doing this?"

Charles, who'd returned to his wicker chair with a fresh beer, didn't even look at her. He flapped a beckoning hand at Kat, grinning, and their fingers brushed as Kat passed him the pipe and a lighter. *And you don't see this any more than you saw us*, Jen thought, looking at Rhonda, who was all eagerness, eyes wide and glittery bright. Charles tucked the pipe stem between his lips, bent the lighter over the bowl, and flicked the flint. For the briefest moment, the small, crackling whoosh of air was more audible than the storm raging outside of the rental house. After a long pause Charles exhaled, then coughed. He tried to laugh, which only made him cough more, and Jen pulled her T-shirt up over her nose and mouth, thinking of all the closed windows, how warm and still the air had gotten without the breeze or even the wheezing output of the air conditioner.

"Gimme," said Rhonda, and Charles, still coughing, passed over the pipe.

Jen wasn't even surprised when Jimmy accepted it next. He was gracious enough to look shamefaced, and he said, lighter poised, "Just one hit, babe. This may be the last time I ever get to do this." He didn't wait for her reply before sparking it. *Sparking it.* Like the Girl Scout salute, the phrase surfaced from a part of her she'd thought long buried, fossilized.

She intercepted the pipe as he handed it across the table to Kat, enjoying the look on his face, on all their faces. The glass was warm and damp between her lips. When she lifted the lighter to the bowl, nervously imitating what she'd seen the others do, Jimmy tried stopping her hand. She shook him off with one hard snap of her wrist. "Fuck you, Jimmy." She had to thumb the wheel of the lighter twice to get a flame. "If you get to do this one more time, so do I."

Rhonda said, "Jen—"

She sucked air through the stem, and the bowl glowed orange. She tried not to inhale much and let the smoke spill out of her lips almost immediately, but the dry tickle hit her lungs anyway, and she coughed painfully into her hand. *Sorry, Baby*, she thought with real sorrow. She handed the pipe and lighter to Kat and met Jimmy's gaze. He looked bitter and guilty, and he looked like he was wondering whether he could have another hit, or if he did, would Jen insist on following him once more, tit for tat, goose and gander, and if she did, was that bad enough to keep him from doing it? Was it really that big of a deal? She watched the candle flames and wondered if she was feeling anything. What about now. What about now. When she was Kat's age, she had thought that adulthood would be dignified. She had thought she would finally know some things.

When she took the second hit, no one argued with her. Maybe they were just high enough by that point not to care. A surge of heat rolled across her chest and passed through the back of her, setting her heart to racing, and at some point she said, "The baby is an eel in my belly," and everyone laughed so hard they fell over sideways.

Rhonda was eating pretzels. "I know what we should do," she said between mouthfuls. "We should stay up and go to the beach for sunrise. We should totally do it."

"Hell, yes," Kat said.

"When's the last time we did something like that?" Rhonda demanded. She swung her head between Charles and Jen.

"I can't even remember," Charles said.

Jimmy reached across Jen and plunged his hand into the pretzel bag. "Eight, nine years ago? After that Lady Antebellum concert?"

And then it seemed that Kat and Charles had been talking about her. It wasn't that she heard them so much as she understood that she had heard them a while ago. She had a summarized memory of the fact. Of Charles saying how ridiculous she had looked in her bathing suit that first day at the beach, and how she wasn't as fun as she used to be, and he was showing Kat something in his wallet, a photograph or a business card, and Kat said, "Oh, wow, that's so neat." The heat receded for a moment, and she knew that they had probably never talked about her. Her throat was so dry that swallowing was painful, so she lifted herself from the chair with careful stateliness and walked to the kitchen, rolling her feet from heel to toe to demonstrate her composure, and she gulped down a tall glass of tap water, then a second, and she thought, *I am coming back up to the surface again, thank God*, and that's when another comber of heat crashed against her heart.

"But yeah," Rhonda said. "Sunrise at the beach. This is happening. I'll be damned if this doesn't happen."

"It's happening," Kat said.

It went on like this for a while, an hour or hours, and Jen saw the pipe go around again but she shook her head against it. She kept having to go to the bathroom, struggling numbly out of her sweatpants to sit on the toilet, tilting her head to the right so she could rest her temple on the cool porcelain of the sink. One of the times, the bathroom stank of beery urine, and she used a wad of toilet tissue to clean the seat and a towel to soak up where Charles's or Jimmy's stream had hit the floor. Each time she left and returned, the scene in the living room seemed to degrade further: Rhonda slid down in her chair, then sideways, then off onto the floor so that her blouse rode up and the bottom of her orange bra showed; Charles went from wheezing laughter to just wheezing, his big face sweaty and red. Jimmy grew increasingly still. Each time he blinked, his eyes stayed closed a little longer. Then he yawned like a puppy. On another night it might have been endearing.

The rain was perhaps letting up. Jen stretched out on the wicker sofa and didn't feel like moving when she realized that the cushion was half out from under her. She peered through the dwindling candlelight at Kat, who had found Rhonda's pack of cigarettes and helped herself. She was using her empty tumbler as an ashtray. She smiled at Jen.

"How's the eel?" she asked.

"Sleeping," Jen said. She yawned so widely that her jaws popped. "What about going to see the sunrise? Is that still happening?"

"It's happening," Kat said.

She awoke to sudden movement and blinding light and nearly fell off the sofa when she tried to sit up. Many things seemed to happen simultaneously: A beep and a sudden roar as the air conditioner kicked on. Charles gasping—*huh wha who*—and swinging out roughly with both arms so that Rhonda had to grab his shoulder steady and say, "Calm down," her voice hoarse. A puff of air from the creaking ceiling fan, sending a scatter of goosebumps across Jen's forearms and thighs, and a thin whiff of smoke as one of the candles blew out. Jimmy popped up from behind the coffee table, rubbing his face, and he said *fuck* with so much heartfelt misery that Jen felt the threat of hysterical giggles.

Her eyes were sticky, the corners near the tear ducts tender. "Lights," she said, squinting. She leaned forward, meaning to shift her center of gravity enough to stand, and her lower back throbbed. "Someone turn them off." She nearly yelled it.

"Hold up," Charles said. There was something in his tone that stopped their blinking and grimacing, and Jen noticed for the first time that Kat was not among them. The pipe and the Advil canister were no longer on the coffee table. Her discarded bandage still was, and it had unfolded itself part of the way in the night so that it looked now like a smiling, toothless, fleshy mouth.

"Goddammit," he said. He was holding his wallet, peeled open, and was flipping through its contents with his thumb. He pulled a bill divider one way, then another. Finally, he shook it in the air and it looked like a black bat attacking his hand.

"She cleaned me out," he said. "Check your wallets. Check your purses."

Frantically, they went through their belongings. Jimmy's wallet, which he'd left on the nightstand beside the bed, was also emptied of its cash, the Discover card, and a twenty-five-dollar Outback

Steakhouse gift card that he'd gotten from his boss for his birthday. Rhonda lost her iPad and all the cash in her purse. From Jen the girl had stolen only a few dollars in cash—all Jen carried—but she'd also found the five or six necklaces Jen had brought along and arranged neatly on the dresser top so that they wouldn't tangle, and swiped them all: the gold chain and cross that was a graduation gift from her parents, the silver horse pendant Jimmy bought her for Christmas a few years back. A couple of worthless costume pieces. A gold herringbone chain Jen had spent a week's salary on back when she and Jimmy were only engaged; she had wanted, the one last time before marriage, to spend her money frivolously and answer to no one. Why care about lost things, she thought, tracing the empty dresser top with her index finger, when you were supposed to be on the cusp of all the happiness a life could offer?

"We need to call the police," Rhonda said from the other room. Jen came back to find her pacing, arms knotted across her chest. "We're on a godforsaken island. She can't have gone far. Not on foot and with that storm."

Jen remembered the boyfriend and the sound, his and Kat's perfect harmony in that still, deceptively shallow water. "I don't think she had to walk," she murmured, but no one seemed to hear her.

"Call the credit card companies," Charles said flatly. "Forget the cops."

They argued back and forth for a moment, and then Jimmy said, "Guys? Did she take the phones?" And then the argument changed again, and Rhonda tried the land line, but it didn't seem to be working. From far, far away, Jen saw her lift the receiver, jab the hook, and slam it back home, disgusted. Then Charles tried. And they argued about that, too.

Jen went to her and Jimmy's bedroom and wriggled between the cool sheets, sighing with relief as her back opened up and the tight muscles in her neck and hips and calves unclenched. Perhaps in the morning she would share her friends' affront, and she'd wonder with them at the girl's audacity, her callous lack of human feeling. But for now she turned her face into her pillow to muffle her laughter. She imagined Kat and her boyfriend wending their way up Highway 12 as the sun rose to the right, cruising past the destruction from last night's storm, rolling down their windows to the fresh damp air. She imagined them kissing passionately, the way they had in the water, and not paying attention to the road, impervious to harm. In the morning, Jen would remember herself and her anger. But for now, she wished the girl well.

machine

Until the squabble about the kitchen, Juliet had been tending a fantasy about the famous photographer that would be lodging with her at the college guest house. She knew that he was a bit older than she was—twenty years, at least—but that was perhaps a good thing at this point in her life, as recently separated as she was, as recently thirty as she was. An older man, an artist, a jet-setter in (she imagined) khaki trousers and vests: she'd seen his self-portrait on the internet and felt very kindly toward him. The image was black and white, the light poetically unflattering, but it was saved from cliché by the smile on his face, a look that had struck Juliet as genuine, as disarmingly vulnerable. In her own most recent portrait, the photograph on the back cover of her book of short stories, she had tilted the corner of her mouth only slightly; a smile, she had thought, just didn't get at the book's seriousness. "I know this look," her ex had said when he wasn't yet her ex, when there were still moments of sweetness between them. "It's your, 'I'm very disappointed in you' look. 'I'm very sexy and very disappointed in you.'"

She was a visiting professor at a private college of about two thousand students, a winter short term that began on January 2 and ended three weeks later, and she was expected to meet with the same class daily for three hours. Twenty-five hundred dollars, a pittance—they should have paid twice that, at least. This is what her thesis director from graduate school told her. He had published five novels, a story collection, and two collections of poetry, and he alternately flattered and irritated her by treating her as a peer, by expressing disappointment when Juliet applied for teaching jobs before she'd finished her novel, teasing her about her self-serving social media presence, though who didn't have a self-serving social media presence these days? Juliet's own mother had a Facebook page dedicated to her essential oil "business," and even Joyce Carol Oates was on Twitter, though it would probably be better if she weren't.

"Wait tables," her thesis advisor had told her. "Get on a house-painting crew. In my day, writers went out into the world. They had experiences. There wasn't all this scrambling to join the middle class right out of college. I don't get you young people. You're healthy, you've got your whole life ahead of you, and all you can think about is getting a shitty cinderblock office in the bowels of a satellite college." He'd said this to her with a Starbucks cup in hand. She hadn't said OK, boomer, or eloquently defended her choices; she'd just made some apologetic murmur about how even the waitressing jobs were hard to get these days—and, about that letter of rec: would he still be willing to write it for her?

That was three years ago, when her book was in contract but not in print, she was all untarnished promise, and her relationship still seemed solid. Her prospects had been dazzling enough that she turned down a decent job offer in favor of an adjuncting situation that suited Danny better, figuring they'd both go on the market again once he'd sold his book, increasing their chances of landing somewhere suitable: in a blue-state city with a light-rail system, indie theaters and bookstores, bars that offered cute things like artisanal bitters and infused bourbon. Since then, her personal times, alongside the national and global times, had changed for the worse. She had let her short-term lease expire in December, after she'd submitted grades at the state college where she taught—it was a small, awful, overpriced apartment, the only one she could find on short notice after things fell apart with Danny—and then she'd cobbled together the rest of the month by pretending one holiday visit after another: former graduate school friends, a former professor (this one female, dry, infinitely practical—"Take the $2,500 and say thank you," she'd instructed). Her mother's back in Kentucky. Always overstaying her welcome by a day or two, so that she and her hosts hardly said goodbye to each other so much as they wiped their hands of one another, weary, nursing grievances. She had brought Ned and Amanda a fifth of Rowan Creek, an expensive treat and one of their favorite indulgences from the old MFA days, and they never once opened the bottle in the week Juliet was there, not even for a symbolic sip or two. "Thank you," they'd simpered, putting it into a kitchen cabinet next to some dry sherry and a bottle of olive oil. "How lovely." Her friend Annie, who was on tenure track with a two-course load, had kept grousing about all the work she had to do—no time to write, no time to think—and did Juliet know how lucky she was, not having tied herself to a city and a mortgage? "This house owns *me*," she'd said, flapping her hands at it: the cozy fireplace and the curved banister and the hardwood floors. "I never thought I'd be this settled. I'm disappointed in myself."

"Don't be stupid," Juliet had snapped. She had gone on the job market again last year, after her book was published, and gotten two campus visits and no job offers. This year, when a new job and relocation would have made the most sense, she hadn't had the energy to make the attempt nor the money to finance a trip to the West Coast for MLA, and she knew her prospects weren't great, anyway—that there was a brand-new crop of shiny MFAs with shiny book contracts, books that might still get a full-page *Times* feature or the endorsement of a celebrity influencer. Her four-course lectureship was feeling more and more like her real job—what she did, not just what she was doing. "For god's sake, Annie, do you know how many of us would trade places with you?"

It had been like this: testy comments and passive aggression, too much wine beside the Christmas tree, the indignity of futons, too many dinners out. "It's on me," Juliet kept saying, plunking her Discover card down before her friends could argue, making panicked mental calculations and determining that she could have lived more cheaply if she had kept her apartment. Why was she like this? She wanted to do the right thing, but she wanted her friends to love her enough to talk her out of it. "You're *our* guest," they should have said. "It's on us." She was sick of their barren refrigerators ("We don't generally eat much breakfast") and their thermostats, always set on sixty or seventy-four, never at a livable degree in the middle. She hated how none of them watched television, though she hated it equally when her parents, who owned a forty-inch flatscreen, wouldn't turn theirs off. She hated how Ned and Amanda, who had a kid now, barely drank anymore, and she hated how they let the kid, a three-year-old boy, climb up into their laps and pinch their lips shut midsentence. "No, you got to be quiet," he kept saying, and they kept smiling and turning their faces out of his grasp, as though he were the adult and they the children and the whole thing was just too funny.

She was self-aware enough to hate all this hate, to recognize how pathetic and bitter she'd become, and the awareness only angered her more, because she couldn't fix herself right now. She was homeless and nearly broke and her marriage had failed, and the only comfort she'd been able to find was through her laptop, on pirated Wi-Fi, looking at the image of her famous photographer and the fantasy of what three weeks with him in a quaint guest cottage would be like. They would be sharing a kitchen, a living room. She imagined that there was a fireplace. It was January, northern Ohio, and perhaps they'd get snowed in, and she'd volunteer to make them dinner, something simple and comforting, like tomato soup and grilled cheese sandwiches. He might be married. It didn't really matter to her. They would talk about writing and art, his interesting travels, and soon enough they'd cap their long teaching days with sex, long, creative evening sessions of it, and (this was the most absurd and best part) when the term was over, he'd invite her to travel abroad with him to Bangkok or Paris or wherever famous photographers went to snap shots of interesting people. No need to come back to two freshman composition classes and two overenrolled undergraduate fiction workshops. No need to find a roommate or an apartment so horrible that she could stay within her six-hundred-a-month rent budget.

She hated exposition. Yes, that too. In her fiction classes, drawing the plot checkmark on a marker board and scrawling "rising action" and "dénouement" in all the correct places, she would mark through "exposition" and write "imposition," a joke, stolen from her thesis director, that always failed to elicit more than an uncertain titter from her very best undergraduates. "Readers don't want to wade through pages of backstory," she would say. "They want to know the problem and know it quick. It's the writer's job to deliver the problem." She was good at delivering problems, she had decided. Good at zeroing in on trouble.

The story of how her marriage ended varied depending on whom she was telling it to. To her mother she blamed Danny's mental illness. He had always struggled with depression and anxiety, and it got much worse after the election (her stepfather, outraged, had declared, "I knew that spineless little wimp would let you down!"), and (she kept this part vague) they both made some questionable choices. They decided, together, a break was in order.

She told her old MFA friends that the central issue between Danny and her had been his book, the collection of stories that his agent had been trying for over a year to sell. In the spring he had started to send it out to the university press contests, and he was surly about it. It was never supposed to be like this. He had published in a glossy and several of the most prestigious reviews, and he'd been in the back of *Best American Short Stories*. In graduate school, Danny was the one that the professors had their eyes on, the one who won the student contests and was first on the list for departmental fellowships. And now here they were, in this bizarro universe where Juliet, whom nobody had watched, had managed to get a contract and even a small advance, which she had put toward the purchase of a reliable used car. How could it be? He alternated between sullen self-pity and a forced enthusiasm for Juliet that was even worse. He would punish her with passive aggression ("Are you sorry that it didn't get a *Times* review?" and "Well, it really is a very particular kind of thing you do, so it makes sense that you'd get some interest just from a marketing perspective"), then try to make it up to her with outsized compliments that bordered on comic, like the time when he told her, straight-faced, that she was going to be the next Alice Munro. She had turned down a decent job offer to support Danny's career, she told her friends, and things had not gone according to plan for either of them. Resentment built up on both sides. They decided, together, a break was in order.

The truth, like most truths, was a little of column A, a little of column B, and a good-size helping of a dozen or more other columns. She could identify the breaking point easily enough: she thought of it as the last supper. They'd driven home from work that day listening to NPR, its parade of catastrophic news, and they were both on edge, hopeless and morose. Danny had dropped his satchel to the floor and immediately pulled a bottle of red wine from the box they kept in the utility closet; they were two thirds of the way through it before sitting down to the dinner she'd made: brown rice, sad, flaccid-looking portabella caps that she'd overcooked on Danny's electric grill, an item that collected the cooking fats in a little trough so you could marvel at all of the calories and taste you'd spared yourself. Perhaps she'd made a testy comment about it, how sick she was of mushrooms, and perhaps Danny had spat back a comment about how she'd be eating pork chops while Rome burned, and somehow the conversation turned, as it always did, to their writing careers, because that, at least, was a category of hopelessness they could wrap their minds around. They were on a second bottle of wine when Danny let slip that the thesis director they'd shared, the man who would later insist that Juliet was too good for twenty-five hundred dollars, had said to Danny at the bar one night while they were still in graduate school, "Juliet writes good sentences, but her stuff's too soft and domestic. The women writers who are taking off now are the ones doing the weird, in-your-face, overtly political stuff. Fabulism, autofiction, that kind of thing. Juliet's still writing like she can have Lorrie Moore's career in the '90s."

"Why are you telling me this?" She tried to keep the warble out of her voice.

"Because you idolize him and you think he has your back," Danny said. "And I don't think he's ever had your back."

"You think I slept with him," Juliet said. She had, a handful of times, before dating Danny. In her first year at the MFA program.

And Evan had let her down afterward so gently and sensibly that she hadn't even been angry with him, or very angry.

"Of course not," Danny said. "But you've got him between your ears, telling you what to do and not to do. Like, this rigid point of view shit, what is that? Like every story has to be third limited. I hate when I see his fingerprints on your work. It's worse than imagining you slept with him."

"You're ridiculous," she said.

Danny sawed at his mushroom with the edge of a fork, frowning. "You know I'm right. Like the way your story about the nurse ended, and how Evan told you that it would be a cheat to get in the patient's head in the last paragraph? He talked you out of the best part of it. That still infuriates me."

"So instead I should listen to you," Juliet said. "And you can tell me the right way to end a story."

"Don't be like that. You're being obtuse."

"I don't think you even know what that means, being obtuse. It means being deliberately dense. But you say it like it means being a smart-ass."

"What if I just say you're being a bitch?"

There was a funny thing about this conversation. Juliet, reading and offering comments for the third and last time on Danny's manuscript, had finally realized that she didn't much like her husband's book of stories. She wasn't sure why it took her so long to be certain—she'd read most of the drafts in grad school, wrote him letters of sincere and effusive feedback, assumed, like everyone else, that he was an extraordinary talent—but there was something about seeing the stories all together, realizing how similar they were, how limited in their scope. They were all about men, mostly in their late twenties or early thirties, mostly with an aspiration that they'd given up because of marriage or a dead relative or a fear about not being good enough: the singer-songwriter who performs as a cowboy clown at children's birthday parties and finds himself doing a gig at the house of his high school girlfriend; the minor league baseball player forced to decide between new love and an unexpected ascension to the next level of play. There was a sweetness and earnestness to the stories that Juliet had at first found winning: the men were smart and self-effacing, the details about work and exercise routines spot-on, the characters' neuroses believable and exaggerated ever so slightly for comic effect. He threw in enough experimentation to keep things fresh: there was a second-person story, a plural first-person story, a story called "Three Hurricanes" that tracked the disintegration of a beach house alongside the disintegration of its owners' marriage. But Juliet also realized during that third read that the women of the book were all blandly noble and long-suffering, and while the man-child narrator worked through his feelings of inadequacy, making such frequent comment about his failings that you couldn't help but think extremely well of him, to believe him enlightened, his girl stood by, full of spunky good sense and patience, never angry, never granted the luxury to be small or selfish. But he was her husband! What kind of wife told her husband these things?

"I could be a bigger bitch than I've been," she said. She poured a teaspoon of peanut sauce out of a bottle sitting on the table between them. There was a dried crust of sauce on the lip of it, and the entire thing came loose and fell onto her plate, diminishing what was left of her hunger.

"Yeah?"

"Yeah."

"You want to tell me something about *my* writing, I suppose. Well, enlighten me, Miss New York Press."

"That's *Mrs.* New York Press," Juliet said. "To you."

"Mrs. then. Enlighten me."

"Evan talked about you too, you know. He said no one's going to want your book now. After Me Too and Time's Up and all that."

Danny's cheeks, which were pocked from very bad adolescent acne, got splotchy. The light beard he grew to hide the scars looked to Juliet against that pink and pitted skin like something painful, a miniature experiment in acupuncture. "What the hell's that supposed to mean? I don't write about—about rape, or whatever. I mean, my whole book is about interrogating toxic masculinity. And what the fuck does Evan know about any of this stuff, anyway? He had his dick in half the MFA program. He's lucky he even still has a job."

"Wake up," Juliet had snapped. "Nobody gives a shit anymore about your nice guys falling out of love."

And this was when Danny, no one's nice guy, told her that he'd cheated on her twice, once with a mutual acquaintance of theirs, a woman who also taught adjunct at the university, and once with an undergraduate, though he'd waited—bastion of ethics and morals!—until almost a full semester after grades were submitted. And Juliet had finally attacked him with the secret of their marriage, the fact that she had, in fact, slept with Evan, that she was still in love with him, and Danny pretended not to care.

"I'm not even angry. It's just sad," he said, scraping most of his brown dinner into the bokashi compost bin he carefully tended, though living in an apartment meant he had to surreptitiously dump it every couple of weeks in a small greenspace behind the complex. "I thought you were smarter than that. No wonder you take his word as God's."

"Don't you dare pretend to pity me," Juliet said. She was shaking with her anger. "Don't you dare. You don't know my heart. You never have."

"I knew you had daddy issues," Danny said. "But this is another level."

The college was in a village with one stoplight, two four-way stops, and a small square with a pavilion and a fountain in its center. There was a barbershop, a coffee shop with an attached bakery, some law and real estate offices, a pub. "The bar's cash only," Juliet's faculty contact told her as they made a quick driving tour around the campus and town, the air outside bitter enough to dissuade even a genuine outdoor enthusiast, which Juliet was not. They'd met at the student union, and Melissa had unexpectedly insisted that they take Juliet's car, which she realized too late was full of old utility bills and half-drunk soda bottles and bags from fast food. "But there's an ATM on the corner, and they have good burgers, I hear, if you're a meat eater. Do you eat meat?"

Juliet nodded.

"I don't," Melissa said. She smiled stiffly. "So I miss out on about a third of what the town has to offer." She was an assistant professor specializing in rhetoric and composition—tall, red-haired, nervous. Juliet, who had driven eight hours from her parents' place and was still dressed for the car in jeans, canvas sneakers, and an old sweater, had been intimidated immediately by Melissa's expensive-looking riding boots and colorful scarf, and the woman's manner, too: she was fidgety, uncomfortable with eye contact. She asked pointed questions with a slight accusatory note: "Have you had a chance to log on to your U-mail yet? It's a good idea" (Juliet hadn't.) "Did you bring copies of your book to sell after your reading?" ("The bookstore won't handle that?" Juliet asked, panicky.) And, "I'm sure that you must know Jeffrey Rosenbaum's work, right? He's such an exciting new voice." To that, Juliet had smiled vaguely, inwardly despairing. "He's certainly provoking a lot of conversation," she said. She'd never heard of him.

The campus would have been picturesque in spring, idyllic in autumn, when the maples lining the main pedestrian thoroughfare went gold and red and the students were sauntering across the quad in their bright knits and flannels. But it was January, the trees bare, the quad empty, and there were only a few crusts of gray snow left over from the month before. The desolation made the cement sidewalks look ragged against the dead grass, the brick buildings, both the old ones and the ones made to look old, grim as prisons. Apocalyptic. There was the requisite modern structure, one of those decisions made in the late '90s with a flush of donor money: a new dining hall, its wall of glass facing the center of campus, high ceilings with fake timber support beams, a Starbucks. Juliet could see only a few people wandering around inside—a lonesome feeling, watching them.

"Most of the students don't come back from break until tomorrow," Melissa said. "The caf has regular hours then until the end of the term, and the meals tonight and at breakfast are continental."

She motioned for Juliet to turn onto a side street and pull up to a limestone cottage with a modest sign rooted in the ground out front: UNIVERSITY GUEST HOUSE. "I'll give you my cell number in case you need anything."

"I'm sure I'll be fine." Juliet didn't like talking on the phone, despised calling people she didn't really know.

"Well, this is it!" Melissa said when Juliet cut the engine, suddenly and unexpectedly chipper. "Home sweet home for the next three weeks."

There was a polite argument over Juliet's suitcase and backpack, which Juliet insisted on carrying, and Melissa contented herself with the two fabric totes of groceries that Juliet had carted in from a quick stop at the Columbus Trader Joe's. They were crossing the threshold to the entryway when Melissa stopped. "You're sharing the space, of course," she said, handing Juliet a key on a ring. "My understanding is that you're upstairs, and Paul Sacca is downstairs. Do you know his work?"

"Of course," Juliet said.

"It's so exciting he's here. Such an interesting person, I'll bet. He's giving a lecture on photographing Syria next Wednesday that you won't want to miss."

It wasn't until Melissa put it this way that Juliet realized how absurd her plan for Mr. Sacca had been, her mission to seduce him with grilled cheese sandwiches and relatively pert thirty-year-old breasts. She was always doing that: spinning such elaborate fantasies that she could keep herself warm with them for weeks, only to have the whole thing suddenly and rudely unravel on her the moment the real world intruded.

"Oh, I'll be there," Juliet said. "I've been looking forward to it. I'm going to require that my workshop go so that they can think about narrative in a different way."

"Excellent!" There was that chipperness again. Juliet wondered whether Melissa were one of those people who had to remind herself to be pleasant—to be pleasant by force of will—and felt an instant of kinship.

Upstairs, Melissa showed Juliet the bedroom, which had two twin beds, and the bathroom, which had a coffee maker on the vanity, like a hotel room. They returned to the first floor, retrieved the bags of groceries from where Melissa had left them, sitting on the floor beside the banister, and headed toward a closed door off the formal dining room.

"This is the kitchen," Melissa said, putting her hand on the knob. She turned it, tugged, frowned. "Hmm. Locked." She jiggled it briskly, making the door rattle in the frame, loudly enough that Juliet winced a little. "Let me try your key," she said, putting her hand out.

Juliet, humbled by her brisk authority, handed it to her quickly, but she noted with a glance that the keyhole was only decorative. "I think it's dead-bolted from the inside," she said tentatively, pointing to the facing plate. "Is there another entrance?"

Melissa went ahead and tried the key, again rattling the door uselessly. "I guess you're right," she said. "I think it opens on the other side to the downstairs apartment. Paul might have locked it by accident. Or one of the cleaning staff."

The door opened suddenly, making them both jump and squawk little high-pitched gasps. Melissa looked at her hand, still extended from where she'd been turning the knob, and seemed to consciously put it away into her coat pocket for later use.

"May I help you?" It was a woman—late fortyish or early fiftyish, petite, olive-skinned, and very thin. Beside her, even Melissa seemed gawky and large and inelegant, her scarf too bright and showy, her boots like something from the mall. The woman—Juliet knew her immediately as Paul Sacca's wife—had the kind of mean chic that Juliet associated with photos of a middle-aged Joan Didion. She was wearing the uniform of a wintering Manhattanite: a very fitted, dark gray wool dress that would have made a woman with even a palm's worth of tummy look plump, dark tights, black flats. Her hair, cut to hang about an inch above her shoulders, was also dark and streaked with white, thick with a very slight wave; it was pulled back from a small, unlined forehead and curled out from where it tucked behind a pretty ear. The visible lobe was dotted with a tiny, perfect pearl.

"You must be Paul's wife?" Melissa was suddenly nervous, deferential, her false cheer gone. She unpacked her hand from its hiding place. "Melissa McPherson—I'm with the English department. I was just showing your housemate around. This is Juliet Page-Watkins."

"Just Page now," Juliet said, smiling in the wry way that she always did when she made this admission, and put out her hand. The woman responded with not a shake so much as a tweeze; her dry fingers rasped against Juliet's.

"Very nice to meet you," the woman said. "I'm Marie Sacca, yes. Pauli's Marie." She remained standing in the doorway, expression polite but not warm.

"And you're here for the term?" Melissa said. "How wonderful."

Marie's smile was squinty; her mouth moved as if she had a lemon candy on her tongue. "Only a week of it, I'm afraid. Then I'm traveling to San Francisco to spend a week with our daughter, and then I have to get back to work."

"What kind of work is that?" Juliet asked.

"I'm a buyer for an architectural salvage."

Juliet and Melissa both stammered versions of "How interesting!" and then for a pregnant moment they all stood staring at one another.

"Well," Melissa said, "I thought that I'd show Juliet the kitchen and let her put away groceries."

"Um, of course." Marie rubbed her dry, brittle fingers together like kindling. "But perhaps she'd like to look at the laundry facilities first?"

Juliet felt her face and neck flush. She shifted the bags of groceries from one arm to the other.

"They're in the basement," Marie added, motioning to a nearby door.

Melissa, a bit wide-eyed now, looked between Marie and Juliet. "Would that be all right, Juliet? Would you want to take a quick look downstairs?"

Juliet set the groceries down. "Sure," she said. Flatly. As she expected, Melissa stayed back when she went to the door, even giving her a little wave when Juliet turned around for one last look. *Really?* she wanted to say. *Seriously?*

Melissa nodded in an encouraging way.

There was nothing to see in the basement. A washer, a dryer. Both boxy late '80s models with coin-operated mechanisms that, Juliet noted with the tiniest bit of optimism, had been dismantled. A shelf with a box of generic powdered detergent and another box of generic dryer sheets. A few wire hangers dangling from a rack like picked bones. The smell was the smell of every old, relatively clean basement laundry room that has ever existed: must and sweet mold overlaid by a sweeter layer of chemical perfumes. A worn couch with blown springs was in the corner.

She sat on it. A murmur of voices traveled downstairs, muffled through the door—they'd closed it behind her—but not totally inaudible. The tone, at least, was clear: Marie's voice was haughty and put upon, Melissa's conciliatory ". . . schedule, perhaps?" Juliet might have heard. And "our privacy." That was Marie. There was a lull, finally, and Juliet took the stairs back up slowly and heavily so that they wouldn't be surprised by her reappearance.

"Juliet!" Melissa said in her stiff chipper voice. Marie had disappeared behind the closed kitchen door. "Can we talk?"

There had been a miscommunication, Melissa explained. You know how it is, two different departments, university red tape, etcetera, etcetera. The Saccas had been promised a private kitchen. Would Juliet be terribly inconvenienced?

"We'll get you a pass to the dining hall, of course," Melissa said.

They also brought over a microwave for her from Campus Facilities so that she could have her oatmeal or a frozen dinner if she would like, and a minifridge. Juliet put a carton of half-and-half and a pitcher of water into it and tried to appear agreeable. In only a few moments, all had been lost: the famous photographer *and* the soup and sandwiches. No fantasy, only a guest room and a sky the color of Marie Sacca's wool dress and a suitcase full of old, wrinkled clothes that all fit her badly, too loose or too tight, artifacts from the days when, in grad school, she'd been briefly stylish. She saw that there wasn't an iron, thought about requesting one, worried about seeming too demanding. So she bought one at Walmart, along with a drinking glass, a microwave-safe bowl, plastic cutlery, and some sandwich meat and cheese. The first night in the room she poured herself a glass of red wine and cooked two pouches of microwave oatmeal in the oven, not wanting to experiment with the dining hall's "continental" supper and perhaps also feeling in the mood to martyr—Danny's term. It was he who turned it into an intransitive verb. "You're martyring," he'd say when Juliet told him to take the last of the cookies she'd baked or when she stayed up late the night before her morning class to help him put comments on his students' composition papers. Hadn't stopped him from taking the cookie, though. Or the help.

And so began the procession of days. She rose at seven, bathed, dressed. She put sneakers on her feet and dressier shoes in her bag, and she walked for half an hour before entering the building that housed her classroom, trying to warm her muscles and her brain, thinking about the stories she'd assigned the students or the stories they'd submitted for workshop, planning a writing exercise, gnawing at anxieties like a ragged fingernail. There was the moody girl who always sat at the back of the class and glared and drew manga cartoons on her notebook while the rest of the students were discussing the reading. There was the baby-faced guy with a beard who thought that he already knew more about writing than she did—and how could she not think of Danny when she looked at him? But they were good kids, finally. Like always. They wrote stories about serial killers and torturing pets and the end of the world, and they sent her emails that opened "Hey" and read as if they'd been texted, but they were good kids, even the manga girl; she liked them, and the hours she spent in workshop were the best of her day. When she left class to walk to the dining hall for her lonely, bad lunch she felt the kind of deflation she'd felt as a child leaving a birthday party or the community swimming pool.

But the students that she liked so much in class—and she thought that they liked her too, at least most of them—were different creatures at the dining hall. She ran into them, whether she liked it or not, again and again: in the hot entrée line, at the salad bar, carrying her tray to a solitary table in the corner, putting her dirty dishes on the conveyer belt and stepping wide to avoid a puddle of spilled soda. Again and again: the furtive glance, perhaps a quick nod of acknowledgment. Sometimes they pretended not to see her at all. And when a student did at last take pity on her—moved, perhaps, at the sight of so many friendless lunches and dinners, at the sight of Juliet's walk of shame back to the line for a dish of soft-serve ice cream, with sprinkles—it was always worse than the silent treatment. Juliet stammered, blushed, blurted. "How's your writing exercise coming?" she'd say, then realize she'd made the assignment only an hour before, so how could it be coming at all? Or, mortifyingly, "How was your Christmas?" to Essie Goldberg, who had only smiled and said, kindly, "Fine. Good." Juliet hadn't even meant December 25! She was an atheist, more or less! She'd just meant the break, had still not gotten over sixteen years of calling it Christmas Break, and anyhow, it had been stupid of her to ask about Essie's winter break when they were a week and a half deep into a new term. She was too lonely, too often alone; she was forgetting how to speak to people.

She had taught a week's worth of classes and begun the first round of workshops when the student she'd been thinking of as Danny Jr.—his real name was Fenton, though that hardly seemed like a real name to Juliet—approached her booth in the back corner of the cafeteria. They had discussed his story today, and at the end, when Juliet always called on the writer to speak—was there anything he wanted to ask or explain?—Fenton shook his head, rocked back in his seat a little, and crossed his arms. "Nah," he said. That was it.

She cleared some papers now from the space opposite her. "Fenton, hi," she said. "Did you want to sit? Do you want to talk about your workshop?"

"Um, yeah." He shrugged out of his backpack and slid heavily across the bench. His lunch consisted of two baskets of French fries, both covered in zigzags of ketchup, and a cereal-sized bowl of chocolate pudding the sickly color of refried beans. "Thanks."

Juliet put her fork down. She wouldn't be able to eat her own lunch—two squares of pizza and a salad—while he was watching her. And that was unfortunate, because she had a feeling that Fenton wouldn't be quick. "What's on your mind?" she said, trying to convey a tone of cool authority. These young men could be difficult, and Fenton had been sizing her up since she first walked into class in her earnest plaid skirt and ruffled blouse, looking more like a middle school librarian, she knew, than the kind of Serious Writer these kids wanted to model themselves after. Where were her cigarettes, her Moleskine notebook?

He was salting his fries, avoiding eye contact. His hair, quite a bit longer than Danny's, hung over his forehead, and he jerked his chin to flick it out of the way. "So, yeah. I guess I just wanted to clarify some things? Some terms and things you said." He shoved three fries into his mouth, continued talking around them. "I was confused by two points specifically."

"Shoot," Juliet said.

"The first was that you said that my concept wasn't original, but, I mean, I thought that it was really original." He blushed. He'd written a story about how, the earth faced with rising temperatures and oceans, with more and more catastrophic flooding, scientists had started splicing human DNA with fish DNA to create amphibious merpeople with gills and dorsal fins. Only the wealthiest could afford the procedures, so the narrator, a young black man from New Orleans, led his band of poor but determined survivalists to Mount Mitchell, North Carolina, the highest point east of the Mississippi.

"I didn't say that the concept was unoriginal," Juliet said. She made an effort not to fidget or pick at her salad. "What I said in class today is that your narrator is a very conventional hero: morally upright, smart, capable. A kind of Mary Sue. You don't dignify him with any weaknesses, so the story is lacking a necessary complexity."

"Okay."

Juliet could tell that he wasn't satisfied. "What was the other thing you were confused about?" she asked before he could launch into another defense.

He took out his manuscript with her letter of feedback stapled to the front. He had, in the hour since class let out, already written all over it, underlining some of her comments, putting angry question marks—?????—in the margin next to others. "This," he said, pointing with a broad, blunt finger at a phrase he'd drawn a box around. "Deus ex machina. I know what it means. But I don't get how my story has one."

"If the story had ended with the flood killing the survivalists, that would have been one kind of thematic comment. If it had ended with the rich merpeople dying but not the survivalists, it would have been another. But the ending you have now is just a random exit strategy." One of the survivalists, a character who hadn't even been mentioned previously, went crazy and killed everyone except the narrator, who decided to continue on to Mt. Mitchell alone. "It doesn't satisfy any of the questions you've set up. It's out of left field."

"I was trying to say something about the darkness of human nature," Fenton said, mouthing a spoonful of pudding. "That you can fight all of these big powers of evil only to get taken down by your own kind."

"If that's what you're trying to say, you need to start saying it sooner," Juliet said. "At the very least, you need to establish this killer as a character before you produce him with a gun in hand. Remember what I said last week about Chekhov."

"I get it," Fenton said. "But, no offense, it sounds to me like you don't think stories should have surprises at all. And that just seems kind of boring to me. No offense."

"I like surprises," Juliet said. "But they should be earned surprises. What if *The Great Gatsby* had ended with Jay Gatsby dying in a tornado instead of at the hands of George Wilson? And Fitzgerald's explanation was that he wanted the book to be about the random cruelty of nature? How satisfying would that have been?"

“I haven’t read that book yet,” Fenton said. He let the veil of bangs fall back over his face, which was bright red again.

“Well,” Juliet said, triumphant. She took a big bite of her slice of pizza. “Anything else?”

She wrote a little. Not much. She’d been working on her novel for four years now, and she was beginning to think it was a bust, that she should scrap it and start over with something new, but she didn’t have anything new, and she didn’t have the courage to be without a project. The separation had only slowed her down more—or maybe that was an excuse. She had burned brightly during grad school, had taken her laptop to coffee shops or to outdoor cafes where she could smoke, for smoking had been part of the life then too, and she had worked for hours, churning out eight or ten pages a day, going home to write more, staying up until three or four in the morning. She kept a bottle of red wine at her desk and refilled the same unwashed glass. She rolled the wine around in her mouth and played with words and thought of Evan, what Evan would like. A sentence, a metaphor, an image—they were secret messages for him. She reread all of Evan’s books, even the poetry, and thought hard about what would please him. Frank sexuality. Over-the-top metaphors. Experimentation with the movement of time. He had a story about a teenage boy who wrecked the car of his father’s mistress, and there was this very good business in it about the money, the social pressures of who owed whom and how the money, not the stickiness of the infidelity, ended both the affair and the marriage; and that was the story that inspired Juliet to write what she thought of as her best piece, the one that became the title story in her collection. She wrote in her acknowledgments that she owed the book to Evan, and it was true. It was her love letter to him. How she had longed for his praise in class—how she loved it when he noticed the lines she wrote for him. “Damn fine,” he’d say sometimes, his highest compliment, and hearing it could set her afloat for a week. Seeing it jotted on her manuscript in his slanted scribble, the sluggish gray ink of those cheap disposable ballpoint pens he favored, could move her to tears. To have it in writing, permanent, irrefutable? Damn fine. There were no better words. She thought that she could finish this novel if only she could know that Evan would scrawl "Damn fine" on the last page of it.

If only he would look at it for her. But he told her he wouldn't. "You know I give what little wisdom I've got to dispense to the current crop," he wrote once in an email. "And besides, love, you don't need the old man telling you yea or nay anymore. You're past that."

But here she was, three hundred pages in, floundering. Fifty pages from a complete draft, but it might as well have been a million. And maybe it was just a dated domestic story, after all.

She went to the famous photographer's lecture on Syria. She didn't want to, but it was in her syllabus, she'd already told Melissa she would be there, so she went and so did her class—she collected their names on a sign-up sheet. Surly, she watched him speak. Paul. Pauli. *Marie's Pauli*, she sneered to herself. He was, it turned out, lithe, petite, but hardened—a Picasso to Marie's Didion—handsome, Juliet had to admit, but vain. He didn't operate his own slideshow. He claimed to not know how. The photos were shocking not for their depiction of war but for their willful serenity. He stopped on a slide depicting a hand wiping a plate clean with a piece of pita bread. "It is a composition," he said, pacing back and forth in front of the screen. "A re-creation of a typical moment. The plate is a blank face, the hand moves from the left to the right. It is time, a countdown. And the image depicts what it does not show, as well as what it does. I cannot say 'Syrian' without making you think of war. You see it even in the clean plate, the soft bread, the buffed thumbnail. The plate is a canvas for what you already perceive to be true. The photograph is transgressive because it is mundane."

There were murmurings of approval. Juliet spotted Fenton texting a few rows ahead of her, the small screen of the phone glowing down beside his hip. She put up her hand.

Sacca pointed to her.

"It's an arresting image," she said. "But it could have been taken anywhere. It could be in a diner here in Ohio. And I get that the universality is the point—" She was blushing—every gaze in the room, including Fenton's, was fixed on her—"but, despite what you're saying about context, it seems entirely without context to me. A detail without a story."

"But God is in the details, Miss Page," he said. She hadn't thought that he knew her name. They had only passed one another a couple of times in the foyer of the guest house, exchanged curt nods. She had adjusted her schedule to avoid him, and now he was staring at her, expression amused and perhaps annoyed, curious.

"So much of what you're talking about is in the title, though," she said. "The adjective, 'Syrian.'"

"And what if the title were *American Clean Plate?* I think you only prove my point, Miss Page. I call the image 'American,' and it becomes a statement on entitlement and gluttony, perhaps innocence. There's an accusation in it. The title is all. Surely you know that, as a writer."

Juliet stumbled forward, unable to stop herself. "I believe that a title should point to meaning, not create meaning where there is none."

"You think the image is meaningless."

"No," Juliet said. "I mean, of course not. I suppose I just don't see the point of flying across the world to make a staged photo of a plate. You said the image was transgressive, but when is transgressiveness just—" She flapped a hand, trying in a panic to produce the word. *Affectation*, she'd think later, but what came out of her mouth was: "disrespect?"

"Disrespect," Paul Sacca repeated. "You seem to be an authority on the subject." His lips were crooked into a slight smile, the expression of triumph she herself had worn so recently at her lunch with Fenton. Fenton was watching her now, deciding, perhaps, whom he agreed with, whether Juliet were worth taking seriously after tonight. Her retort would be all.

She cleared her throat, which was very dry. "Perhaps," she murmured. There was a hush as people waited for something else—an apology, perhaps. Paul Sacca retained his look of amused disdain, but most of the people in the audience were frowning at her. "Perhaps I am," she said, a bit louder this time, and Paul Sacca nodded and motioned toward the student operating the slideshow on a laptop. The image shifted. He resumed his monologue.

She practically ran out of the auditorium the moment the lecture concluded. She had come off as a bully, a troll, she thought miserably. Paul Sacca and his Marie had provoked her with the kitchen stuff, but no one else in that room had known that, and perhaps the Saccas' slight hadn't even warranted Juliet's reaction. They were good photographs, really. She liked his work. But a dinner plate? Meditations on American entitlement and gluttony, from the guy who couldn't even deign to share his kitchen appliances for a few weeks? Too much.

There was a light snow falling. She shrugged on her coat, zipped it. Lifted her hood and hunched her shoulders so that her face was obscured. She walked briskly toward the village cafe, thinking that she'd stop in for a coffee or a hot chocolate for consolation, a talisman against the cold, but some students from the lecture—they must have driven—had beaten her there. It was a lovely night, the sky clear, the snowflakes large and damp, and there was no breeze, so the fall was remarkably still, like a photograph. She felt the snow melting into her suede boots, a splurge from last winter, when she was still part of two incomes, and noticed that the ATM Melissa had pointed out was one storefront down. She withdrew two twenties and wandered to the bar, ordered a Wild Turkey, neat, and retired to a booth near the front plate glass window.

She had two more bourbons and a glass of wine, sipped slowly, and felt the relief of drunkenness take hold—a measured, calculated drunkenness, the kind that wasn't gotten so much as made. She had class in the morning. For now, she didn't care. She listened to the creak of the bar's wood plank floors, eavesdropped on a conversation or two, considered with sleepy bliss the calm and faultless snow, how her footprints into the bar had already disappeared. There almost certainly wouldn't be snow in North Carolina right now, but she thought about her twenty-eighth birthday, when things between her and Danny were still pretty good, and how—it was December—it had snowed like this, thickly and sluggishly, and the streets, unplowed, had emptied. They had walked half a mile to their favorite Italian restaurant, drunk two martinis apiece and a bottle of wine, and talked without self-consciousness to the few other diners and waiters, united against the cold, all of them friends suddenly, sharing appetizers across the tables. When they found out it was Juliet's birthday, they had all sung to her, and it was nice, actually, genuine, and the chef came out, a beautiful old man, and joined them: *Tanti auguri a te, tanti auguri a te, tanti auguri a Juliet, tanti auguri a te.* The restaurant was an old family joint, nothing fancy, plastic table runners and a mustachioed cartoon man on the menu. Christmas lights strung around the windows. Tony Bennett low on the speakers. She and Danny had left it wrapped around one another, laughing, slogging through a rare ankle-deep drift. She remembered kissing him, tasting his tongue, which was still sour from the wine. Snow in her collar, his hot fingers scrabbling against fabric to find her waist. Then home, bed, his skin against hers and a light sleet starting to spatter the window, the best night of her life, maybe, though she hadn't known it then, had only known that she loved and was loved, the love still good enough for them both to take for granted.

She took out her cell phone, jabbed the Contacts tab, and there he was, still topping her list of Favorites. There was a ringing, and she imagined him in bed, reading or maybe napping now, the book spread open on his chest, glasses slipped to the end of his nose as he nodded over it. She had always wanted to see him this way, the way that a loving wife would.

"Juliet?"

"Hey," she said, knowing that the single syllable gave away her drunkenness. "Hey, you."

There was a long pause. A throat clearing.

"I asked you not to call me," he said. "At home."

She felt herself mugging, as though he could see her—blinking back tears, contorting her face into something like a grin, a breezy, confident, independent woman's grin. "But it's tough right now, Evan," she said hoarsely. "I've had a real bad night."

"Cynthia's downstairs. Watching TV."

"I won't keep you."

He sighed. "You just need to know that I might have to let you go in a hurry or even hang up. I don't want you to take it personally if that happens."

"I don't take anything you do personally." She stopped, pinched the bridge of her nose. She wasn't saying what she meant. "I understand you, is what I'm trying to say. I know you. You've never hurt me on purpose."

"I've never meant to."

"Danny told me this thing you said one time. About my writing—my stories."

There was a pause, a smooth breath. "Go on?"

"My domestic stories. My soft domestic stories."

"Well," he said. She knew the look that would be on his face—knew, so well, the face itself: the high forehead and widow's peak, his bright blue eyes, the way his hair, always a little too long, swept back as though he had just finished raking his fingers through it. "That was a long time ago."

"After we slept together?"

"Yes."

"And you still believe it?"

"You wrote a fine book," he said. "A damn fine book of stories. Some of them are domestic stories. I don't know that I feel about those the way that I once did. The mind's a flexible thing, and that's an amazing discovery to make when you're on the downhill side of your sixties."

"It doesn't even matter, I guess," Juliet said. "It's out there. I'm content with it."

"How's Ohio?"

"Cold and lonely."

"Are they at least taking care of you? They're lucky to have you there, you know."

"They've been nice," Juliet said. She thought about it. "They're covering my meals. I've saved a fortune on groceries."

“And you have a place lined up to live? For after you leave?”

“Uh huh,” she lied.

“Spoken to Danny lately?”

“Not since before Christmas.” They’d talked on the phone for a couple of minutes, long enough to make arrangements for him to ship her a box of old papers she’d left behind at their apartment. “We didn’t say much.”

“So you don’t know about his book, then,” Evan said.

“No.” She felt a trembling inside her.

“It was a finalist for one of the university press contests, and his agent used the leverage to get him a deal.” He mentioned a publisher in New York. “She wrangled him some advance money. You probably ought to know that, as stuff gets official. When will you be divorced?”

“We can file in June,” she said. “After we can prove a year of separate residences.”

“Well, then. Make him disclose the particulars.”

There was another exchange or two, nothing that mattered, nothing that she would remember. She closed her phone at some point, tilted back her glass, sucked the last of the whiskey off an ice cube. The snow had stopped, finally.

“Ma’am?” the bartender said. “We close at midnight during the week.”

She nodded, stood. Swayed a little in her boots. “Thanks.”

On the sidewalk outside she stopped, hot suddenly, and dropped onto a snow-covered bench. She leaned over and retched between her legs, splattering the suede, and thought about how Evan was right, that she needed the details of Danny’s deal, but the money didn’t matter at all to her. If only it had happened the night of her birthday, that snowy evening two years ago, when nothing had gone so wrong that they couldn’t have made it right again. When she still loved his book, all those bumbling young narrators and lyrical endings and obvious symbols.

A car crunched to a stop on the road in front of her, engine humming smoothly. It was an impressive machine—silver, boxy, German—and when the window rolled down she saw that it was, inexplicably, Paul Sacca, and the passenger seat was empty. Marie, she remembered, had flown to San Francisco over the weekend.

"You need a ride," he said. It wasn't a question. "Let me take you home."

He waited for her answer, godlike, his face glowing with success and good health. She didn't know whether he wanted to sleep with her or take care of her. When she nodded her assent, he stepped out of the car, grasped her hand, and led her, so she wouldn't slip in the snow, to the passenger side.

"Watch your head," he said as he opened the door, and so, obedient, she tucked her chin into her chest and gripped his forearm, dropping inelegantly into the bucket seat. The warmth of the car was fierce and startling. She gasped for breath, then exhaled slowly through pursed lips.

"You okay?" Sacca said. He was leaned over with his hand propped against the roof of the car, appraising her, his voice rich with disdain and doubt. She had noticed at the lecture that his handsomeness, so elegantly aged and hardened—a lucky stroke of genetics that had probably made him more attractive at forty-five than he had been at twenty-five—was just starting to fade. It was most noticeable in the hunch of his shoulders, a little hump in the upper back. In the shadow he'd cast against his slideshow, she had made out the silhouette of his future elderly self, and she'd felt for a moment the power of her youth and strength. But now, under the force of that assured masculine gaze, his blue eyes so bright beneath those distinguished, shaggy brows, she cowered.

"I'm fine," she managed to say.

He smiled a little, almost kindly this time, and came suddenly toward her. She quivered for a second with uncertainty, thinking he meant to kiss her, but he was only pulling the seatbelt across her chest and lap, then locking it into place.

swallows

This was the year she had the job at the elementary school on the south side of town. At the end of each day Robin would tidy the art room and prepare materials for tomorrow's projects, stab out lesson plans into the spreadsheet on the old desktop computer at her teaching station, and peel out of the parking lot with a podcast called *Catastrophe* playing through her phone. On it, two white women around her own age, one an environmental scientist and the other a comedian, infotained on the topic of the world's worst natural and environmental disasters, then offered recipes for craft cocktails. The rhythms of their familiar, infuriating, endearing So-Cal accents, their lighthearted accountings of tsunamis and reactor meltdowns and volcanic eruptions, had the perverse effect of lowering her blood pressure as she drove to the Teeter for dinner fixings and (too often, because she was a cliché) a bottle of white wine. Food preparation for one was a daily dismay, and six years of it had barely removed the sting. The key to survival for Robin had been not planning ahead too much and not buying too many prepared foods, and she very rarely made big comfort meals that would turn into a week of leftovers. There were few things sadder than eating, by yourself, a bowl of four-day-old chicken pot pie. Well, except for Chernobyl—*Catastrophe* season 2, episodes 5 through 9—of course.

So Robin became something of a regular at this Harris Teeter, a low-traffic location hemmed in between a Planet Fitness and a Hobby Lobby. Seagulls—confused, hundreds of miles from shore—pinwheeled above the cracked parking lot and its freight of economy cars and bent shopping carts. She could navigate the store's aisles by heart, had learned the rhythms of its sales—when to catch the Dave's Killer Bread for a still pricey $4.99—and recognized most of its staff, including the checkout guy whose nametag read SCOTT, a man (late thirties? early forties?) so genuine-seeming and agendaless in his friendliness, so apparently content to be scanning and bagging groceries, that Robin had reached the conclusion he must be a little slow—or "differently abled" was probably the better phrase to use.

That guess was complicated (somewhat) when, standing in the checkout line one day, she listened in on the checkout guy's conversation with an elderly shopper. When Scott-the-checkout-man's earnest interrogation on the quality of the old man's morning had earned him a reciprocal "How was yours?" Scott-the-checkout-man responded, "It was good. I mean, it was really good before I came to work. I got up. I read some poetry. I had some eggs and toast. I went for a walk in the woods near my apartment. And work has been fine so far too. Thank you for asking. Thank you very much."

Now Robin wondered whether he was coming on to her—if he'd seen her in line and unloaded that poetry-reading, walking-in-the-woods spiel to try to impress her. She pushed her cart up into the awkward little niche behind the *People* magazines and *Soap Opera Digest*. What kind of hipster nonsense was he trying to spew? Read some poetry. Sure you did.

"Hey, how are you?" he asked her, smiling as if she were an old friend. He started pulling groceries out of her cart. "I see you in here a lot, don't I?"

Yep, she thought. Coming on to me.

"Yeah, I usually come in after work," she said. He was—and she'd noticed this, uncomfortably, even when she theorized he might be mentally challenged—not bad looking. He reminded her a little of Amy Schumer's husband. She followed Amy Schumer on Instagram and had tracked her progression from singlehood to marriage to motherhood with cynical interest. To say she was "obsessed" with Amy Schumer's husband would be way too strong, but he intrigued Robin enough that she'd actually lay in bed one night reflecting on why, and the conclusion she reached was that he was handsome but a little schlubby in a way that made him seem plausible, like a man Robin herself might have dated if she'd done something less masochistic with her life than settle in central North Carolina and work in public education. This Scott guy was a slightly schlubbier version of Amy Schumer's schlubby husband. Maybe ten, fifteen pounds overweight, cheeks starting to hollow, the first suggestion of what might become jowls in another ten years. His grayish brown hair, worn just a bit too long to look neat but not long enough to seem fashionable, gave him the guileless affect of a second grader on picture day. But his eyes were a startling pale blue, and he had a truly lovely smile. It was the smile, she realized, that made her doubt his intelligence. What could a smart person possibly have to smile about these days? You'd have to be a bit dim to feel that kind of happiness.

"Can I please see your ID?" he asked, holding up the wine bottle.

"Sure." She fished it out. The request never ceased to flatter her.

"1980," he said. "The same year I was born!"

"Yeah?"

"Yep. Okay, ma'am, do you need help getting this out to your car?"

It was one cloth bag of groceries, and this too seemed like a possible come-on or a robo-line delivered by a person who lacked the social acuity to recognize when that part of the employee script might not apply to a situation and could therefore be eliminated. Unsure how she felt about either scenario, Robin said, neutrally, "It's okay. I've got it."

"Have a great day!" Scott told her, beaming his sweet smile. She felt almost shaken in its magnitude. Like he was laying on her something she didn't deserve or didn't have the fortitude to bear. She nodded, waved a little.

The car, once started, picked up her phone's Bluetooth signal and immediately started blaring her podcast where it had left off, on a commercial for Blue Apron, order code DISASTER.

She found herself thinking throughout her workdays about her coming trip to the Harris Teeter and then, later, aiming her cart for Scott's line. She told herself that he cheered her up, which was true.

Contemplating an array of salmon filets on Styrofoam trays, smelling their saline-fishy musk, she told herself that the poetry he read was probably something truly mortifying, like Jewel or James Franco, not that she was any kind of poetry expert herself, and in fact the only poem she could remember off the top of her head was the one she'd had to memorize for eighth-grade English, "Invictus," which gave her slightly embarrassing goosebumps, even now, as she mentally recited its last two lines. She asked herself what a man in his late thirties was doing working as a checkout boy—his badge wasn't even marked with the little Management star—and why he wasn't married. (He could be divorced like you are, she chided herself—but he didn't seem like a person who'd be divorced. Again, his sweetness, his warmth, his overall contentedness, seemed to exclude this as a possibility.)

YOU THOUGHT HE WAS SLOW! she screamed to herself as he once again unloaded her cart, making little observations about her bag of oranges, her jar of garam masala, and had she ever gotten these frozen gyoza before? Were they worth the money? She wondered what it said about her, that she could go from that assumption to possible romantic interest. It couldn't be good.

"I haven't even asked, how was your day?" he said, running a box of spaghetti noodles across the scanner.

"It wasn't great, to be honest," she found herself saying. "I teach art. To little kids. And the fourth graders, they were a handful today. Something must have been in the air. Like a gas leak."

"Well, a natural gas leak would probably cause unconsciousness rather than hyperactivity," Scott said.

"I didn't mean it literally."

"Oh. I got you." He smiled widely. "I'm sorry that was your day. You seem like a nice person. And teaching children—that's important work. Holy work, even."

There it was! She felt almost as relieved as disappointed, finally being able to put her finger on the thing she couldn't understand about him, the reason he was indisputably unsuitable. He was a religious nut.

"I'm not a holy roly kind of girl, to be honest," Robin said.

Her cart was empty, her debit card already processed, and the receipt had spat itself into a curlicue. Scott ripped it off and tucked into the grocery page, then paused, holding the bag upright gently by the straps. He offered them to her. "Now you're taking *me* too literally."

No one was behind her in line. Her heart hammered. "Was I? I apologize."

"Absolutely no need," Scott said. "We're starting to understand each other. That's all that matters."

"I'm Robin," she said.

"I know. I've seen your ID a lot."

"And you're Scott."

He was grinning now. "I guess that means you can read mine." He flicked his nametag.

"Scott, do you want to go do something with me sometime? Like, a walk? Or we could get coffee. Or a drink."

"I don't really drink," Scott said. (Dear God, Robin thought. Worse than a religious nut. A teetotaler. But it was too late now, the thing was in motion.) "The rest of it sounds good, though. I'd love to."

"Are you sure?"

He laughed. "Why wouldn't I be?"

And that was how it started between them.

He was not simple in the air quote, wink-wink sense, but there was something simple about him, after all, though Robin came to believe it was the simplicity of a Shaker chair, a crisp white sail, a—she was preparing one of her solitary meals as she thought this—green salad dressed with good-quality vinegar and oil. On their fifth date, he came to the apartment bearing tickets, of a sort; they'd been photocopied onto neon orange paper and cut unevenly in rectangles. BYE BYE BIRDIE, they screamed—Central High School William T. Powell Auditorium, October 25, 2019, 7:00 p.m.

"You're taking me to a high school play?" she asked. She'd put more than a little effort into her appearance, straightening her hair, then waving it with a heat wand, applying foundation and highlighter and not just her usual thin scrawl of eyeliner and mascara. Her jeans, a pair of Ksubi she'd thrifted for the astonishing total of $3.99, were (this was the real cost) perhaps a size tighter than, well, ideal, and she didn't relish the idea of sitting in them, in a wooden folding auditorium chair, for two hours. She'd thought they might sleep together tonight. She'd thought she might not have the jeans on for long. Not for certain, but maybe. She was receptive to the possibility.

"Um, well. Is that a bad thing? You sound like you think it's a bad thing."

She shrugged and twisted the toe of her boot in the rough pile of her entryway carpet. "I don't know. I guess I just didn't expect it. It's not a thing I'd ever think to do."

"Hmm. It's actually something I do fairly regularly. We always get the flyers for the plays at the store, so I figured one time, why not, and it turned out to be pretty good. And it's not like we have a professional theater company anywhere close."

"That's true," Robin said.

"I mean, it beats Netflix."

Robin was certain *that* wasn't true, but she nodded again, murmured an unenthusiastic affirmative, and grabbed her light jacket off the entryway hook.

"Why don't we just go to a movie instead?" Scott asked as she locked her door. He scratched the side of his head, sheepish. "I wasn't thinking. Things seem like a better idea in my head sometimes than they are when I put them in motion."

Now she felt bad. "No, let's go. It could be fun. It's something different."

So they went to the school play. It was opening night, and the mildewy auditorium was packed with parents and grandparents and clusters of high school students with their feet kicked up on seats in front of them and smart phones propped against their thighs. Robin realized, following Scott to some open seats near the aisle on the right wing, that they blended in. They too could be a couple of middle-aged parents, settling to watch Jenny or Johnny warble their way through a rendition of "Lot of Livin' to Do." She'd always assumed she'd have kids, probably at the fashionably late (but not too late) age of thirty-three or thirty-four, and then the divorce happened, and that was that. Her job was her job, and she actually didn't feel pangs of maternal longing much at work—she had steeled herself against such sensations there; as the school's principal would tell them, "You've got to leave it in the classroom or you'll end up quitting"—but melancholy descended on her now as she pressed her bottom into the spring-hinged seat, which was (at least) nicely padded. She listened to the gentle roar of conversation around her, the coughs and throat-clearings, the squeak of opening and closing seats, and she watched the velvet curtain that hid the stage ripple gently, as if an open window were behind it, and a gray haze shrouded it all. Warm pressure found her hand, and she looked down to see Scott's fingers woven through her own, and from what seemed suddenly like a long way away he asked, "Are you okay?"

She nodded.

"Do you want to leave?"

"Of course not," she said, a little harshly. "We just got here."

Then the lights dimmed. Around them, screens continued to glow, rectangular luminarias, and then the faculty director got onstage and made the obligatory comment about turning off your cell phones, and most of them winked out, at least temporarily. Over the speakers, the prerecorded orchestral overture started to play.

The performance was surprisingly entertaining. Not good, or at least not consistently good; there were perhaps two students with genuine talent, and the young woman playing Rosie was luminous, revelatory, in a way that ought to suggest a future full of great things, though Robin knew (from experience) that high school successes meant jack shit in the real world. Still, the girl could sing, with skill as well as feeling, and Robin found herself moved by the character's longing and vulnerability, even though Rosie's 1950s' ambitions were no greater than seeing her long-term boyfriend-slash-boss become an English teacher. As if that were something to aspire to.

After the play, she and Scott drove back to his apartment, talking about Rosie and also a bit about the kid who'd played Conrad Birdie. He wasn't as good a singer, but he had an electric quality, charisma-with-a-jet-pack, that reminded Robin of a young Tom Cruise, before he went and ruined it with his craziness. They decided, together, that the best thing about the play was seeing young people put away their phones and care deeply about something. "In general, though," Scott said, "I like the millenniums or zoomers or whatever you're supposed to call them. Most of the teenagers we get working at the store are good kids."

"Do you ever wish you had them?" Robin asked. With another man, she wouldn't be able to bring herself to just ask this question outright. She'd be afraid he'd see it as an angle, an invitation, a thirty-eight-year-old woman's last-ditch attempt to secure a sperm donor.

"Kids?"

"Yeah."

He pulled into the parking slot marked with his apartment number, 8. He turned off the ignition and rested his hands on the steering wheel. Squeezed it, released it. "I do, honestly," he said. "I think I would have been a good dad."

"I think you would have been a good dad, too."

"But—" He shrugged. "That's life."

"Same," Robin said, thinking (but not saying) that he could still have them if he wanted, that he and Robin were the same age, but their situations weren't really the same. Because, well, that was life. Aloud, though, she added, "I had to decide at a certain point what I wanted more: kids or to love the man I was married to. And I found that kids were less of a priority for me. But the pangs don't go away, even if you know you made the right choice." Again, she knew that another sort of person wouldn't understand her, and she felt a moment of exhilaration, sitting in the car with this man she barely knew but somehow trusted.

Scott pulled his key from the ignition, and the dome light blazed. "Upstairs, then? I've got stew in the crockpot."

"Sounds good," Robin said.

And that was the night, after all, when they first slept together. It was, for Robin, as if they'd started this part of their relationship a year or so in—past the nerves and awkwardness, before the arguments and tedium, at the point where they understood each other's preferences and bodies and committed to the act with an absolute lack of self-consciousness, with only tenderness and mutual respect. The third time at his house, she reached into his bedside table to grab a condom, and she noticed the box she pulled it from was more than half empty, emptier than it ought to be if he'd bought it specifically for use with her. She stared at the little foil package, its 2021 expiration date, and she ripped it open without comment, but wondered. After, though, with the bland rubber smell of the spent condom still faintly lingering, she could not stop herself from asking, "When was the last woman you slept with? How long ago?"

She was lying on her side, ear against his chest, and he shifted his arms just a little and resettled so that his fingertips rested against her elbow. "January. So, what is that? Nine months ago."

What she felt wasn't jealousy, exactly, but the emotions were related. Second cousins. She'd thought Scott was a treasure for only her, hidden in plain sight, and she couldn't imagine the woman who would have seen in him all the things she now saw—though that thought, in those words, was much crueler that the truth in her heart.

"What did she do for a living?"

"That's what you want to know about her?" Scott asked. "Her job?"

"A person's job says a lot about them," Robin said.

"I think my job's the very least interesting thing about me," Scott said, and Robin almost flinched, because she now knew, consciously, the reason she'd asked him that question. She wanted to picture the woman who had slept in this bed, nestled in this man's arms. She wanted, through some kind of fucked-up sexual trigonometry, to measure her own value by assessing that of this other woman. She recognized this, but that didn't stop her from saying, "That's true. It's just a starting point. You don't have to tell me if you don't want."

"She was a lawyer. Is a lawyer. I assume she's still off lawyering somewhere else."

Huh. That was a curveball.

"What kind of lawyer?" She was forming a picture in her mind: a family lawyer at one of those nonprofits for people who can't afford legal aid. She'd have bad shoes and ill-fitted suit dresses with shoulder pads.

"She did estate planning."

"You met her at the store? Like me?"

"Why do you want to know this?"

"No clue. So, did you?"

"Yeah. I checked her out."

"I bet you did." This she said with exaggerated innuendo, an attempt at humor. "Did you ask her out or did she ask you out?"

"I honestly don't remember," Scott said, and it was the first time Robin suspected he was being insincere, though she also knew she deserved that from him right now.

"Because I was the one who asked you out," Robin said. "If you recall."

"I do recall. I liked that about you. I would have asked you eventually, but I liked that you beat me to it."

Later, she would wonder what masochistic impulse caused her to blurt out what she blurted out—if she was punishing him for having a sex life that preceded theirs, if it was a childish guilt response, the logic that had once caused her to declare to her father, unprompted, as he held her in his lap and hugged her, "Daddy, I think I love Mama more than I love you." What she said was, "I thought you were slow the first few times we met."

"What the hell does that mean?" Scott asked. He pulled his arm out from under her, gently but decisively, and scooted back a few inches. From his side, he assessed her. "Like, mentally disabled? You thought I was that kind of slow?"

What in the love of God was she thinking? She colored, hesitated. Swallowed hard. "I didn't think you were seriously . . . I mean, severely. Or maybe one of those things where the social cues are off. I'm sorry. I was stupid to even bring that up."

He sat up, tucking the covers almost fussily around his bare waist and raking his free hand through his graying brown hair. He shook his head in wonder. "Social cues. You—" he pointed at her—"telling me about social cues!"

"I'm sorry!" she said, and now tears threatened. "I am not going to be able to explain this in a way that will justify it. It's just, you were always so happy and so nice to everybody. You never seemed to have a bad day. You're never off in your own head and out of patience. You just scan people's groceries and act like it's exactly where you're meant to be. I couldn't wrap my mind around it. So, in my head, I belittled it. I assumed you couldn't be too smart if you could live in the world that way. And then I knew better, and then I asked you out."

"So you think a happy person can't be as smart as you are."

"Look around! Look at how things are! It's like people who say they're not political. You either have your head under a rock or"—she stammered, flustered—"or I don't know what."

"Maybe I'd be deeper if I thought about tragedies all the time? Or if I stayed up till midnight getting mad at Tweeter?"

"Oh, you know it's called Twitter," Robin said. "Don't play dumb."

"I guess I'm lucky you decided you could lower yourself to my standard," Scott said.

Now the tears spilled. He'd think they were calculated. Were they? What she knew is that she'd had a good thing, been part of a good thing, and she'd ruined it, maybe. To the extent she'd thought this through—and she hadn't—she'd expected more of his serene aplomb, maybe a philosophical bit of reflection like, *I am slow, and that's a good thing. I don't get in a hurry.* And then, her conscience clear, they could go forward, and maybe she'd take him to Thanksgiving back in Kentucky in a couple of weeks, and when her parents and older sister asked him what he did, how he spent his days, and he favored them with his bright kind smile and explained he was a cashier at Harris Teeter, she'd stand confidently at his side, their fingers interlocking, and her family's doubts wouldn't touch her.

"I mean, it's one thing that you thought it," Scott said. "But why did you have to tell me about it?"

"I'm so sorry," she said again. Now she, too, had sat up, and she pulled the comforter stiffly around her chest and held it in place under her arms. She hadn't felt ashamed of her body with him before, but the thought now of slipping naked from bed, fumbling for her shed clothes under the emanations of his anger, if not his gaze—he would look away, she knew that—almost sickened her.

"You struck a nerve," Scott said. He sounded tired. It was an "I'm not mad, just disappointed" voice, which was almost worse than outright fury would have been. His generosity undermined any defense she could wage. He traced his index finger in a curve over his left ear. "Did you notice the scar?"

She shook her head. She had run her fingers through his hair but not looked closely at his scalp. Scott leaned toward her, and she put out a hand, tentative. She hadn't expected this. That he would invite her, after what she'd said, to touch him. He took her hand and pressed it against the side of his head and under the slightly shaggy thick hair, running her fingertips along a thick, scythe-shaped seam. How had she missed it?

"Meningioma. Which is to say, it was a brain tumor. I was in college when I got the diagnosis, and I dropped out for the surgery and recovery. Then just didn't want to go back. Didn't care. My language was impacted for a while. I had no trouble understanding people, but when I'd speak, I'd do weird things, like forget words I used all the time or use the wrong word. And it still happens every now and then. I have to be careful. So, for you to think I was stupid, it hit me." Wordlessly, he knocked his knuckles against his heart.

"Jesus," Robin said. "I'm sorry, Scott. I wish you'd have told me."

"I actually don't think about it much. It's another part of me that just doesn't strike me as very interesting."

"But it had such a big effect on your life. Your whole trajectory. What were you studying in college?"

He peered at her. "Does it matter?"

"I don't know. It must have at one time."

"Anthropology," he said. "And believe me when I tell you that I could be saying anything to you right now and I'd feel about the same level of emotional investment. It could have been business or philosophy or welding for all it matters now. I'm not the same person."

"Because of the tumor? I mean physiologically. Not, you know, psychologically."

He shrugged. "My mother would say so. It was hard for her, and I don't think she understood me very well on the other side of it."

"That's just fucked up," Robin said.

"You're the one who thought I was slow," Scott said, a little sharply. "Put yourself in my mom's shoes."

"Okay. Point taken."

"She thought I gave up on everything that mattered to me, lost my ambition. I got the job at the grocery store, and she thought, well, it's temporary, he'll go back to school next semester. Then another semester went by, and the semester after that. And then she started telling me jobs she heard about, places where I could get my training on-site, and then," he laughed, "she started asking me about Teeter's management program, and that's when I knew she'd all but thrown in the towel. I don't want to say you're like my mom, because that's half a dozen different kinds of messed up, but you two might understand each other. She thinks being happy is being hungry, like your happiness is supposed to be predicated on something you haven't achieved yet. And I'm just not built like that anymore."

"What does that mean, then: you're hungry for nothing?"

"I'm glad to be alive. I feel like they cut that thing out of my head, and maybe they took something that was part of the old me, but if they did, I don't miss it. I'm glad it's gone. And before you told me how when we first met you thought I was slow, I was happy holding you and starting to know you and having the luck of you coming through my checkout line and asking me out. But if you're wondering about my application to the Teeter management program, I can at least save you that suspense. I'm not interested."

"Fair enough," Robin said.

"Is it enough?" Scott asked. And as answer she put her arms out. Another kind of man might have held back, enjoying her doubt, but Scott returned her hug, and they sank back under the covers, protected from the chill of the room, the chill of the world.

Every day, between her podcasts and NPR, entombed in her little sedan from home to work and the grocery store and back again, the car's aging speakers rattled, and the world made its violent intrusions. *Catastrophe* did a deep dive on Love Canal and paired it with a spin on a gin and tonic that featured a thyme-scented simple syrup. The impeachment probe continued. Theories circulated about Jeffrey Epstein's suicide. A couple of students out in California were killed in another school shooting. At Robin's school, a city cop circled the parking lot a couple times a day, and she found herself wondering whether he was here to protect the children or to keep an eye on them. It was less than either of those things, she decided—a gesture, a superstitious ritual.

Robin hadn't really wanted to be a teacher. To call it a backup plan, though, would be to suggest she had a plan at all, when in fact she'd just passed her four years of college in a happy bubble, spending her parents' money on tuition and art supplies, experimenting with edibles, and falling in and out of love, all of it culminating in a self-important senior thesis, a series of clay monoprints that were now stored in a crumbling stack under her bed. It occurred to her that her college experience, her one-time aspirations, were no more real to her now than Scott's were to him. How little it had all prepared her for the misery and tedium and occasional exaltation of her workdays.

Late November. The leaves were finally starting to fall. She photocopied maize-shaped outlines for the kindergarteners to color, replaced October's pumpkin collages with the first graders' horns of plenty. She sifted through the bins of chalk pastels for the little pieces too broken to use, soaked paintbrushes in soapy water. *Catastrophe* covered Mount St. Helens and the classic Dark 'n' Stormy. It rained for almost two weeks straight and the music room flooded, so the school, which was built in the '20s, reeked of mold, and the fourth graders' value studies contracted into waves on the drying rack. There were times, working with a student—like six-year-old Isaiah, who navigated his classes in the oversized body of a third- or fourth-grader, racking up disciplinary notes, his eyes so young and soulful and desperate for tenderness that Robin almost couldn't bear looking at him—and she'd be guiding the child's hand on the safety scissors or showing him how to blend the acrylics, and she wanted to cry because everything seemed both precious and already lost. What good was living, or loving, in the face of that?

She was trying one Sunday morning to find the words to ask this of Scott. She lay on her side, looking at him. Even this, she thought. What we have here, in this bed. You, propped up against pillows against headboard, wire frames perched on your very straight, slightly long nose. Your mouth shaping itself silently around the words you're reading. And my love for you, nestled tenderly and secretly within me. Even this. What good is it?

Instead, she asked, "What are you reading?"

He placed his finger in the book's spine, folding it most of the way closed, and showed her the cover. "Wendell Berry's poems. He's a Kentuckian. You'd like him."

"I've never been able to get into poetry," Robin said. "It's one of my many failings."

"I didn't like it, either, before this." Scott motioned to his scar. "I'd always been a reader. But then, you know, for a while there my concentration was affected, and I got headaches. I felt stupid. And poetry had always made me feel stupid, so I figured why not try it again. I had nothing to lose."

"And you suddenly understood it?"

"No, but it made sense to me."

"There's a difference?"

Scott pulled one of his pillows loose, tossed it on the floor, and wriggled down, mirroring Robin. Even his morning breath was dear to her. "After the surgery, when language got weird for a while there, it was like everything I thought I knew, everything I thought was solid and real, it wasn't. Even words. The bottom dropped out of them. There were these gaping holes where they'd been. And that's a problem if you want to read a novel, but it's kind of an advantage if you want to read a poem. You read a poem and you can just sort of embrace the unknowing."

"Embrace the unknowing," Robin said. "Sounds like a Pink Floyd album."

Scott laughed, hard. "Okay," he said, tapering off. "Can I read you one?"

"You want to read a poem to me?"

"You don't have to sound so alarmed."

"I don't think we're there yet, Scott."

He laughed again. "It's not a love poem, I promise."

"Okay," she said. She rolled onto her back and looked at the ceiling. "Lay it on me."

He cleared his throat a little, and she heard the pages of the book rustle:

There are seasons enough for sorrow
but best be sorrowful in spring
when the martins at last return
to their houses near the porch
the barn swallows to the barn.
You can't be entirely sorrowful,
watching the swallows flying
to live, and ever delighted
to be flying. They know perfectly
that they are beautiful. And the good
never is made less good
by subtracting badness from it.

"I wouldn't know a swallow if I saw one," Robin said. "But I like that poem. I think."

"I'll find you a swallow this spring. We just need to track down a barn first."

She couldn't bear to meet his eyes, but she fumbled across the covers and found his hand, gripped it, thanking him for the promise. The promise of spring.

"You're going to make me take a hike, aren't you?" she managed to say.

"You love it," Scott said. "You love it."

gratitude

Acknowledgments don't seem to suffice as I write this list in the waning days of 2021. So here's my gratitude, sprawling, indulgent, and deeply felt.

Thanks to the readers who offered me feedback on stories in this collection: Danielle Lavaque-Manty, Elena Makarion, Erin McGraw, Michael Parker, Drew Perry, and Julia Ridley-Smith.

Of course, readers are often also dear friends. I dedicated this book to Erin McGraw, whose friendship I treasure and whose opinion I value above all others. Thank you. Our Zoom drinks with Juliana Gray—and thank you, too, Juliana—kept me sane. Other sources of light and sanity, via text message or email or Zoom or the occasional precious neighborhood walk: Risa Applegarth and Matt Loyd, Mike Croley, Jennifer Whitaker, and the aforementioned Danielle Lavaque-Manty.

To my colleagues at UNC Greensboro, past and present. This year has made me more grateful than ever to have such a great job. And the students in our MFA program are a huge part of that. They inspired me to experiment with fabulism, which helped me find a way, finally, to write about the "persistent strangeness" of the last four years.

I want to thank Counterpoint for granting me permission to use Wendell Berry's poems and Wendell Berry for putting words to the seasons of sorrow and hope I wanted this collection to encapsulate. I could not imagine this collection without them.

To Gail Hochman and Jim McCoy: thanks for all you do and for your belief in these stories.

I'm grateful for the educators and childcare professionals who put themselves at risk to care for my kids. I'm grateful for the doctors and nurses who treated my father when he was hospitalized. I'm grateful to the writers whose books sustained me and for the sweetly hopeful animated fantasies I started watching during lockdown with my family each night before bedtime.

I lost my brother Johnny on December 24, 2018, and my father died on September 10, 2021. They were both honest, selfless, loving men in a world desperately in need of honesty, selflessness, and love, and as I write this, the loss of my father is still so raw that I can hardly convince myself it's real. I miss them both terribly. Dad, I hope I did a good enough job while you were here of showing how grateful I was to have you. To my mother and my brother Eric, who are mourning along with me, I love you both so much.

And to my sweet little family: Brandon, Selby, and Raina. Even in the midst of loss, I am still the luckiest person I know, and you three are the reason. As I once told Selby, you fill my heart with joy. And Selby told me, "That's because I'm the boy you get." I'm so, so grateful you're the ones I got.

Stories in this collection previously appeared, sometimes in different forms, in the following journals: "Antipodes" in *Colorado Review*; "Exhaust," under the title "One For the Road," in *Epoch*; "Stars," under the title "The Farmer Takes a Wife," in *Joyland*; "Fortress," under the title "You Have a Beautiful Home," in *Cincinnati Review*; "Distancing" in *You Are the River* (NC Museum of Art); "Axis" in *Southern Indiana Review*; "Ark" in *Epoch*; "Shelter," under the title "Sound Side," in the *Southern Review*; "Machine," under the title "The Right Way to End a Story," in *Tin House*.